BLACKER
THAN BLUE

VAMPIRE SORORITY SISTERS BOOK 2

By the Author

The Fling

Better Off Red: Vampire Sorority Sisters Book 1

Blacker Than Blue: Vampire Sorority Sisters Book 2

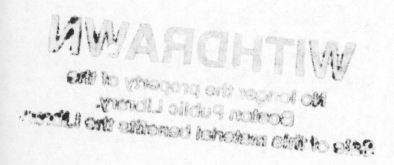
Visit us at www.boldstrokesbooks.com

BLACKER THAN BLUE

VAMPIRE SORORITY SISTERS BOOK 2

by

Rebekah Weatherspoon

2013

BLACKER THAN BLUE

ISBN 13: 978-1-60282-774-5

This Trade Paperback Original Is Published By
Bold Strokes Books, Inc.
P.O. Box 249
Valley Falls, NY 12185

First Edition: January 2013

Credits
Editor: Cindy Cresap
Production Design: Stacia Seaman
Cover Design by Sheri (graphicartist2020@hotmail.com)

Acknowledgments

I must thank the following people:

Summer Youngblood for her all around awesomeness.

My editor, Cindy, for trying her hardest to make me a better writer.

And Radclyffe for letting there be a book two.

To Tecora Arnold, for holding my hand from far away.

PROLOGUE

Benny
Freshman Year, Thanksgiving Break

I pulled Gus onto my bed with me and switched my phone to my other hand. On the other end of the line, my girlfriend, Cleo, sighed in my ear. "You were able to escape?" I asked.

"Fuck yeah," she replied. "I swear my mama invited people just because they have the last name Jones. There were three dudes who I know aren't my uncles, just kicking it. I'm getting some gas now." Maryland University only gave us a week off for Thanksgiving, but it was long enough to make me miss being away from my few friends at school, the girls in my sorority. It was too long for me to be away from Cleo. I thought about telling her, but I kept the thought to myself. Still, I was enjoying my time with Mama and Daddy, and soon I'd be back with Cleo again.

We'd been together for a little over two months now. I never thought I'd fall in love. I wasn't sure I believed in it anymore, especially since my parents were bound by something greater. Yes, Mama loved Daddy, but he was a vampire, one of the strongest demon-bourne vampires of his kind. They were bound together by blood, and that strengthened the affection between them. I knew Daddy would find me a demon to serve one day, and he had. Camila was wonderful, and I couldn't wait to see her once I got back to the Alpha Beta Omega house, but what did I have with Cleo? I never thought our love, a love that allowed me to serve her willingly and fully, would come for me.

It was more than the fact that she was a junior and I was only a freshman. Or that she was so beautiful, so physically perfect, and I was just a notch above dumpy and plain. It was that she wanted to be with me too, even when I explained what I really wanted in a girlfriend, if I ever got one. Cleo understood that I wanted, needed a mistress, someone to mold and control me sexually. She'd more than lived up to the task. She didn't even mind that I wanted to keep our relationship a secret. She understood why. I held in my sigh and shifted Gus in my lap just as he decided to taste my hand.

"Ouch. No biting." I pulled my finger away from Gus's puppy teeth to inspect the damage. He didn't break the skin.

"Playing with your new dog?"

"Yes. He's a little menace, but he's so cute."

"I can't believe she gave you six dogs. Is that what they give for Thanksgiving? Dog meat?"

"No." I laughed. "Dalhem and his bound-sisters have these gift-giving cycles. It was Paeno's turn." Daddy and his demon family had a number of bizarre traditions. Mama and I had learned not to question them.

"It's strange, but whatever. What time you coming back?" Cleo was heading back to the Alpha Beta Omega house early to get a jump on studying for her anthropology final. Aside from the six vampires our sorority fed—the only real reason for the sorority—and our housemother, the house would be empty. A perfectly quiet place for Cleo to get some studying done, away from her large, loud family. I was heading back a little early as well. I wanted to spend some time with Cleo alone.

"What time am _I_ coming back? You know that's not up to me," I said. My heart fluttered as I stroked Gus's thick silver fur.

"How about you're ready for me at nine?"

That early? I wanted to ask, but I couldn't deny the sparks the act of obeying set off between my legs.

"I'll be ready at nine."

"That's a good bunny." I did sigh this time. Lightly, but away from the phone. It was one of the things we were working on. I needed to be more up front with my feelings. Keeping things in was something I'd learned to do well in the last eighteen years. It was a hard habit to break.

Someone knocking at my door stopped my response. "Come in," I called and smiled instantly as Mama poked her head in the door. She shrank back bashfully, just for a moment, when she saw I was on the phone.

"How long do you need, angel?" Mama whispered. We had Christmas shopping to do.

"An hour," I mouthed.

"Is that Cleo?" She smiled as she nodded toward my phone. I nodded back, matching her grin. I hadn't told her much about my girlfriend or my first relationship. Still, she knew how I felt. I didn't feel comfortable opening up to the girls in the sorority, even my good friend Ginger, who was so easy to talk to, but I could tell Mama anything.

"Good morning, Cleo," Mama called across the room before she ducked back out the door. Cleo's deep laugh sounded in my ear.

"Tell her I said hi. When am I gonna meet her?"

"Soon. I need—"

"I know."

Cleo and I had come a long way. She had been very patient with me, but I needed more time. I still needed to keep parts of my personal life separate.

"After spring break. Come stay with us," I said, uncomfortable with the suggestion. I tried to lighten my tone and the mood between us. "We'll take you to the blossom festival. I still can't believe you haven't been yet. Richmond isn't that far from D.C."

"It's far enough." I heard a few clicking sounds and then the rusty squeak of her car door opening. I'd offered to replace the old Civic for her, but she was so attached to the thing, a gift from her mama. The door slammed and Cleo huffed an exhausted breath through the phone. I was anxious to relieve her stress.

"Well, let me get off this phone before I wreck or get pulled over," she said.

"Okay. Study hard."

"Yeah, the hardest." Suddenly Cleo's voice was soft. "Benita?"

"Yeah?"

"I love you."

I hesitated for a moment before I replied quietly, "I love you too."

"Bye, babe." Cleo hung up as I said good-bye. I gave myself a moment to think about what Cleo had said and a few minutes longer to consider what Cleo expected of me the following morning. It was true, I never thought I'd find the love we had found together, but it was deep and it was good. Even though parts of it still scared me, I knew every time Cleo gave me an opportunity to submit, that love would last forever.

CHAPTER ONE

Benny
Senior Year, Second Semester

I looked over at the iPod docked on my mahogany nightstand. The final notes to my favorite harmonious tribute to love lost played through the speakers, and the clock on the square display snapped over to 9:55. The music was perfect for moments like this. Sometimes, the girls didn't feel like talking, but they still had their hour. Marvin would fill the silent moments while Ashley decided whether she wanted to confess to more bingeing or purging that week, or when any number of the freshmen needed a few minutes to come clean about their own issues. Ron Isley would give Maddie something to hum along to while she wasted time rolling around on my comforter. In a professional office, playing music would be unprofessional, but it was perfect for sister counseling.

The Dixie Chicks strummed in a beat later, and Maddie laughed.

"You have the weirdest taste in music." Her hand slid down the mahogany post and she sighed as her fingers sought out a crack in the clear finish that wasn't there. Mama had found the queen-sized bed frame at an auction in Raleigh. I'd appreciate it if my sorority sister didn't chip its finely coated surface. I took my attention off the curious hand and gazed over Maddie's body. Her flat stomach was perfectly toned. Spray-tanned skin dusted with nearly invisible hairs peeked out from under the hem of her racer-back tank top. Her hard nipples poked at the red cotton. She didn't have a bra on, and from the tightness of her skimpy shorts, I could tell she didn't have any underwear on either. The black spandex barely covered the junction of her thighs.

I had shed a few pounds, but dropping from a size twenty to a size sixteen didn't give someone license to wear hot pants in front of the other girls in the Alpha Beta Omega house.

"I love this bed," Maddie muttered, lifting her legs in the air. Her tiny dancer's feet pointed to the gossamer canopy above. She looked over to me, but I watched as the ruby pendant on her chest slipped to the side and slid between the strands of her heavily highlighted hair. Absently, I adjusted my own necklace.

"You must hate this. Listening to us complain every week."

I didn't hate the peer counseling sessions that were now mandatory twice a week. I simply didn't want to hear about all of the ridiculous things my sorority sisters thought were important. I knew these sessions served a purpose. I knew firsthand how secrets kept, big and small, emotions hidden, never led to any good. I knew the same to be true about the truth itself. I still hadn't perfected the balance, but I knew when to keep quiet about my own business. I'd mastered the poker face and the art of being a steel trap when it came to information, whether it was useful or not.

Oddly enough, my refusal to gossip or show real emotions made my sisters in Alpha Beta Omega trust in me that much more. You could tell me anything and it would never get around, but not because I wanted to keep the secret. It was because I didn't care. I had my own classes to study for, my own demon to feed and please. I had my own problems to deal with.

I didn't care about the petty things, but I had to listen. Every time I thought of Sam, my friend, sister, and occasional bunk-buddy, and every time I thought of Ginger, my best friend, a loving girl, turned vampire queen at nineteen, I would pause and stop myself from tapping the clock.

Both Sam and Ginger had been tortured in various ways by the same boy, and if someone had been there for Sam as her boyfriend had taken his hands to her, things would have been different. Greg could have been stopped before he forced himself on her over and over again. An alarm would have been sounded as his sick feelings for Ginger continued to fester. Sam wouldn't be so ruined and Ginger wouldn't have faced death only four months into college.

Madeline and Ruth would make up in an hour, fall right back into each other's arms, and tear each other's clothes off. Things for them would go back to normal, but if Maddie or Ruth came to me with a real problem, I had to be ready to listen.

Every week, twice a week, from nine to ten, Amy, our chapter vice president, and I opened our doors to hear all gripes about school, parents, boyfriends, and girlfriends. Mostly girlfriends. Living with forty-six girls who were perfectly comfortable sleeping with one another brought up some interesting instances of jealousy. And there were other things.

A few small incidents had been avoided since my term as chapter president had begun. We were getting help for Ashley, but mostly it was bullshit. It was the bullshit that made me resent these sessions. That, and with the exception of Samantha, Ginger, and Camila, I hated having people in my room. I didn't like people touching my things, and I hated people asking questions. I didn't have pictures of Mama and Daddy around my room for a reason.

"I don't hate it," I said. "You'd rather talk to me about it, though? Right?"

"God, yes. Ugh. She's such a little bitch."

I kept my eyes from rolling. Ruth had said the same thing about Maddie a few weeks before. The two of them had behaved like this for a while now. Always in and out of love.

"And after graduation?" I wanted to get back to the point before our time was up.

"She wants us to move to Miami and I want to stay here. I can get a tryout with the Ravens, but she's all, 'The Heat have a squad too, blah blah.' But I'm over basketball players."

I understood that part. I couldn't stand the members of the Maryland University men's basketball team. The "men" part was always up for interpretation. But they weren't the focus of this conversation.

"You need to weigh your real happiness, Maddie. What do you want?"

"I don't know. I love her. Just—" She broke off, chuckling. I added a tight-lipped scoff. Maddie liked going in circles. "Such. A bitch."

"You have four months to think about it. If you want a real fresh start once school's over, you need to consider if what you two have has run its course or if you really belong together."

"I know. What about you? What are you going to do after graduation?"

"This isn't about me." I flashed a tiny smile.

"I know! It's never about you. Okay. Whatever." Maddie swung herself upright and hopped off the bed in a graceful leap—graceful until she reached behind herself and tugged her Spankies out of her ass. "You're coming to the game, right?"

"Yes. I will be there."

"Good."

A knock on my door had us both turning. "Come in," I called out.

Amy skipped through the doorway, her notebook tucked under her arm.

"Hello, ladies." Amy's blue eyes sparkled as a smile lit up her whole face. She was already dressed for bed in a thin black camisole and red flannel pajama pants. The red polish on her toes matched mine.

I liked Amy a lot. She was too enthusiastic, but she was genuine. She reminded me of my mama.

"Ruth is waiting for you in the hall," she told Maddie.

Maddie took a deep breath then marched toward the door. "I'll see you guys later."

Amy wasted no time. She crawled up onto my high mattress into the newly vacant spot, mumbling about her fondness for the four-poster bed. "Anything good?" she asked once she was comfortable leaning against the wall.

"No. The usual with Ruth and Maddie. Same stuff with A.J. and her little sister. You?"

Amy bit her lip, holding in a laugh.

"What?"

"Jill."

I groaned quietly. It was the same thing every week. "What did she say?"

"Baby B, she's in love with you. What do you think she said?"

"I've already told her no."

"She doesn't care. She's got it bad."

"She'll have to deal with it."

"Oh, but she can't, Benny. You're just so, unf, you're so irresistible."

"What did you tell her?"

"This time I told her—" Amy giggled. "I told her you'd decided to go into a convent after graduation."

"Amy."

"I told her that your stepdad got an e-mail from God, and a life married to the church is your calling." Tears threatened to stream down Amy's face.

"Great. Now she'll ask a million questions about which order I'll be joining."

"I'd tell you to slip her a pity fuck, but she's too smitten to handle it."

Last time Jill had come to Amy, talking of her love for me, Amy had told Jill that I was still a virgin and was saving myself until I met the right man. Three weeks before that, she'd told the gullible girl that my parents were in the process of arranging a marriage for me to be carried out right after graduation. I was supposed to remain celibate until the binding ceremony to this mythical person. Every week, Jill bought the excuse and sulked in her room for a few hours before her will to love made her think she could convince me to pick her over whatever life I had planned otherwise.

Jill couldn't be swayed. There was nothing that I could say, and I wasn't willing to do anything that would actually scare away someone with such an intense infatuation. My single status gave the obnoxious freshman hope. No matter what Jill decided was the truth, a relationship between her and me, sexual or otherwise, was not going to happen. I physically couldn't bring myself to do it. Though I wasn't completely against sleeping with others, I'd only given my heart to one person, and that was the same person I still lusted after and longed for. That person was not Jill.

I put my heartsick sorority sister out of my mind and shuffled off my bed. I smoothed the hem of my thick cable knit sweater around my hips and checked that my tank top was in place under the low-draped neckline.

"Let's go," I told Amy. "They're already waiting."

Our weekly meeting with our queen and her seven vampire sisters was a certain kind of torture a small part of me yearned for. Dalhem, my father, had selected six of his most treasured demon children to patiently nurture future generations of willing human feeders. The blood my sorority sisters, the boys of Omega Beta Alpha fraternity, and I provided kept the rest of mankind safe from what could have devolved into hordes of lecherous vampires. The night dwellers had been brought to the earthly plane between heaven and hell by my father and true protector, and his hell-spawned brothers and sisters. It was an honor for me to serve them.

The original six sister-queens of his Alpha nest had entered my life nearly four years ago. I had been bound to the former queen, Camila, three weeks into my freshman year at MU. She respected my wishes and never took our feedings beyond anything but a simple drawing of blood, and I loved her for that graceful show of love and appreciation.

The other sister-queens all cared for me, and I loved them all equally in return. Faeth, a proud farmer's daughter from New Zealand; Omi, a survivor of the Bajan sugar trade; Natasha, the czarina of the last Russian imperial reign; Tokyo, a reborn indentured servant and lover of all things leather; and Dalhem's eldest demon child, Kina, a Mi'kmaq Native American from the north. All were examples of what us girls of Alpha Beta Omega could someday be.

But it was the seventh sister who meant the most to me. My ex-girlfriend, my ex-mistress, the former love of my life.

I saw Cleo around the house plenty of times during the week, here and there on the weekends. Cleo joined the nest only a week before Ginger was turned. Ginger was married to Camila; Cleo was Camila's best friend. Best friends of lovers, lovers of best friends. It was impossible to avoid her. Running into Cleo in Ginger and Camila's apartment or in the hall was one thing, but during our weekly meetings, sitting across the room from my ex for over an hour was almost unbearable. Almost.

Everyone who had the nerve to ask me always wanted to know the same thing. Why would I put myself through the torture of being in the same room with the only person I had ever loved and now the one person who truly hated me?

There was no reasonable answer. The feelings I had for Cleo couldn't be met with logic. We were broken up and had been since the day after Cleo died. It was over, but I only had a few months left to savor the pain of being in Cleo's presence. After I walked across the graduation stage, there was a chance I would never see Cleo again. I knew if Cleo had things her way, that would definitely be the case.

"Are you sure you want to do this? I can go down alone," Amy offered. The new girls had no real idea what was going on between Cleo and me, but the seniors knew. Amy knew.

I grabbed my leather-bound portfolio off my mahogany desk and opened the door.

"Let's go."

Amy kept quiet until we were inside the house elevator. The lift was hidden in the pantry and was the only access point to the sister-queens' quarters from above ground. The ability to vanish through walls made fire exits unnecessary for the immortal beings who lived below the colonial mansion at 1444 Milson Avenue. I punched the code into the keypad on the wall, and the elevator began its smooth descent.

"You know what I want?" Amy said as she cocked her hip against the wall. "I want to be there when you go mental. When your repressed feelings force you to just snap and flip out on your boss or when you climb that clock tower and just start picking off poor, defenseless people. I want to see that."

I had gone through all the stages of grief and cycled to jilted and bitter in a little under two days after Cleo dumped me. I'd been sitting in that particular spot ever since. I was hurt. I could admit that to myself. Sometimes I was angry and even jealous, but I would never lose control. No one was worth making stupid decisions over.

"We both know that won't happen."

"You still talk to Ginger, right?"

Ginger and I talked about a lot of things, but never my real feelings. That was why Ginger and I got along so well. She knew not to push. She understood that sometimes talking about your pain did absolutely nothing to ease it.

The elevator door slid open.

"I'm going to talk to her tonight," I said.

"Good."

I took a left and continued down the dark corridor, loving the feeling of the cool marble under my bare feet. The black walls were bare, lit every few yards by dim light fixtures hidden in the crown molding. This floor of the house was a virtual maze for unwanted visitors, but I had always felt at home in the rooms behind these black walls. Most of them, anyway.

We turned the last corner to the sister-queens' quarters. Our demon keepers took turns hosting the weekly meetings they held with us. Omi's apartment was the favorite. She had altered the lighting and furnishings in her quarters to give the effect of being at a beach resort. I didn't care where we met, but for me, anything was better than the apartment Cleo shared with the sister-queen Tokyo.

Tonight, we were meeting in Kina's rustic setup. The log cabin motif was warm and comforting, highlighting Kina's longing for a life in the wilderness. Tokyo's place was a den of pleasure. No couches or chairs, just large pillows and comfortable mats surrounded the television. I had never entered her bedroom, but I'd imagined it. I'd envisioned Cleo beyond the black bedroom door, shackling Tokyo to the wide bed they shared. The two had been close friends and lovers since Cleo and I had parted ways. I remained on good terms with Tokyo. She had nothing to do with our breakup and she was always kind to me.

I fought the twitch that gripped my cheek as the image of the two of them together came into clear focus in my mind. Cleo's feeders couldn't help the attraction they felt for her. It was part of the bond. The connection brought demon and feeder together in a deep, caring relationship built on sacrifice and devotion. The vampire's bite carried with it an instant, amazingly intense orgasm that even I couldn't withstand.

The difference was I knew how to keep my physical passions under control, the strong emotions I felt for Camila, even if they were fleeting. And I never acted on them. I couldn't blame Laura or Melanie for the way they felt about Cleo. I couldn't blame Andrew, the only male who was under Cleo's protection, for openly admitting to how much he lusted for her.

Cleo was a master shifter. I had overheard, hundreds of times, how Cleo could make her body bend and stretch in the middle of sex. She could even alter her anatomy at the flicker of an eyelash. That was how Andrew liked her best. Her clit would grow to a nine-inch length and she would take him from behind.

Tokyo liked her that way too. She and Cleo were both demons, so their closeness had nothing to do with a blood bond. Tokyo liked sleeping with Cleo, plain and simple.

That, I hated.

I took a deep breath and subtly stretched my neck before knocking on Kina's door.

"I'm telling you. Clock tower. Short scope. Long rifle," Amy whispered beside me.

"Amy. Shut up."

The door opened with a light click and opened wider at Ginger's will. Amy and I were almost the last to arrive. Amy called out a cheerful hello.

Cleo was there, sitting across the room, beautiful and perfect as always. Her skin was like warm milk chocolate, her perfect lips plump and full. Years ago, the change had caused her afro to grow so long, so quickly that her ebony locks began to spiral. They were secured away from her face by a red ribbon that Cleo had always worn. Her legs were spread wide and Tokyo was lounging between her knees facing Cleo's lap.

Tokyo turned quickly. "Hey, guys," she said before turning back to Cleo. Or more importantly, Cleo's crotch. Her long cock was hard against her thigh, held tightly in place by the leather pants she'd taken from Tokyo's wardrobe. I hated how good she looked in those pants.

I hated the white wifebeater Cleo wore too. I knew a burlap sack wouldn't dull Cleo's amazing features and her erotic curves, but it would do something to cover up the seams of the red pushup bra that were peeking out from under the white cotton. I missed those breasts.

Cleo didn't look up from Tokyo to greet me or Amy. She watched Tokyo with a blank expression, letting her trace small circles across her knee.

"I have to feed first, but let's go to Tens," I heard Tokyo say. Another night at the strip club was just what they both needed.

Cleo didn't respond. I knew Cleo treated Tokyo well, as she did all the other girls, but both Cleo and I had the same walls up around our hearts and our true personalities. Once, I had the power to breach Cleo's well-constructed façade of confidence, but Cleo hadn't let anyone in since the accident.

I had no control over the way my body reacted to Cleo's indifference. My skin grew hot and the moisture flowed between my legs whenever I was near Cleo, and now was no different. I swallowed before taking a deep breath. It had taken some practice, but now I was able to keep my lips from parting whenever I caught Cleo's cherry blossom scent. Most humans didn't recognize a demon's scent for what it was, but I did, and Cleo's scent permeated the room.

Amy gently tugged on my pinkie. I ignored the gesture, but I appreciated the support. A familiar, powerful, masculine voice came from Kina's art studio, and the baritone sound was enough to put a stop to my arousal.

My legal father, the only full demon in this part of the world, stepped into the living room. The sister-queen Kina was a step behind him. I was used to his black wings that protruded from the smooth fabric of his gray suit. When he was comfortable, the scaled feathers would extend from his back as they did now. A man's fingers were in place instead of his natural talons. His onyx horns blended naturally into the copper-brown skin of his forehead. His white hair was shaved close to his head now. Mama liked it better that way.

"Daddy?"

"Ah. It is my Benita. Hello, my darling princess." Daddy crossed the room in two easy strides and took me in his long arms. My mood instantly lifted as he kissed me on the forehead. He was deadlier than he appeared and one of the most gentle, caring beings I had ever encountered.

Beside me, Amy stared in wide-eyed shock. Daddy knew exactly who she was and who she fed, but none of my other sorority sisters had seen him before.

He reached out and gently chucked Amy's chin with his large knuckle. "Hello, my child."

Amy's jaw flapped before she answered. "Sir."

Daddy's golden eyes shone as he smiled at her.

"What are you doing here?" I asked him.

"I have dropped in to check on my queens. The truth lies in the element of surprise." He winked. "I will leave you to your meeting now." He leaned down close to my ear. His strength was undeniable, but I could hear the humor in his tone. "Young lady, call your mama." I laughed at his perfect impression of my mother's Southern drawl. The smile was back in his voice as he went on. "She is lonely for you."

"I will."

Daddy turned with a graceful nod of the head in Ginger's direction. She returned the acknowledgment with a curtsy and a giggle touched with sarcasm. Anyone else would have found it disrespectful, but Daddy loved Ginger. She got away with more.

His golden eyes flashed briefly as they connected with Cleo's light brown stare. No one missed his anger as he vanished from the room. As his essence dissipated from the air completely, Cleo still refused to look at me.

"That's your dad?" Amy gasped.

Natasha appeared before I answered. "I have missed our master?" Her white-blond hair swayed as she slid to the floor beside the coffee table.

"Yeah," Ginger replied. "And yeah, Amy. That's Benny's dad." Ginger crossed the room and took my hand. I followed her to the couch. Camila settled down on my other side and murmured her sweet hello.

"Let's start. It's getting late," Ginger announced.

"Please, a moment." Natasha held out a rectangular box. "Sweets from my husband." I resisted taking more than one as the chocolates circulated around the room, and passed the box on to Ginger. I gently bit into the dark square and savored the slightly bitter taste. It was all I could do to ignore the piercing glare that was suddenly focused on my slightest movement.

I opened my calendar, then peeked up long enough to watch Cleo take a piece of the chocolate Rodrick had sent over. Cupping the back of Tokyo's head, Cleo ran a thumb over her porcelain cheek. I shivered.

"Open up," I heard Cleo murmur. Tokyo did as she was told, her light pink lips parting easily, exposing her sharp fangs. Cleo slid the chocolate into her mouth and let Tokyo suck her index finger. Cleo waited until the square was gone before she slowly drew her finger out and licked the traces of the candy with her own tongue. I had to look away.

"I want your cock tonight," Tokyo purred. Her light citrus scent spiked in the air. For a second, it overpowered the other smells in the room, even the dark flavors that lingered on my lips.

"We'll see if I want to give it to you," Cleo replied as I glanced their way again.

"But you're hard." Tokyo slid her hand across Cleo's abnormal erection. "I want to take care of that for you."

My eyes closed for a moment before I turned most of my attention to Ginger beside me. She smiled again, her fangs biting into her lip before she dropped her head onto my shoulder, rubbing my arm to banish the shivers away. I couldn't stop myself from listening for Cleo's response. I saw as she wiped Tokyo's bottom lip.

"I said we'll see. Don't ask me again."

Tokyo would get sex, no matter what. She had her feeders. The sister-queen Faeth, who was always ready to screw, and there was Moreland, the demon across town who let both Tokyo and Cleo have at her stock of slaves and well-trained submissives whenever they wanted. But for some reason, Tokyo seemed to crave Cleo's attention the most and, just as she had with me, Cleo loved making her work for it.

Cleo glanced up and we looked at each other. This was part of the pain, the part I actually looked forward to because something in my brain was broken. These fleeting moments where Cleo and I would pause to ignore everything around us and do a quick mental undressing with our eyes. I would remember everything we had been to each other, the way her fingers felt across my lips, and every sinful command she gave me.

I could see it in her eyes, in those few heated moments, that she remembered the afternoons in my dorm room freshman year. How she learned to command me and felt her own delight in how easily I would obey. In those moments, she took stock of every inch of my body, the bits of skin she liked the most—my blue eyes, my breasts with their overly sensitive nipples, and most definitely my butt—and like that, her eyes would turn cold. She glared at me, but now we weren't alone. I felt Ginger tense beside me as she lifted her head and Camila, on the other side, reached for my hand. They had chosen my side from the very beginning, but that didn't change the way Cleo felt. She told me with that single stare, she still fucking hated me.

To Cleo, I was overconfident and a bitch. Both points I agreed with. Cleo almost died two days after Thanksgiving. Her body was badly damaged in a car accident on her way back to campus. She was returning early from her parents' home in Virginia to study in an empty sorority house for her anthropology final and to spend a few uninterrupted hours with me on my knees. To save her the agony of a painful recovery, or death, Camila made the decision to turn Cleo to the vampire she was now. Knowing she was alive and safe, I couldn't hide my joy in discovering that Cleo was now an immortal. I wanted to share the joy of a blood bond and the ecstasy of feeding with someone I loved, with my girlfriend, my mistress. Not that I didn't appreciate my bond with Camila, but it wasn't the same.

I also saw Cleo's immortality as an escape from her family. Her mother would never accept Cleo as she was, human or otherwise, because Cleo was gay. Her mother, her church, and her family would have shunned Cleo if they knew the truth, if they knew about us. Cleo had told me early on that I was the one for her. We'd made plans, plans for our future with both of us remaining mortal. There was marriage and a family on our horizon, things we could still have, but once Cleo saw how happy I was, when I made it known that I was glad that fate had intervened and given me Cleo as I had ultimately wanted her, Cleo was done. She hadn't looked at me with love in her eyes since. Lecherous intent from time to time, glimmers of lust, but never love, and that's what caused my pain. It was all we had anymore, and I knew I would have to take the steps to let it go.

"All right." Ginger spoke up. Her voice pulled me back to myself. "Give me the bad news first."

"Jill's still having a hard time. I know we thought moving her into the house would make things easier, but the other girls just aren't taking to her," Amy told our sister-queens.

"It's 'cause she's Canadian and proud of it." Cleo laughed. She only spoke up because she hated Jill.

"Hey! That's my little Canadian." Ginger scowled playfully. "Besides, Kina's from Canada and we like her just fine."

"It wasn't called Canada when I lived there," Kina muttered from the opposite armchair.

"We'll spend some time with her," Camila said.

"I think it's Benny she wants to spend time with." Faeth had to say it. The way Jill felt about me was no secret, but Faeth didn't need to bring it up.

"Between German class and studying with her, she gets enough of my time," I replied.

"What's wrong, B? She's not your type." Cleo glared at me again, challenging me.

I felt Camila shift beside me, and I knew she and Cleo were sharing some mental back and forth. Demons could communicate through telepathy, and due to our blood bond, Camila would want to stick up for me. But I could take care of myself. Jill was beautiful, but much shorter than me. I liked my women tall. She had a vibrant personality, but I tended to go for someone with a little more backbone, someone with more of an attitude.

"We both know she isn't," I answered as calm as ever. Cleo's gaze shifted back from Camila to me, but it was Ginger who broke up our staring match.

"Okay. So Jill. Check. What else? What's on the Calendar, B?"

"Zetas' Valentine's Day auction this Thursday. Gwen is putting herself up. And Saturday…" I paused before I delivered the horrible news. "Men's basketball has a night game."

"Not it," Tokyo yelled as the others grumbled. Our sister-queens loved all of us, but they didn't like changing form to go out in public, especially Cleo, who grumbled the loudest. She couldn't risk someone recognizing her at a university game.

"The whole chapter is going," I went on. "I think Maddie would appreciate it if a few of you would come."

"It's my mom's birthday this weekend. We have dinner at my parents'," Ginger replied. She was telling the truth. She and Camila had been shopping for Linda's presents for weeks.

"Faeth and I will go," Cleo said. Faeth groaned and rolled on the floor. "What the fuck? Maddie's your feeder. You ain't weaseling your way out of this."

Faeth grimaced. "We'll go."

"Thank you," I replied.

The meeting dragged from there. More boring business, a recap of the monthly calendar. A reminder from Ginger of the coming spring break. In a few weeks, we girls were off to the Caribbean for vacation. The sister-queens would draw straws to see who would chaperone.

"Okay. I'm hungry and I know Camila is too. Anything else?" Ginger asked.

Cleo coughed and looked pointedly at Natasha.

"You are a rat." She scowled, her Russian accent thick over every word. She turned back to Ginger. "My Rodrick has rescued a puppy for the boys."

"Oh, come on!" Ginger yelled.

"I know, my queen, but—"

"That is so unfair," Amy whined. I kept my mouth shut. I was only an hour away from my dogs and could see them anytime I felt like taking the drive.

"See." Ginger motioned frantically between Amy and Natasha. "And he thought chocolate would cover his ass? We're not getting you girls a dog."

"Why?" Amy whined some more.

"'Cause Florencia is not having that shit," Cleo answered. Our housemother was understanding and kind, if not slightly standoffish, but she didn't like dogs, period. "Even if you guys housebroke the shit out of it, Florencia wouldn't trust you to take care of it."

"No dogs. I'll think about other pets. Maybe a hamster or something," Ginger said.

"Yeah. We'd love a hamster," Amy said.

"Good. We'll keep him in your room." With her foot down, Ginger ended the meeting. I closed my calendar and tried to ignore Cleo's eyes following my movements with cold focus. Camila led me out of the room, but as we went, I was still able to catch a bit of Tokyo's voice as she crawled into Cleo's lap.

"You're still hard, you know," she said.

"I told you not to ask me again."

CHAPTER TWO

Benny

My thoughts bounced between German verbs and the backless shirt Tokyo had worn to the meeting. My test tomorrow would be easy, but I wanted to review the material at least one more time before class. The flawless pale skin of a particular sister-queen continued to invade my mind. At that very moment, Cleo's hands were most likely all over that particular back. Or somewhere lower, around to the front. I grumbled softly to myself. Cleo was never so easy. Tokyo was a joke, and in truth, a whore. Not Cleo's type at all. She needed a challenge, not someone who begged shamelessly and openly to be fucked as if that was all that mattered. She needed someone with a full brain and not just a strong libido.

A yawn escaped, and as I released my irrational grip on the arm of Camila's leather couch, I looked over my shoulder to see her smiling down at me from behind my seat.

"Is there a problem?"

"Benny, you're too tense." Camila gently stroked my neck. I felt my pulse jump against her warm fingers. We had the apartment to ourselves. Ginger was feeding from Anna-Jade upstairs. I was comfortable, settled on their worn leather sectional. The usual slow-tempo house music Camila loved pumped through the room, serving as the perfect ambient noise. Still, I was having a hard time getting my mind and my body to settle.

"Breathe, *mi'jita.*"

I let out a deep sigh and closed my eyes, breathing in and out.

"You ready?" Camila asked with a gentle smile.

"Yes." I slid down a little farther into the rich leather and pulled my sweater off my left shoulder, making Camila growl softly. For all of her loving instinct, I imagined the demon inside Camila had very little control when it was brought face-to-face with its life source. I didn't want Camila to wait any longer than she already had while I was busy reviewing my mental notes and plotting vampericide. I offered my neck.

It was easy to believe in their magic whenever Camila's fangs bit through my skin, right into my vein. There was never any pain. Only pleasure. The cool piercing of my neck shot right between my legs, and I came harder than I had in some time. My tongue braced against the roof of my mouth to hold in my whimpers, but a moan still rumbled in my throat. I focused on Camila's presence to keep my hips from moving.

This time, as with every feeding before, Cleo's face was back behind my eyes, her voice in my ears. This time, Cleo muttered softly, sweetly, making perfect demands. Her phantom hands stroked me through my clothes. Her invisible lips sealed over my breast, tracing my nipple.

I didn't like it, but I didn't fight this part of the feeding. My pleasure centers were linked to Cleo. Fighting my desires and my memories only made things worse. Camila drank slowly as always. Her warm tongue massaged the pulsing vein, coaxed more blood to the surface with every heartbeat. I continued to come. Over and over. Every time, I came for Cleo.

I glanced at the clock just as Camila began to seal the punctures in my skin. "Thank you," she purred softly. Slowly, I slid to the edge of the couch. My legs felt like Jell-O and my crotch was still clenching in time with my thumping heart. When I stood, Camila handed me a bottle of water from the bar.

Then she said, "What can I do?"

There was nothing Camila could do. As much power as she had, I wasn't weak-minded enough for her to toy with my memory, and I wasn't foolish enough to think that sort of thing would work in the long term. I was feeling sad and lonely, and that's when Cleo always decided to show up in my mind.

"I'll be fine."

"Okay," Camila said. Pushing was pointless. She started toward her bedroom. "I'll let Red know we're done." There was still a rumbling purr to Camila's voice, and even though I hadn't been paying attention, being distracted didn't dull the fact that Camila's thick cinnamon scent now filled the room. Thanks to our blood bond, Camila had felt every ounce of my pleasure during, and usually after, our feedings. Ginger was typically waiting in their bedroom, naked and willing to fully sate Camila's other physical needs.

"Do you mind if I use your restroom?"

"Not at all. Take your time. I think Ginger wanted to speak to you anyway."

I quickly moved to put myself between Camila and the bedroom door, as if Camila couldn't vanish right through me. More proof that I hadn't been thinking clearly. "About what?"

I stepped back when Camila smiled that smile that told me there was no discussion to be had, then I watched my sister-queen drift into her bedroom. I had a few moments before Ginger would come walking through the door or magically appear by the couch. I took advantage of those moments and went to the bathroom to freshen up a bit.

I turned on the water and pushed up my sleeves. My wrists were looking thinner again, but that wouldn't last long. Some cool water splashed on my face helped with the light flush that spread across my skin during her feeding. I'd have to wait a little while to change my damp underwear, but I'd survive. I adjusted my camisole again, and my ruby necklace. Camila was expert at drawing blood. There wasn't even the slightest red speck on my white sweater.

When I came back to the living room, Ginger was there.

I liked that my best friend hadn't changed. She was a very powerful demon now, in charge of many of her kind, richer than any other twenty-two-year-old on the planet—until I turned twenty-two, that is—but nothing other than her sleeping habits and her diet had changed. Her bright red hair was almost always in a ponytail. She still wore the same V-neck T-shirts every day, the same jeans. She'd added a little more black to her wardrobe, but that was Camila's doing. Almost everything she owned was black. She still wore the ruby necklace she'd gotten from Camila before they'd even started dating, when Ginger was just a bookworm freshman. After all this time, Ginger just wanted to be a good daughter, a good wife, and a good friend to me.

"Cookie?" She pushed herself off the back of the couch and held out a plastic container filled with large chocolate chip cookies. A small voice in the back of my head, a voice that sounded exactly like Lamont Wilkes, suggested I keep my hog finger out of that box. Where was the ghost of my real father when I'd eaten that chocolate, and all that pasta at dinner?

Ginger rattled the box and took a bite of one herself.

I crossed the room, lowering my voice even though Camila could still hear us in the bedroom. "Whatever you want to talk about can wait. I know you and Camila would like some time to yourselves. We can do this tomorrow."

"Are you done being ridiculous? Great. Have a cookie."

I grabbed the huge piece of chocolate chips and sugar out of the Tupperware and took a bite. It was still warm.

"Mmm, these are good. Florencia made them?"

"No." Ginger snickered. "Jill."

You could have heard my eyes roll.

"She's so sweet, B. Just give her a chance."

"Fuck you, Ginger," I said with a slight shake of my head, but I didn't stop eating the cookie. I finished it and reached for another.

"Come sit with me. Let's chat." Ginger handed me the cookies, then tugged me back around to the other side of the couch. Just then, Camila came from the bedroom. She had changed to go out, wearing her full biker gear: a motorcycle jacket, tight jeans, and her riding boots. She didn't own a motorcycle, but the clothes and her badass spiky haircut would make her fit in just fine with any biker crowd.

She stroked my cheek with gentle affection before she rounded the couch. Then she leaned over her na'suul, her hands resting on either side of Ginger's shoulders, their lips close together. The demon marriage bond allowed them to read each other's minds over any distance. It allowed them to share emotions that no human would ever know. At heart, they were still two young lovers, trapped in eighteen-year-old bodies, going through what seemed like a never-ending honeymoon phase. I wanted what they had. Instead, I had Jill's cookies.

"I'm going out," Camila said.

Ginger tilted her head up and kissed Camila softly on the lips. "You driving or flying, my *Mila*?"

"Flying. I have a few places to go." Then Camila looked over to me and said, "Benny. I'm here, okay? I mean it." I nodded in appreciation, but we both knew I would never take her up on the offer to talk.

"You..." She pointed at Ginger. "Don't go anywhere. I'll be back soon."

"I'll see what I can do. Come here."

I looked away, but Ginger was sitting so close it was hard to ignore the passionate way their lips moved together. The kiss was tame for the two of them. Considering they had both just fed, it was extremely tame.

I could only imagine the thoughts and fantasies they were sharing in that single kiss. Plans for later.

Plans for forever.

"I love you," Camila whispered as she pulled away.

"I love you too."

Camila vanished from the room with a playful wiggle of her nose.

Ginger purred gruffly and stretched. "Sorry. She has that effect on me."

"I understand."

"Okay. So where were we? Oh, right. I was going to force you to do that thing you hate," Ginger said with an unnerving smile.

"What thing?"

"I'm gonna make you talk."

I sighed and rolled my eyes. Like Mama, it was hard to shut Ginger down completely. She was such a good friend and so honest. When she came to me about something important, I knew I could trust her. "What do you want to know?"

Ginger grabbed another cookie and curled up on the couch to face me. "You okay?"

"Yes. I'm fine."

"Listen, we all saw Cleo during the meeting. I just—"

"Cleo isn't bothering me."

"Benny."

"She's not. She acts like that all the time. And it's been three years. I've had plenty of time see her with Tokyo. It doesn't bother me."

"What about what she said about Jill? I know Cleo too. I know when she's trying to start something."

"Well, she didn't."

"Anything else bothering you? You look worn out. Do you want Camila to feed you when she gets back?"

I finally sighed. Camila's blood would definitely ease the fatigue, but that was about the only cure it could offer me right now. "No, it's just been a long day. I have a German test tomorrow and a UGA meeting tomorrow night. I just want to go home."

"You should. Go spend time with your mom. Go see the master on his own turf." I returned the silly smile Ginger flashed when she mentioned Daddy.

"I know," I replied. "I will soon."

"Well, good. Now go to sleep. And send Amy to the UGA meeting.

You know they're just going to finalize things for spring formal. She loves that crap."

Ginger was right. Amy got sexually aroused over the idea of planning any sort of social event, but I only had a few more weeks left as chapter president. I didn't believe in handing off my duties on the final lap. ABO had enough trouble with its wild ideas about mixing races. Being a lesbian-friendly sorority tested the tolerance of enough of our fellow Greeks. I didn't need to give bitches like Kimber Knowles, the chapter president from Tri Pi, more ammo when it came to nominating officers for the University Greek Association come fall.

"I'll be fine, and I need to go to that meeting."

"Okay, well, for now go to bed."

"Okay."

"Now."

"Okay, your highness."

Ginger stood and walked me to the door. "Sunday. Me and you vegging on the couch?"

"As long as Jill doesn't show up."

Ginger chuckled. "I am making no promises." She shoved the last of Jill's cookies into my hand and nudged me out the door.

The house was relatively quiet. Florencia was busy doing a final sweep of the kitchen. She had a kiss on the cheek and a pat on the back for me as I passed out of the pantry. A few of the freshmen were still up studying together. Anna-Jade's TV was on. There was music coming from Hollis's room. Maddie and Ruth were fucking with their door cracked open. I just wanted to shower and lie down. I needed a new day. I needed to get out of my jeans. I wanted anyone but Jill to be waiting outside my door.

The girl was cute. Really, she was. Her two dads had farmed the Canadian gene pool for the perfect egg donor and then came Jill. She was half African-American, half French-Canadian, pouty lipped with braces, and adorable. She barely cleared five feet, but unlike our other pint-sized resident, A.J., her spunk made up for her size. She was smart, kind, and giving, and she had a quick sense of humor. And horrible timing and no sense of personal space. She also cried on a dime. I had to be nice to her.

"Hey, Jill. What's up?"

"I thought if I brought you some cookies you'd quiz me." She was much too cheery for after midnight, but Jill was always like that. There was a white box wrapped in a purple bow balancing on top of her German book. It was sweet that she knew my favorite color, but...

"Ginger already got me." I held up the plastic container. There was only one cookie left.

A scowl started to spread across Jill's forehead, but it vanished a moment later. "Oh. Well, I made these for you anyway."

"You didn't have to, but thank you." I took the fresh box and opened my bedroom door and headed straight for my dresser. Jill was right behind me. My sleep music was already on, a mix of jazz and techno that Camila had made for me. And as I glanced over my shoulder, I saw there was a horizontal lump under my comforter. Sam. Her brown hair, streaked with blond highlights, was spread out over my pillows.

"Listen. I'm exhausted," I told Jill as I rummaged for fresh underwear and a washcloth. "Maybe tomorrow—"

"I just want to make sure I have my—"

"Jill!" Sam rolled over and sat up. "What the fuck? She said no."

"Sam," I chided her.

"What? She's not deaf; she's just choosing to be. You said you were tired, so lie down and let's go to sleep."

Jill's bottom lip started to quiver. Tears lined her eyes. "I'm sorry."

"Don't listen to her." I sighed, annoyed with them both. "Come get me at six. We'll study, then go get breakfast."

A bright smile broke out across her face. "Really?"

"Yeah."

"So, Jill," Sam said. "She said yes. Get out."

"You should get some sleep." I patted her on the shoulder and gently guided her toward the door.

"I will. Thanks, Benny. I'll see you tomorrow."

"Night." I forced a smile and closed the door before she worked up a second wind. Then I turned on Sam. She'd rolled back over and pulled the covers back up to her head. Sam was incapable of sleeping alone. Things with her had been that way for a while. I didn't mind helping her with her insomnia, but she had to meet me halfway when it came to my responsibilities as chapter president.

"You should be nice to her," I said.

"Yeah, whatever. Hurry up. I'm cold."

I didn't hurry. I took a long, hot, completely ineffective shower.

My back was tight and my whole body still tense from my feeding with Camila. I didn't have the energy to masturbate in the shower, but I played with my clit some. Made a lazy effort to scrub away the wetness from between my legs. When I came back to bed, I was clean but not relaxed. I thought of sending Sam to Amy's room so I could stretch out, but I was too tired for another conversation. I dressed in the dark, then slid under the covers with Sam.

CHAPTER THREE

Cleo

I sat on the Montgomerys' porch swing, watching my parents' house, wondering what in the hell was taking Nat so long. Mama and Daddy came home from worship hours ago. Maxwell and Tina had been by and left for home. Despite the shitty, icy weather, the roads were clear. There was no reason for my little brother to be drifting around the countryside at midnight. Mama wouldn't have let him skip out like this before I died. Lately, though, I noticed he was coming home later and later. I tried to stay out of my parents' thoughts and their home, but I noticed other things were different. They weren't grieving together anymore. Daddy pushed Mama away. He'd started drinking again. Mama found her refuge in the church. Not sure which option offered more comfort.

They were still the perfect couple on the outside, made stronger by the loss of their only daughter. I saw little things, though, like he still opened doors for her, and he listened when she talked, but they didn't touch anymore, and Daddy almost never smiled. When I watched them, that is.

There was nothing I could do to help them. I couldn't ease their minds to let them know that I was safe and not in a jar above Daddy's TV. Even if I could reveal myself, I think their relationship was too far gone. Daddy was doing the right thing and sticking around. No church folk can resist the scandal of their preacher's husband walking out on her. They'd think he was cheating, or worse—gay. He was just heartbroken. Again, there was nothing I could do about it, but I did watch them. Somehow, it made me feel better. Now, if Nat would just get his ass home, I could get on with the rest of my night.

My phone vibrated in my hand. I looked at the text message from Tokyo and hit Ignore. I liked her, but it pissed me right off when she acted like that. There's nothing sexy about a disobedient bitch. I pocketed my phone, then rubbed the extended length of my clit through my pants, still hard, and I thought of Benny. Hate and lust went so well together, especially when it came to her. I wanted to choke the shit out of her the moment she started talking tonight. She didn't give a shit about Jill or Maddie's dance team. Benny was just playing a part. Always playing a part until she got what she wanted. No fucking clue what that was these days, and I didn't care to find out, but I still wanted to fuck her.

I pulled up my phone again and went to Amy's Facebook page. Benny didn't have one, but she couldn't duck her way out of every sorority photo, and Amy loved posting pictures of her against her will. Only a few flicks of my thumb and I found the picture I wanted— Benny with Amy and my Laura at our Christmas party. I glanced at my Laura for a second, with her jet-black hair and bleached white bangs. Her blood was so fucking sweet. I licked my fangs just thinking about it, but my gaze strayed back to Benny.

It had been torture watching her body change over the years. I like my girls thick, and Benny had been about the thickest when I snagged her, but that was before she really developed and grew some adult curves. I looked at the red blouse and black trousers she wore in the picture. She defined tits and ass these days, and her aqua blue eyes had somehow come to be more sultry. She knew I still watched her. She knew I still wanted her, but I knew better than to mess with her again. I might have been dead, but I wasn't stupid or heartless enough to deal with Benny's soulless approach to life and me.

I stroked myself harder, thinking about her bound beneath me in ways she hadn't let me enjoy before. Gagged properly for once with no safe words or boundaries. Though it was just a fantasy, it was better than the reality we had spent together. In my fantasy, I had some say.

People would never believe the truth about Benny if I told them. They knew now that we'd secretly dated for the first two and a half months of my junior year, the last seventy-three days of my life, but they had no clue how it had started, how one afternoon following initiation, Benny had invited me back to her room. How she'd laid out her plans for me, plain and clear. We liked each other, that much was obvious. But she wanted me to be her girlfriend, officially. She wanted me to dominate her. She offered to teach me how. And all of this, our play, our relationship, and eventually, our love, was to be kept a secret.

"I'm not ashamed of anything I do," she'd said. "But we have to share everything with our sorority sisters. I don't want to share this." I liked the idea at the time and I loved how freaky Benny turned out to be, but I should have known something was off. No eighteen-year-old should be that focused and calculating. No human being should be that cold. I was glad we were over. Still, echoes of what we were—Benny herself—haunted me everywhere. Tonight, it was definitely that tight, white sweater and how wet she got when I fed Tokyo the chocolate. It felt good to play them both, if only for a few seconds. I stopped rubbing myself. I didn't want to come thinking about her. Not tonight.

I looked up from my phone, feeling a certain stir in the night air. I caught Camila's scent just before she arrived. My sister-queen appeared before me on the Montgomerys' lawn.

"Want some company?"

I shrugged before I nodded to the empty spot on the swing beside me. She reappeared at my elbow and crossed her heavy boots up on the porch rail.

"Who are we stalking tonight?"

"Just waiting for Nat to get home."

"Is it insulting to say I'm proud of you?" she asked.

"A little, 'cause it shows you still don't trust me." I was only half-kidding. Camila had offered me a proper good-bye with Mama shortly after I died, but Ginger died too a few days later. My family got lost in the shuffle, and I was too tired and frustrated to try to mend the breach. I regretted that decision every day. And every day since, Camila silently worried I would snap and approach my family, who thought all that was left of me was a pile of ashes. I missed them, but I wasn't stupid. Exposure was a one-way ticket to hell, and there was no reason for me to make that trip.

"I trust you," Camila answered. "But I wouldn't trust myself in your shoes."

"Yeah," was all I said.

Camila had showed me her memory of her little boys, murdered the same day she died. I pitied her loss and envied the children she'd had all at the same time. Picturing her kids, I couldn't help but think of Benny again, how she'd ruined everything we could have had. A life. A family. It was better in the end, though. She was too selfish for both.

Camila and I sat in silence for a long time. I didn't have anything to say, and she knew small talk was unnecessary. I hung my head and closed my eyes, thinking of sleeping and a good time to feed again. We both looked up when the side door to my parents' house opened and the Montgomerys' cat, Tabby, sprinted across the street through the cold. He stopped short of the door and came to Camila's side.

"Hey, kitty." She scooped him up and purred back as he rubbed his head under her chin. Being able to whisper to animals or whatever comes in handy when you're a demon.

"My daddy's been feeding him," I told her, scratching Tabby's thick back.

"He looks fatter."

I reached over to my other side and rang the doorbell twice and again when Mr. Montgomery didn't come to the door. "Who is it?" he yelled. Tabby jumped off Camila's lap and meowed back. Finally, Mr. Montgomery cracked the door open and peered out. He stepped on the porch, swatting at Tabby with his foot.

"Get in here, ya fool cat."

Tabby scurried inside, but Mr. Montgomery lingered just outside the door, no doubt feeling our presence, but blind to us as we hid under my cloak, our power that rendered us invisible. It was amazing how much humans could notice if they just took a moment to see, to feel.

"Watch this," I whispered to Camila. I shoved my feet off the railing and sent the swing flying backward. We crashed into the white siding of the house, then forward. Mr. Montgomery literally screamed like a little girl then froze, clutching his robe to his throat. Man, the way his eyes bugged out of his head. I crumpled on Camila's shoulder, laughing hysterically. She waited until he slammed the front door behind him before she joined me.

"Have you done that to him before?" she asked.

"No, I swear," I said. "But don't feel bad. He's cheating on his wife. He deserves a little terror in his life."

"Well, don't do it again. Dalhem will not be pleased if he goes crazy."

"Whatever." I laughed some more, thinking it wouldn't be much to spare the asshole's sanity. "He'll be all right."

It took us both a few moments to calm down. I couldn't stop laughing and Camila was having trouble controlling her own snickers. But eventually, I yawned. I tried to hold it in, but it was a big-ass yawn. I covered my mouth as it slipped out, then tried to stretch all casual like, but I wasn't putting one over on anybody.

Camila asked, "Have you slept recently?"

"Nah. Not much. I will tonight."

"Good." She sighed.

My phone vibrated again. I have no idea why I checked it.

"Lord Jesus." I almost threw my phone in the street.

"Who is it?"

"Tokyo."

"What are you doing with her?" Camila asked as if that question wasn't loaded as hell.

"Man, I don't know. She wants to go out."

"Tens?"

"Yes! I like strippers. I really do, but damn. She and Kina should just buy the fucking place. They're up in that bitch every night."

Camila shook her head. "Sometimes a house full of girls isn't enough."

"I won't even ask if you want to go 'cause I know Ginger isn't having it."

"Wise move." It wasn't a jealousy thing. Ginger knew where she stood with her wife, but Ginger's birth mother had lived and died by the pole. Ginger wasn't a fan of any of us hitting up those types of establishments. She didn't try to stop us, but she definitely wasn't a fan, and Camila wasn't the kind of woman to show just to spend time with me and Tokyo.

Just then, Nat's Ford came down the street, but he didn't pull into the driveway. He stopped several dozen yards before our house.

"Don't," Camila said with a hand on my knee before I could read his mind. "Just wait." There was movement in the car and a moment where Nat's face was lit by his phone. A gust of wind blew his scent in the opposite direction, stopping me from picking up anything but the forest behind the Montgomerys' home.

It looked like Nat was texting, but soon the light on his phone went off and he drove into our driveway. I waited until he was inside the house, then I turned to Camila.

"Get back to your lady."

"I think I will." Camila stood, but before she left, she gave me a long, lingering kiss on the forehead. I felt how much she cared about me in that kiss, as more than my friend. More than my maker. There was concern and understanding and the love she'd had for me since the day we were first bound together as feeder and queen. Our relationship was so different now, but better. I was too tired to hide how much the gesture moved me.

"Get out of here," I said, giving her a gentle shove. She winked at me and then she was gone.

I watched Nat as he moved through the house. He stopped in the kitchen, then Daddy's den where he'd most likely passed out with a brandy in his hand. When Nat's bedroom light came on, I vanished across the street and double-checked that the doors were locked, stopping myself before I vanished to the roof to peer in on Mama. Back across the street, I found myself pacing, debating my next move as I did my best to ignore my exhaustion.

With one last look at Tokyo's pleading text, I sent a message to my brother-king Rodrick to let him know I'd be spending the night at the Omega Beta Alpha house. Tokyo would have to find someone else to fuck with tonight.

❖

I don't know what it is about frat houses. It doesn't matter how clean they are, they always have that smell. Something about these boys living together, compounded by all the fucking they do. My senses were overwhelmed for the few moments I waited for Andrew to open his door. The smell of sweat, aftershave, layers of cologne and body spray, and piss had my nose burning. The new puppy—nowhere near housebroken—wasn't helping the situation. I had no idea how my brother-kings could stand it.

I knocked again on Andrew's door. He liked to study with his headphones on. There was a light shuffle and the sliding of his chair across the thin carpet before he opened his door.

"Hi," Andrew said with his prime-time heartthrob smile that made most of his frat brothers weak. I loved that smile too. His scent was fresh, like soap from his recent shower. I didn't wait for an invitation to step inside.

His room was clean and the biggest in the house. He'd turned down the offices of president and vice president, but the boys insisted he take the president's suite. He'd spent five years out of college, and at twenty-six, his frat brothers thought he deserved the biggest space. Perfect, because it gave us both someplace to spread out. I stroked his toned stomach as I passed him on the way to his desk. I glanced at the window on his laptop before I sat on the wooden surface. Andrew stepped between my legs and exhaled as I gently tugged on his nipple rings.

I'd thought about our bond a million times. Before I died, I'm not sure we would have been friends, but now he was easily the best thing in my life. Easy on the eyes too. Andrew was tall, with brown hair, gorgeous eyes, and a big bubble butt. But I wasn't straight and neither was he. I wasn't human, but thanks to our blood bond, I was able to see beyond all the reasons we had no business hanging out. I could have traded him for a female feeder at any time, but I didn't want to. We meshed together. Strange how that works. I wondered what it was about him, beyond his blood and the fact that he was a well-worn submissive, that made me trust him and crave his company. He didn't know me before. He didn't know what I was like without the demon. Somehow, though, the moment we were bound, he knew exactly what I needed. He knew I was broken.

"What are you working on?" I asked.

"Nothing. I was just messing around."

I breathed him in again before I sighed. I loved the smell of him and the taste of his blood. When Moreland gave him to me, Andrew reeked of leather and lube and confusion. Now he had his own scent, and of course, he carried traces of mine. I thought I'd done all right by him. He was perfectly healthy when I got him, but after I followed Camila's instructions and gave him his human life back, gave him back to the sun, he seemed stronger. Happier.

"Are you hungry?" he asked as he leaned into me. I shook my head. I could always feed. Always. But I fed from both of my freshmen babies before our meeting.

"Tired?" He tried again.

"Yeah. I'm worried about my brother."

"I wish I could help."

"I know, honey."

His arms wrapped around me. That was the only place I could go. His warmth was the only thing that didn't drain me. My girls needed my support and wanted my attention. Mel and Skylar were very clingy. Laura and Hollis were insatiable. Tokyo wanted everything and didn't know when to stop. Andrew was my only break in the night. The only person who didn't want something from me. So I gave him everything I had plus some pieces I shouldn't have spared.

Mama wasn't much for affection, but my daddy had this thing he used to do that I never told Andrew about. It was just another thing he picked up on. I sagged closer, letting my cheek rest on his shoulder. In response, he undid my ribbon, then ground his fingers into the base of my scalp. My hair was thick as shit, but Andrew had quickly picked up on the difference between kneading and tangling. He found the perfect spot, making me purr. My eyes squeezed shut and I groaned even louder. A vampire shouldn't have to ache like that.

"How many days has it been?" he asked.

"A full night? I don't know," I said before I reconsidered the truth. "Five months."

"Dude."

"I know." I felt the moisture leave my eyes and looked down just in time to see the blue drop roll down his bare chest. It was moments like this I hated Benny the most. Hated who she truly was. Why couldn't she be like Andrew? Why couldn't she give a shit?

I wiped my face and then his chest. "We'll camp out tonight. I'm ready." I looked into his deep brown eyes and saw how worried he was. I kissed him then to silence any more questions. I enjoyed his soft mouth for all of five seconds before we were interrupted. Van, this adorable freshman from Atlanta, poked his head in the door. His family was originally from India, but they'd relocated to the States just before Van was born. He was scrawny and baby-faced and still in the closet to his parents, who were so happy he had joined a fraternity. If only they knew how much he loved my Andrew.

"Hey—oh. Sorry. I can come back," he said.

"It's fine. Come on in, man," Andrew replied. "What's up?"

"Nothing. I can come back," Van said again, but he stepped into the room anyway, eying me nervously. Most of the boys respected us sister-queens, but a few others like Van were freaked out by us.

I stared back at him, offering a knowing smile. Aside from the lustful scent oozing off him, it wasn't hard for me to recognize why he'd stopped by. A booty call was a booty call. Andrew and I waited for a while as Van figured out what he wanted to say. He looked at the floor, back between Andrew and me, then considered the door again. The small tent in his shorts made him rethink the exit.

"Is it okay if Cleo watches?" Andrew finally asked.

Van bit his lip, probably weighing the embarrassment factor of having me look on. "Yeah, that's fine."

Andrew nodded toward his bed. "Come on." Van nearly bolted across the room, stripping out of his shirt and his shorts as he went. He was naked and facedown on Andrew's comforter before his boxers hit the floor. I laughed to myself and watched Andrew as he moved around his room, locking his door then digging up some condoms and lube.

I stopped him as he passed his desk one last time. I took him gently by the chin and shoved my other hand into his shorts. I worked his cock, feeling it grow hard in my palm. He shuddered as I barely pricked his neck with my fangs.

"You come for me, okay?" I instructed him.

"Yes, Cleo," Andrew replied. Eager to be alone with me, he walked to the bed, ditching his own shorts as he went.

When we see our feeders fuck, it's like a switch is thrown inside. We want to feed and we want to participate, though I had no interest in touching Van. I watched Andrew as he pounded away with sharp thrusts. It only took a few minutes. Van came quickly, and just as fast, he kissed Andrew on the mouth, grabbed his clothes, then ran back to his room.

Andrew discarded the condom.

"We'll go down to Moreland's soon," I said. "I need to have you properly."

"Yes, Cleo." I growled softly at his tone. He was such a good boy.

"For now." I stood and unzipped my pants. I reached below my clit and spread my juices up along the shaft. "I want your mouth."

Andrew came across the room and knelt before me. He was good with his tongue.

I fed from him and fucked him for a good two hours, giving him my wrist periodically to help replenish his drained fluids. Once we were finished, I stripped completely naked and waited in Andrew's bed while he cleaned himself up. Cum covered his stomach and his thighs.

"Honey, set your alarm for four forty-five," I told him before he settled with me between the sheets. Andrew reached for his clock while I set another alarm on my phone. I'd take another form for my own safety if I slept past sunrise, but I wasn't in the mood to chance it. I ignored another text from Tokyo—*Where are you?*—and cuddled up next to my feeder to sleep.

CHAPTER FOUR

Benny

I turned in my German test and went outside to wait for Jill to finish with her exam. She was the only freshman in our German IV class, but she was doing very well. Almost as well as me. I headed for the rotunda at the front of the building and continued walking the moment I saw a group of basketball players occupying the sitting area.

I found a seat outside on a raised ledge by the stairs and pulled out my media and culture book. It was still cool out, but the sun was shining and most of the recent snowfall had melted. There was still time before the bell tower chimed off the hour, but soon students started trickling out of the building. I tucked myself farther out of the way and continued to wait for Jill. I wanted to ditch her and enjoy lunch by myself, but she knew where I lived. As I turned the page, a shadow blocked the sunlight coming through the winter clouds.

"Mmph. Benny, Benny, Benny." I didn't have to look up to know De'Treshawn Boss was standing over me. The point guard for the Maryland University men's basketball team had been sniffing around various girls all year, but recently I'd been honored by his attentions.

I nodded, my lips pursed.

"No hello for me?"

Realizing that reading was futile until he left me alone, I peered up at him. De'Treshawn wasn't attractive. His head was too small for his body and his teeth were too small for his mouth. And his breath smelled. He overdressed in this obnoxious way where everything matched, from his hat to his shoelaces. Today's motif was brown and gold, with a faux designer pattern. Where he found brown jeans with that much sag, I'll never know.

I stared at him a moment more, wondering what would be the best way to shake him. Politics. Feminine hygiene. Literature.

"Sorry. I was just so wrapped up in my book. Chinese marketing keeps me busy."

His eyes glazed over momentarily as he looked at the cover of my book. I wasn't entirely sure how well he could read. There were several girls who actually did the team's homework and papers. But in this instance, he couldn't be swayed.

"You coming to watch me hoop this weekend?"

"I will be in attendance. My sorority sister is on the dance team, remember?"

"Word. So when are you gonna let me holla at you? A good-luck kiss before a game can work wonders for a nigga's jump shot. And I know you don't want to spend Valentime's weekend alone."

He said Valentime's.

Though I never looked forward to being alone at any point in the year, the question didn't dignify an answer. I tried to make my point clear to De'Treshawn. I wasn't now, nor would I ever be looking to spend time in his company. De'Treshawn took this as some sort of challenge and tried harder with what he thought were jokes and compliments to get me to see why I would be a fool to go on living without his penis inside me. We'd done this dance before, though never with a steadily growing audience.

At first, it was just a buddy of his who appeared at his side. Then two more and then two members of the women's basketball team, one of whom, Trea, was actually a very attractive butch who I wouldn't have minded a romp with in another time and place. She seemed to understand that I wasn't playing hard to get. Unfortunately, she was enjoying the show and didn't step in to tell De'Treshawn to shut up. But what would have been a stupid and forgettable exchange turned into a full-on scene the moment I saw Jill marching toward us with marked determination. She didn't care for De'Treshawn any more than I did, but only because she thought he was encroaching on her turf.

"You ready to go?" I said to her the moment she approached, but she was focused on my gentleman caller.

"Why don't you just back off, De'Treshawn!" she nearly screeched. That caused a few more people to stop and stare. Mostly because his name sounded adorably ridiculous with her accent. "She's not interested in you."

"Oh yeah?"

"Yeah," Jill said. "Benny doesn't even like boys, so you don't have a chance."

"How you know all that, shorty?"

"Because she's my best friend and I know she's gay." This conversation between Jill and me had never taken place, but still she let those words burst out of her mouth. The president of the Tri Pis, Kimber Knowles, and three of her lackeys walked down the stairs just in time to hear that little confession. They stopped to watch the rest of the show as well. I ignored Kimber's snide smirk.

"I told you, stupid," Trea yelled over De'Treshawn's shoulder. I glared at her. Trea just smiled in return.

"Is that right?" De'Treshawn saw this as a challenge.

Trea broke in again instead of letting me answer for myself. "I have a better chance than you, dumbass." She slid between De'Treshawn and me, brushing my shoulder gently as she went. "Benny, when you get tired of this fool barking up your tree, you come holla at me."

"Yeah, I'll think about it," I muttered as she and her teammate walked toward the cafeteria, all high fives and laughs as they went. I was ready to go myself, but De'Treshawn wasn't ready to let me leave.

"Whoa! Whoa! Wait," he said, grabbing my wrist. He'd crossed the line.

"Let her go," Jill yelped, giving him a shove. He stumbled back a half step, chuckling at Jill as he recovered his footing.

I paused and looked at his fingers digging into my skin. "Let me go," I said quietly. De'Treshawn dropped my wrist. I fixed my jacket and tucked my book into my bag. I'd planned to give De'Treshawn a piece of my mind, but then Micah showed up.

Micah was a good friend. As president of our brother fraternity, we did a lot of Greek-related activities together. He cared about all of the girls in Alpha Beta Omega, not just his girlfriend, A.J. I appreciated his chivalry when it came to our whole chapter, but the moment he stepped into this situation flanked by Jim and Tim, the Tongan twins, two massive football players who had pledged OBA in the fall, it escalated a now-uncomfortable conversation to the workings of a fistfight. The fact that Micah, Tim, and Jim were wearing their OBA letterman's jackets made it look like a basketball versus football throwdown was about to break out. I'd say it was a situation akin to something else I'd experienced in high school, but I went to an all-girls school where I was rather invisible.

"Can I help you?" De'Treshawn said.

"That depends," Micah replied, thankfully keeping his cool. "Is he bothering you?"

"Yes! He—" Tim slipped a hand over Jill's mouth and dragged her out of the fray.

"No, Micah. He's not bothering me."

"You heard her, white boy. You and the faggot patrol move along." As pasty and blond as Micah was, he also met De'Treshawn at an even six-four and he definitely wasn't gay. He also wasn't the kind of guy who thought being called gay was an insult. Micah laughed and I may have snickered a little as his girlfriend A.J. walked up and slid her tiny hand into Micah's massive palm.

"Hey, baby," A.J. said as she looked cautiously between Micah and De'Treshawn. "What's going on?"

"The Boss here just throwing his slurs around and harassing Benny," Micah replied.

"It's not harassment if she like it, playa," De'Treshawn said.

"And I don't," I finally spoke up. "De'Treshawn, good luck on Saturday, and please feel free to never speak to me again."

"Was that clear enough for you?" Micah asked.

"Whatever, man." De'Treshawn licked his lips and stared at my breasts. "I'll peep you later."

I grunted dismissively and took the polite elbow Jim offered me. "You okay?" he asked sweetly.

"Yeah. I'm fine." Pissed, but fine.

We headed to the cafeteria with Micah and A.J. Tim followed with Jill tossed over his shoulder. When she giggled through her protesting I knew he'd gotten her to relax. Once we were a safe distance away from De'Treshawn Boss and friends, Micah sprang back to his normal cheerful self.

"You wanna come by and see our puppy later?" he asked.

"Benny, he's so cute," A.J. added.

"Can I come too?" Jill asked.

"Of course, Jilly Bean," Micah teased her, winking at me.

"Don't call me that," she pouted.

"Did you guys pick a name yet?" I asked, preparing myself for even more time with Jill.

Micah broke out in a huge smile. "Motherfucker."

Right, because what else would you name a puppy?

❖

That Saturday night, I found myself in the front row of the students' section of Madison Arena, with Jill chattering my ear off on the right and Samantha on my left, seemingly exhausted from the night before. Most Friday nights were movie nights in the Alpha Beta Omega house, and every movie night, the viewing quickly devolved into an orgy/feeding frenzy for my sorority sisters and our sister-queens. Rather than sit by and try to watch the movie or sit by and watch Tokyo try to weasel her way between Cleo and her feeders, I waited until the first half of *Dirty Dancing* was over before I offered Camila my neck. She was full, of course, but I always felt rude running from her the one night of the week every girl in the house gave from her vein.

I swallowed my orgasm with quiet dignity, thankful that Jill was busy feeding Ginger, and escaped back to my room unnoticed. I called Mama and thanked her for the Valentines and chocolates she'd sent me, finished some homework, then decided it was time for bed. Now in the middle of another night out with the girls, I tried to get comfortable in the narrow plastic seats. I regretted the thick sweater I picked for the walk over from the house. I'd peeled off my jacket, but I was still sweating.

There were a few announcements over the loudspeaker and the other team's players were announced as they took the court. I pulled out my phone, trying to ignore Jill's constant comments. Luckily, someone thought to save me.

"Jill." I looked up, shocked to see our sister-queen Faeth in her natural form, standing beside our seats. She looked nice. She'd straightened her usually curly hair and pulled it back into a ponytail. A gray mock-neck sweater, loose dark gray jeans, and a pair of white sneakers rounded out her outfit. She'd been a demon for over thirty years, but her constant trips back to her former home in New Zealand kept her accent in place. Tonight, though, she covered it, opening her *O*'s up in a perfect impersonation of a Baltimore native.

"What?" Jill replied.

"Skylar and Hollis want you to go sit with them." Faeth nodded up in the stands.

"Really?" Hollis and Skylar had been giving Jill the cold shoulder all year. They'd nicknamed her Jaws due to the metal in her mouth. They refused to give up the cruel name, but maybe Ginger had finally had a talk with them. I glanced behind us to see the two freshmen waving Jill up to their row. I looked up a little farther and caught Cleo's gaze.

She was in a different form, of course. Her hair was hanging longer, down to her shoulders, and was held back by a ruby-studded headband. Her face was similar to a Nigerian runway model I'd seen in a few magazines, but whose name I couldn't remember. She looked different from the neck up, but her body was the same. And Cleo had a way about her that would never fade. Plus, she had on another leather jacket she'd taken from Tokyo and she was sitting beside Andrew with her hand in his lap. She snarled at me with a cold grimace until I turned around. Just three more months and I'd never have to deal with her and her lack of social graces again.

"Yeah, go. Sit with them," Faeth said. "I'll keep Benny company." Jill weighed her options for a moment. A chance at friends, possibly for the next three years, or a few hours next to me.

"Do you mind?" she asked me.

"No, not at all. Go hang out with them. I'll see you back at the house." I mustered half a smile and patted her on the leg. She kissed me on the cheek, then squeezed around Faeth to get to the aisle. Faeth made herself comfortable beside me, propping her feet up on the railing that separated us from the first row of public spectators below. She draped her long arm on the back of my seat. I caught her scent, a light hint of fresh grass. It was an odd smell, but pleasant, and it suited Faeth.

"You're welcome," she said, nudging my leg. "I know she's been driving you nuts."

"Thank you. Your voice sounds too strange this way." I smiled at her.

"Just trying to fit in with the locals. Can I be your Valentine for the evening?"

"I'm not much for company, but sure."

The lights in the arena dimmed, and hip-hop music blasted above us. De'Treshawn and his four teammates were introduced, slapping hands and bumping fists with the rest of their team as they ran onto the court in their Maryland University warm-up suits. The purple and gold was a great combination, but the scheme did nothing to improve De'Treshawn's appearance. I watched him as they warmed up, fixated on his showboating and his small teeth. He really wasn't attractive.

"I'm pretty good at basketball, you know," Faeth said.

"Are you?"

"Yeah. You should see me. I'm all legs. I can dunk and everything."
Faeth laughed. I rolled my eyes, chuckling back at her. Considering
her strength, she could probably rip the hoop out of its supports. Our
conversation was interrupted by the team's equipment manager. I had
no idea what his name was, but he was out of breath and waving a
T-shirt from the aisle near us.

"Benny?" he panted.

"Yeah?" I frowned at him.

"This is for you." He held up the T-shirt closer to my face. A
sweaty Maryland University Basketball shirt, I guessed had been worn
at some point earlier in the evening. "From De'Treshawn."

My body temperature spiked with rage and my cheek twitched.
What the hell was his problem? "I don't want it."

"Please just take it. He'll give me so much shit."

"Kid." Faeth leaned forward. "She said she doesn't want it."

He looked Faeth over. Even though she was sitting, he could tell
that she was taller than him, and anyone could see, much stronger. And
even though I didn't check, I'm sure the rest of my chapter and the
OBA boys were watching. This wouldn't end well if he pushed the
issue. "Shit. Fine," he grumbled.

We watched as he shuffled his way back down to the court.
De'Treshawn took a warm-up shot, made it of course, then ran to
the bench to get the dirt on my response. It would be too much for
him to drop dead right there on the parquet floor and completely out
of the question for him to realize that maybe it was time to back off.
De'Treshawn looked up at me, unfazed as Faeth tightened her grip
around my shoulders, and blew me a kiss. I looked away.

"How long has that been going on?" Faeth asked.

"Doing recon for Camila?" My sister-queen would want to hear
about this. I just hadn't planned to tell her.

"No." Faeth laughed. "Just because you're not mine doesn't mean
I don't care."

"Four weeks, but don't worry about it. He'll realize I'm serious
when I don't cave before graduation." It was enough that Micah was
watching my back without my asking. I didn't need our sister-queens to
be paranoid. De'Treshawn was on my nerves, but he wasn't dangerous.
Just stupid.

"Okay." Faeth accepted my explanation with a shrug.

I watched the first half of the game with mild interest. The
starting five were severely lacking in basic teamwork fundamentals,

but De'Treshawn was untouchable from the three-point line, and his teammate, Ron Michaels, was just as skilled under the rim. By halftime, we were up by twenty. Finally, both teams left the court and the arena went dark.

"Ladies and gentlemen, your Maryland University Eagelettes." Our section erupted in hoots and calls for Maddie before the spotlight hit her. Maddie and her dance team did a three-minute routine to a pop mash-up. She made us all very proud as she executed her twists and flips in her sparkly purple unitard. I looked over at Ruth, a few seats down. She had tears in her eyes, watching her girlfriend dance her behind off. I joined in the cheering once they finished. Maddie waved up at us as she ran off the floor. The game sucked, but it was worth it to be there for her.

There were some announcements about a halftime shoot-out competition. Two lucky winners were called from their seats to match free throws with two recovering patients from the children's hospital.

"I'll be right back," Faeth said as she stood up. "You want something to drink?"

"Get me a Coke," Sam said.

"I'll have the same," I replied.

"Okay." Faeth smiled. "I'll be right back."

Cleo

Faeth slowly walked down the whitewashed cinder-block hallway under the guise of my cloak.

"You sure you want to do this?" she asked as she met me under an intense fluorescent light just outside the men's locker room.

"Yes. Take over." Faeth sighed, but took over the force of the cloak. I needed all my concentration to deal with De'Treshawn.

"He's just a harmless kid," Faeth said.

"Was that shit with the T-shirt harmless?"

"Yeah. Annoying and dumb, but harmless."

"Well, Andrew said he put his hands on her, so we're doing this. If Camila finds out, I'll tell her I worked alone."

"She won't believe you."

I smiled, flashing my fangs.

Soon, the team started filing out of the locker room, yelling and stomping as they rushed back to the court to seal the second half of the game with a victory. A few slapped the ceiling and pounded the walls as they went. I moved my head to the side to keep some senior from punching me in my invisible face. After a few seconds, I spotted that piece of shit De'Treshawn. He jogged past me and Faeth, a goofy grin on his face. I wasted no time getting inside his head. He was chanting the lyrics to some hype song they'd warmed up to, but not much else was going on inside his pea brain. I shifted deeper and planted the thought.

De'Treshawn stopped right in his sneakers.

"You okay, man?" his teammate asked, smacking him on the back.

"Yeah, I'll be right there. Just gotta take a piss right quick." De'Treshawn walked back toward the locker room, but I stopped him before he entered. Faeth checked the hall and the locker room for me one more time.

"You're clear."

I backed him against the wall with a hand on his throat. He gasped, feeling my skin on his, but he was blind to the source. And he didn't believe in ghosts. His breath fucking stank, but I convinced him to close his mouth before I puked from the odor.

I looked him in the eye, making myself completely visible. "Nod if you hear me." He obeyed. "De'Treshawn, nod if you understand." He nodded again dully, searching my eyes for answers.

"Do you know me?" I'd been long dead before he'd enrolled in Maryland University, but a bench near the center of campus had been dedicated in my name. People talked. People Googled.

"No." He shook his head.

"Good. You know Benny Tarver, though, don't you?" De'Treshawn's head flopped against the wall. He wasn't all that intelligent, but his mind was strong. He wanted me out of his brain, and he was exhausting himself trying to shake me loose. "Look at me." His eyes focused back on mine.

"Do you know Benny Tarver?"

"Yes," he replied.

"Stay away from her. Do you understand me?"

"Yes."

"Good. Stay away from her. If you don't, I will find out and I will kill you. Do you understand?"

He swallowed nervously. "Yes."

"Good, because I will kill you. Also, I'd like it if you never put your hands on another girl again," I told him, releasing Andrew's memory of his fingers gripping Benny's wrist. "You know what I'm talking about, right?"

"Yes. I won't do it again."

"Good. Now, when you get back out on the court, I want you to miss five shots in a row."

"Cleo!" Faeth yelled. I fucked up, but it was my ass, not hers. I held up my hand to hush her protest. She kept her opinion to herself, but she kicked the wall, hissing at me.

"How many shots are you gonna miss?" I asked De'Treshawn.

"Five."

"Good." I cleared all memory of me out of his head, leaving my simple instructions and very serious threats in my wake. "Now go play with your friends." I shoved him toward the court and watched as his stumbling turned into a casual jog. He'd be fine.

Faeth punched me in the shoulder. "Threatening to murder him wasn't enough? You want him to fuck up the game?"

"Why do you care?"

"I don't, but Dalhem said—"

"Our master doesn't give a shit about college basketball, okay? It's fine. Baby Dick Boss will be a little bummed 'cause he fucked up the game, but that's it. It'll be fine. Come here." I led Faeth down the hall to the vacant handicapped bathroom.

"What?" she asked as I locked the door behind us.

"Give me your form."

Her mouth popped open to argue, but it was useless. I was stronger than her, my blood much more powerful. But suddenly Faeth's shoulders sagged as she figured out what I'd planned to do.

"She'll know it's you."

"Just do it." I didn't know why—yeah, I did. I felt this bizarre need to be the last person to touch Benny. The girls in the house didn't count. I wanted to mark her in some way. I knew De'Treshawn would follow my orders, but I had to erase him from Benny's mind or at least try to distract her. I couldn't explain the urge. She didn't deserve it, but it was just something I needed, the control.

Faeth and I grasped palms, and when she closed her eyes, I took her complete form, including her clothes, and gave her mine. I opened my eyes and looked down at my new body. A few inches taller and a little wider. The jeans she picked were actually pretty comfortable. The ponytail she was sporting was a little too tight. I repeated the word "home" a couple times to check the accent she'd been using with Benny.

"She and Sam asked for Cokes," Faeth told me.

"Okay. Don't try to fuck Andrew. He'll know it's you."

"Asshole."

Faeth headed back to the stands while I waited in line at the concession counter. The game was about to start when I got back. Benny stared at me curiously as I handed her and Sam their drinks. I paused a moment to look at Sam. She looked like shit. Meanwhile, Benny was eying me.

"What's up?" I said, trying to imitate Faeth's usually light demeanor.

"Nothing. I...nothing." Benny looked behind us. I glanced back and watched as Faeth's subtle behavior slowly gave me away. She had a hand on Andrew, but she was a little tense. I was never tense with him. And she didn't react to Benny's stare. No matter what, Benny always got a reaction out of me. She turned back to the court and drew in a deep breath through her nose. She froze and I knew she had my scent. Oh well.

I settled in and slipped my arm around the back of her seat. A second later, I found myself touching her shoulder. It had been a while since we'd been this close. Her callousness had a physical presence of its own, and I didn't like to get near it. I didn't want it to rub off on me. But De'Treshawn changed the game, changed my needs, so I savored the moment, let my fangs drop behind my lips as they throbbed. Her smell. Her body heat. She was hot and uncomfortable, I could tell, but she would never let on. And she didn't ask me to move my arm. No one could ever see Benny squirm. That wasn't part of her plan.

De'Treshawn did exactly what I told him to do. Three tanked three-pointers and two horribly missed lay-ups. After the last shot, his coach pulled him out of the game. With him on the bench, Maryland University barely won by three points. We filed out slowly and waited for Maddie outside the arena. After she bought my Faeth routine, I shot a text to Andrew, telling him I'd be back to sleep with him later, and joined the girls as they walked back to the house. They were all a-titter about some party the Sigma boys were throwing after the game. I'd pop in and check on them throughout the night, after I checked on a few other things. They didn't notice that Benny and I were slowly lagging behind.

Before we reached our yard, Benny grabbed my hand and held me back. It took everything I had not to growl at her or laugh in her face. Her bravado was hilarious.

"What did you do to him?" she seethed.

"Exactly what you wanted me to do...princess." Something in her blue eyes wilted my anger away, along with Faeth's guise. I watched Benny's face as her fears were finally confirmed. She hadn't imagined my smell. Faeth hadn't been acting a little strange. She'd been with me for half the night and she'd hated it. I leaned down and, foolishly, I licked her neck. She tasted better than I remembered, like sweet cream. She shuddered and wobbled closer to me.

This was the part she couldn't fight. For everything Benny thought she knew, she was never able to grasp one simple fact. She needed someone to love her and to touch her in a certain way. I was the only person who could give that to her, and she'd fucked it up. Would she admit that to herself? No, never. Benny was never wrong. Still, her body betrayed her. Her tits remembered how well I'd sucked them. Her clit hadn't forgotten the loving treatment it got from me. Her whole body remembered how hard I could tug and spank. Her footing gave way and she stepped a little closer. Sweet almonds and vanilla flooded my nose. I embraced her, another stupid move, grasping her ass with both my hands. I couldn't say what I was thinking. My pussy was in control.

My fangs pricked her skin, and my tongue and lips followed, easing the pain away. I wanted to bite her. My fangs ached with the need. And in that same moment, I wanted to snap her neck. *She doesn't deserve this*, I reminded myself. She didn't deserve me. I repeated the motions, my lips, my tongue, my teeth, feeling her blood pulse harder against its hold in her vein, until a slight whimper escaped from her mouth. It would be so easy for her, if she would just take a moment to see. If she could just understand where we went wrong, I would have ended her suffering right there and then. But that was asking too much from a version of Benny that never existed. A version of Benny I used to love. A version I'd made up.

"I have to go," she whispered tightly, right on cue. We'd reached the limits of her control.

"I'm sure you do." I released her and watched her quickly walk back into the house.

CHAPTER FIVE

Cleo

I lounged in Tokyo's den on the mountain of pillows and cushions she liked to call a couch, throwing in the air a baseball I'd taken from one of the boys across the street. It thudded against the ceiling above my head before dropping back down into my palm. It wouldn't be long before I made a nice dent in the black plaster. Andrew was catching up on his own much-needed sleep. I'd sent Tokyo down to Moreland's, just to get her out of my hair. She wouldn't come back quietly, but she would at least be somewhat sated. I needed time to think.

I'd been avoiding all contact with Benny for a few days, but I couldn't stop thinking about her, even when I was with my girls. De'Treshawn had followed orders nicely and left Benny alone, so the boys told me. There was something more I felt I should do. It was the clock and the calendar. In this body, I had all the time in the world. I didn't age. Rarely tired, as long as I had blood. I would always be this way. Doing something about De'Treshawn Boss's efforts to step to Benny reminded me how stupid I was for ever caring about her. She couldn't even thank me for getting that piece of shit out of her hair. Instead...instead nothing. We were back in the same place.

I needed to acknowledge how worthless my life had become. Immortal, and all I can think about is this bitch that never cared whether I lived or died.

As the baseball slammed into the ceiling again, Camila appeared on the other side of Tokyo's door. I was surprised that she knocked.

"Come in," I said. Ginger appeared beside her before they opened the door. They came and sat on the floor beside me. "What's up?"

"You tell us," Camila said.

"Uh, I'm just lying here. You came looking for me."

"De'Treshawn Boss?" Camila said. I got that Ginger and Camila were demon-bound. I got that they were married and took this whole queens-in-control thing very seriously. Technically, I had to answer to them both, Ginger as queen of our nest and Camila as my maker, but I really fucking hated when they did that good cop/bad cop/Mom/best friend shit. I saw them glance at each other out of the corner of my eye. One last silent meeting of the minds before they laid into me.

"Who ratted me out?" I asked.

"No one ratted you out. We're just worried. What is going on with you?" So Ginger would be friend cop this time.

"Nothing," I replied.

"It's not nothing. Listen, Cleo. I know your breakup with her was difficult, but you need to deal with this situation with Benny," Camila said. "You don't have to coddle her like the other girls, but you can't threaten guys who show an interest in her."

"Whatever. He did more than show interest in her and you know it. Shouldn't *you* be protecting her from guys like that? She's your pet. Isn't that your job?" I ignored Camila's growl and threw the baseball at the ceiling again. This time it made a little dent in the plaster.

"My job is to protect her. De'Treshawn wasn't going to hurt her and *you* know it. You aren't protecting her. You're screwing with her head. You're practically stalking her."

"I'm stalking her?" I looked Camila right in the eye. I couldn't top her in a fight, but she was tempting me to try. Ginger glanced at us both, then slid her hand into Camila's lap.

"Both of you, stop."

I looked away and fired another shot at the ceiling. Camila sighed. "You know this isn't about me. That's not why we came here. You know how important Benny is. We can't help you if you cross Dalhem."

"Fuck Dalhem," I muttered.

"Oh, fuck Dalhem?" Camila's dander was right back up again.

"Yes." I let the baseball drop to the floor behind me as I sat up. "Fuck him. He doesn't give a shit about me, so why should I give a shit about him? All he cares about is Benny's precious feelings. I could have ripped De'Treshawn's head off his spine and licked his face like a lollipop. Dalhem would have slapped me on the wrist for getting blood on the floor, but just because it has something to do with Benny, you two have to come in here so we can have a very special episode of *Everybody Loves Benita*. Why do you think I hate her so much?"

"You don't hate her," Ginger replied.

"Whatever. It's his fault she acts like an entitled princess. It's his fault you let her do whatever the hell she wants."

"Is that what you really think?" Ginger asked.

"Yeah. It is. You said it yourself." I motioned toward Camila. "We have no control over these girls. Once we're bound, they walk all over us. We give them whatever they want, whenever they want, as long as they are safe. But with Benny, neither of you can even say no to her, even when she's being a complete dick. Which makes no sense for you, Ginger. You're not even bound to her. If it weren't for Dalhem, you'd tell her when she's acting the ass out, but you don't. You're afraid of the holy master, so his little brat gets whatever she wants. She's president of this chapter and she could give less of a shit about the sorority or the girls and *you* both know it."

"So who do we blame for you?" Camila said "Who's turned you into this out-of-control asshole? Who told you it was okay to behave like this? We know you have Andrew following her around during the day, Cleo. I know that you fucking licked her. I could smell you all over her neck. I won't even get into how not okay I am with that. And that has nothing to do with Dalhem."

"Who the fuck told you about Andrew?"

"Faeth," Ginger replied. "She's worried about you too."

"You say it like I'm a junkie. I know what I'm doing. Just leave it alone. Okay?"

"No. We won't. You could have fucked up De'Treshawn's brain forever, not to mention his basketball career. What would you have wanted us to do then?"

I laughed. "De'Treshawn's basketball career? Are you serious?"

"We all have a responsibility here," Camila said. "But you can't see past your own selfish feelings. This has nothing to do with Dalhem. I know I gave this life to you, but you made a choice to stay in this house, and that choice did not include threatening or harming our feeders or innocent students."

"Well, which is it? Am I a life ruiner or a stalker?"

"Cleo." Ginger let out a deep breath. "We know you love Benny."

"I don't."

"Cleo." Ginger gave me that look. I know how my behavior came across, but that didn't mean she was right.

"No. You have no fucking idea what I went through with her.

You think you do, but you were human when it all went down," I told Ginger. "You still can't get inside her head. She let me in. I know what makes her tick and I know what she did to me. So don't tell me how I feel and how I should act."

"But I can tell you that we *care* how you two act to each other. Jesus. I just wish you two would get back together," she said.

I laughed so loud I was surprised none of the glass in Tokyo's apartment shattered. "Yeah, I won't be doing that."

"Well, you have to do something. You can't keep this up," Camila said.

"You're right."

"What does that mean?"

I stood and grabbed a change of clothes from Tokyo's closet. You'd have thought I'd grabbed an AK from the way Ginger and Camila were cautiously eying me when I came back into the room.

"It means you're right," I said. "I'm sick of this shit. I don't want to live like this anymore. I don't love Benny. That shit is just crazy, but I have to deal with her, and the sooner the better."

"What are you going to do?" Ginger asked.

"Don't worry. I'm not going to kill her. Just an honest conversation. Once and for all."

"Where are you going?" Camila asked.

"Not far."

I vanished to the Montgomerys' porch and made myself comfortable on their swing. All was quiet across the street in Mama and Daddy's house. If only I could get the same peace in my head. I texted Benny the address and told her where to meet me that weekend. She didn't answer, but if I knew anything about her, I knew she'd show.

Just to be sure, I called Faeth. She owed me for squealing. "Hey," she answered on the first ring. "Is everything all right?"

"Yeah. I need you to do me a favor."

Benny

I couldn't focus on media and culture, or my reading. I'd been doing my best to move on from what had happened the night of the game. Once again, Cleo had to turn my life into another one of her sick mind tricks. Our run-in had nothing to do with De'Treshawn, though

I was glad he'd backed off. Cleo wanted to hurt me. De'Treshawn merely presented an opportunity for her to insert herself where she didn't belong. This had been her game for years now, but after that night I knew I couldn't make it easy for her anymore. I wouldn't allow myself to care about what Cleo said or did any longer. I should have stopped her before she touched me or kissed me. It was a moment of weakness I vowed never to repeat again. She was sick, and I couldn't continue to feed into her behavior.

I had decided that moving on was all I could do. Trying to process my feelings would just make me more upset while Cleo went about her life with Tokyo in her lap and Andrew under her thumb. It was a kind of numbing ordeal, trying to push the emotions aside. I was slipping deeper into this state that crept over me recently. I cared less than I thought possible, wanted less. In truth, all I wanted was out. I wanted out of school and I wanted to move on from Alpha Beta Omega. I'd served my purpose. Camila had been fed and I knew how to live as a feeder. Now I wanted to get on with the rest of my life away from the silly, immature group responsibilities and away from Cleo.

But that would be too easy. I looked at my phone again. The text from Cleo was still up on the screen.

We need to talk. This Saturday night. Faeth will bring you.

The address was for some place in Virginia. Once I was alone, I'd Googled the place she'd planned to lure me so she could murder me once and for all.

"Where did you get this angled brush?" I glanced up from my homework and looked at Amy sitting at my vanity. She was busy digging through my makeup case.

"My mother orders them from some place in New York."

"She needs to hook me up with that info. My brushes? They suck."

"You can have that one. I haven't used it yet."

Amy smiled at me over her shoulder. "Thanks, B."

"You're welcome. And speaking of my mother…" My cell phone started vibrating in the crack of my textbook. I scooped it up and hit Answer. "Hi, Mama."

"Hello, angel. Are you busy right now?"

"Just hanging out with Amy and semi-studying. What's going on?"

"Your daddy and I wanted talk to you about something. Do you have a few minutes to video chat with your poor old parents?"

"Sure." I politely kicked Amy out, with the angled brush as a parting gift. Then I opened my laptop and pulled up my video chat client. A few moments later, I was face-to-face with my parents. My chest nearly seized up, I missed them so much. Mama was already in her pajamas, sitting up in bed sandwiched between Daddy and her favorite of our Chow Chows, Boomer. My Gus was probably under the bed.

"There must be some big news if we need to video chat," I said, trying to keep any hint of loneliness out of my voice. "What's going on?"

"It's about your love life, angel," Mama said.

"What?"

When Daddy smiled, his large fangs seemed to shine through the screen. "As you can see, your mama has failed my class on diplomacy for the fourth time."

"And your daddy seems to forget how much he hates sleeping alone," Mama jabbed right back.

"Diplomacy is nice, but what does it have to do with my love life?" *When we all know I don't have one.*

"Before we came to you with this proposal, your mother wanted to confirm that you were not in a relationship that she didn't know about."

"And you told her that there was no way that I would start dating someone and not mention it to her at all?" I said.

"Those precise words, my princess."

"Hey," Mama said. "You two be nice to me."

"No. I'm not seeing anyone. Is there some horrible senator's son you want to set me up with for diplomatic reasons?"

"Not exactly."

I was shocked to be having this conversation. My parents had always let me make my own choices. A setup was not something I expected. Mama's reply didn't put me at ease. It must have showed. "Now, baby, I told your daddy that this was your decision, but I agreed that he should at least have the chance for you to hear him out."

"Okay."

"Our next tu'lah is nearing. This year marks the hundredth year in our cycle." I was familiar with the gift-giving practices of Daddy and his demon-bourne brothers and sisters. Often large pieces of antiquities, lost treasures, and at times, pets were exchanged. Daddy's sister Canaan once sent him a set of bagpipes because she knew he loathed the sound they made. Every one hundred years there was an exchange of humans.

"You want to offer me?"

"No, baby—" Mama started.

"Paeno has asked for you. She would like you to go live with her in her palace in Beijing," Daddy said. I'd never met Paeno or any of his other siblings. The six of them rarely gathered, and when they did, it was in a secret location. I knew Paeno was powerful, the most powerful of their kind. I knew Daddy had to bend to her will. What I didn't understand was what she wanted with me, so I asked.

"My sister has always expressed an interest in you. She wants you for her mate," Daddy said so calmly I felt like I should be annoyed.

It was times like this I hated dealing with demons. Their lives weren't complicated by human emotions or daily stresses, but it was hard to understand their motivations and desires. I understood Daddy's love for Mama and that he cared for me, but there were many moments that I simply had to accept the things he did. I was foolish to think I would get a real explanation about Paeno and her desire to have me. I couldn't imagine that she wanted me for my looks. I could only think that she wanted me because I was the closest any of them had to a mortal child. Keeping it in the family, I supposed.

But that element of why was second on my list of concerns. She didn't want me as a feeder. She wanted me as her wife. I knew I'd be bound to another vampire after graduation, but I never thought I would mate one. Mating a human is the closest a demon can get to marriage, albeit one large step from a na'suul bond between demons. When I thought about becoming someone's mate, I envisioned being at Cleo's side. It bothered me that after all this time, after the shit she'd pulled recently, that I still wanted those vows to exist between us. They never would. They weren't a part of either of our plans.

"What are you thinking about, angel?" Mama asked.

"Uh, I'm just thinking about seeing you guys again. China is far."

"Your daddy can come to you in a kitten's blink and I'll only be a plane ride away."

I dropped my pen and looked at Mama on the screen. "Do you want me to do it?"

"I want you to be happy."

"And you don't think I'm happy now." The look on Mama's face said it all.

"I think you deserve something different and special."

"Paeno does sound different." I sighed and shuffled my pen around on the smooth pages. "Daddy, what do you think?"

"I think there is no better demon I could offer you. Camila is the best of my children, and she is not truly mine. Paeno will treat you like the princess you are, and she will give you everything you could ever want or need."

"No other reason?" I asked. I had a feeling there was something he was leaving out.

Daddy let out a deep breath through his nose, and though it was only a slight movement, I could see his horns shifting under his skin. I knew what was coming. "I don't want you to hold on to the idea that you and Cleo will ever be together."

That time, I felt like my chest did cave in. I swallowed and tried to blank out my emotions. "I don't think that."

"Baby, we know you still love her," Mama said.

"I don't love her."

"You do not speak the truth," Daddy replied.

I looked away from the screen and bit down on the inside of my lip as hard as I could. I wasn't about to argue with my parents about this. Daddy had never liked Cleo, and Mama was nearly as devastated as I was when she dumped me. Another conversation about our end and my emotional demise would get us nowhere.

"I thought maybe…I thought being with Paeno would help you forget about her," Mama said.

So it was that obvious, I thought. Cleo had done me in to the point that moving me halfway around the world to bind me to the most powerful demon on the planet was the only thing my parents thought would clear Cleo from my mind. I wanted to toss my pen across the room and slam my laptop shut.

"When does Paeno want an answer by?" I asked Daddy.

"She seemed to think graduation should give you enough time."

"That's plenty of time. I'll think it over."

"Remember, baby. It's your decision," Mama said. I tried not to snap at her when I answered.

"I know. Thanks. I'm going to finish studying. I love you."

"As we love you, my princess," Daddy said.

I closed my laptop and my book. Studying was out of the question. I grabbed another box of cookies Jill had left outside my door, oatmeal raisin this time, then crawled into bed. I had no idea what Cleo had planned to say to me once I arrived in Virginia, but I would tell her that I was done with her, for good. I couldn't let her affect me anymore.

CHAPTER SIX

Benny

It was a long three hours to Richmond. Clear skies turned to a light rain and then a light snow as we made our way south, which was pretty backward. Faeth sang along with every single seventies rock and pop song she could find on the radio. She seemed partial to Fleetwood Mac and the Eagles. I sat beside her in silence. Emotions I'd worked hard to ignore worked themselves up inside me. Several times, I felt the panic nearing the surface, but I pushed it down. I had to keep it together. Cleo was not worth losing control over.

Finally, we slowed on a heavily wooded road. I could see some lights up ahead, a break in the trees, but Faeth pulled my car off to the side, then stopped.

"She said she'd meet us here," Faeth said. Right on cue, Cleo walked out of the trees into the path of the headlights, bundled warm in a gray hoodie and her leather jacket, not that she needed the heat. Faeth killed the engine and the illumination and handed me my keys.

"Just call me, right? I'll come pick you up."

"Thanks."

She vanished, leaving me in the car alone. I looked ahead, and once my eyes adjusted, I could see Cleo silhouetted against the darkness and the falling snow. I climbed out of my SUV. As I approached her, I had to fight back tears. I'd been preparing for this talk for days. I had no answer for Paeno, but I was sticking to my plan when it came to Cleo. But seeing her again made me miss the Cleo that used to be. I loved that Cleo, her smile and her laugh. This Cleo's whole presence swirled with a menacing anxiety, spiked with anger so deep nothing I could do or say could extinguish it.

I took a deep breath and straightened my shoulders. I wouldn't cry.

"Come on," Cleo said. "It's just up the street."

I didn't say a word, just followed her fifty or so yards to the clearing. There stood a church, old and brick. Beside it was a smaller brick house. A few cars were parked around, not really in designated spaces. There was no clear parking lot or even defined boundaries to the land.

"What are you thinking?" Cleo asked me quietly. We'd stopped walking. She let me take it all in.

"I thought it would be bigger," I told her honestly.

"You didn't Google it forty times?"

"No." I still didn't like thinking about Cleo's family, especially her mother, so I didn't look up anything about their lives or their church. I didn't want to know.

"You surprise me every day." Cleo's sarcasm made me withdraw even more. "Saturday worship ended an hour ago, but my mama is still here."

I almost turned around and went back to my car, but Cleo grabbed my hand. I didn't want to see Cynthia Jones. The last time I'd seen her was the day she came with her husband and Cleo's brothers to clean out her room in the ABO house. Cleo had already kicked me out of her life, and I had to pretend my tears were for mourning the loss of their daughter and not my lover. I had to nod somberly when Mrs. Jones thanked me for being Cleo's friend when all I wanted to do was tell her the truth. I loved her daughter and her daughter loved me. *We had plans before the accident*, I wanted to say. *Plans you wouldn't approve of, but I don't care what you think*. I'd skipped Cleo's funeral. I couldn't pretend with her family anymore.

Cleo hid us beneath her cloak and we waited until two women came through the front door.

"Did you see the way he was weaving and slurring?" one said to the other.

"Drunk as a skunk on payday." They both shook their heads and laughed as Cleo pulled me inside.

The sanctuary was empty but for Cynthia Jones, who stood up in her pulpit. A worn Bible was open in front of her. Her words were quiet, but her gestures were animated. Cleo favored her, their faces very similar, but gray was starting to streak Mrs. Jones's hair, which she had done up in an elegant, outdated French twist.

We sat near the back in a wooden pew, surrounded by the familiar smell of used hymnals and prayer books. I fought the urge to strip off my jacket. It was a million degrees in there, the furnace pumping against the cold outside, mixed residual heat from the hundred people who had recently praised their Lord. Of course, I started sweating. I didn't belong there.

Suddenly, Cleo's father came from a door off to the left. He held up a glass of water to Cleo's mother.

"Here you go, my sweet lady," he said. His words slurred together.

"Go lie down downstairs," Mrs. Jones suggested, but Barry made his way up the pulpit steps and laid a sloppy kiss on Mrs. Jones's cheek.

"I think I will. The spirit of your sermon tonight? Girl, you wore me out," he said. She gently pushed him away.

"I'll wake you up when I'm fittin' to head home."

"Whatever my girl wants." Barry slowly made his way out of the room, singing Al Green as he went. It wasn't a smooth exit.

When he was gone, Mrs. Jones sagged against the wood surrounding her, probably praying that her family didn't have that kind of secret to keep. Sucks being like everyone else, I thought. Eventually, she went back to her scripture and what I assumed was preparation for the Sunday morning service.

"Why did you bring me here?" I asked Cleo.

"I wanted you to see what I can't touch. Every night I come to see my mama, and I can't say anything to her. I can't hug her. I wanted you to see what I lost."

I couldn't fight being pissed. I thought we'd talk about us, maybe the sorority and De'Treshawn. I didn't want to rehash the past like this. I knew what Cleo had lost, but I also knew exactly what she had gained. Her freedom.

I looked at the burgundy carpet and my boots. This church didn't have kneelers.

"What did your mother know about us?" I asked.

"She knew you were my best friend."

"Exactly." I stood and walked to the door. Cleo quickly followed me. I walked outside back into the cold. I didn't care if Cynthia Jones saw the entrance to her church swing open and closed without anyone coming or going. Maybe she needed to believe in ghosts.

I only made it as far as the road before Cleo stopped me with a hand on my shoulder. I turned to face her.

"I told you I wasn't ready," she said. "But I was going to tell her. After graduation, like I promised you."

Cleo used to have a lot of qualities I admired in a person. She was brave and confident. She was kind and selfless. She didn't let anyone boss her around, anyone but her mother. We would have gone on forever as friends and then roommates and then secret lovers when Cleo finally caved to her mother's pressure and married some man of her mother's choosing. I loved her enough, though, to hold on to the hope that she would follow through on that promise.

"No, you weren't. You wanted to, but I saw how things were, Cleo. You were never going to tell her."

Her nostrils flared as she clenched her fangs to her bottom teeth. Her anger as a demon was frightening, but I wasn't afraid of the human who controlled the vampire inside. It was the human you have to fear, Daddy had told me. Not the animal.

"How was me not being out to my mama any worse than you keeping us a secret? Why couldn't I meet *your* mama? Why couldn't we tell the girls and Camila? We were both feeding her. We could have enjoyed that together," Cleo said.

"Because what we did was none of their business."

"But do you see how that made me feel, Benny? You shoved me right back into the closet. For two years, I kept telling myself that I was fooling around with Paige and Barb because of our blood bond with Camila. But I fell in love with you. I knew for sure I was gay and then you made me hide."

I shoved my hands into the pockets of my coat and walked closer to the car. Cleo was getting louder and louder, and I knew her cloak had dropped. The last thing we needed to do was alert whoever was left in the church to our presence.

"Dammit, Benny," Cleo growled as she trailed behind me. "Why don't you get it? Joining ABO, that sorority, that was the first time in my life I ever felt like myself. I wasn't hiding. I wasn't pretending. And then I met you and—"

I turned and gave her a dramatic shrug. "And I ruined everything. I ruined your life. I killed you." I was sick of her blaming me.

"No, Benny. Lord Jesus, will you just listen to me? When you told me you wanted to be my girlfriend, you have no idea how that felt. You were nothing like Paige or Barb or Danni. I wanted to tell everyone."

"And did you ever think of what they would have said about us?" Cleo looked at me, confused. "You could have had any girl in that house, except Ginger, but you picked me. And it would have taken Samantha five seconds before she started telling people that Daddy had Camila force you, or pay you, to be my girlfriend. I know what I looked like, what we looked like together. You were with the fat girl, and no one would have taken that seriously."

"You think I saw you as the fat girl, not the most beautiful girl I ever laid my eyes on? Not someone whose intelligence and independence blew me away?"

"I know what people say."

"Who gives a fuck what people say! It's just gossip."

"Gossip's screwed up my life before, and I wasn't going to let it happen again. I keep what I love closest to my heart. I didn't want you to meet my mama because you matter to me, and I couldn't stand the thought of you judging her. I told you. I told you I was sick of being judged and I didn't want to even think of all the bullshit that would be whispered about us. I'm not a fan of speculation. I don't handle it well, but you seem to love it. Everything has to be high drama with you."

Cleo's face suddenly scrunched up. She was going to cry. "Do you know what happened to me that day?"

I swallowed the pain in my throat. "I don't—"

"My body caught on fire, Benny. I was crushed between a car and truck and I was on fire. I was in pieces for *hours* before Camila got to me. You have no idea—" Cleo covered her mouth and she tried to pull it together. "I was driving back to you. And I died, Benny. I wasn't knocked out. I died. And to be given a second chance like this…I knew I would get to see you. I knew you would be happy that I was a demon. I didn't forget what you wanted, but you didn't even give me five minutes. You didn't ask me if I was okay. You knew I was changed and you didn't call right away to ask Camila how I was. All you wanted to do was feed me. All you cared about was yourself."

"That's not true," I muttered.

"How was it, then, Benny? My memory is crystal clear. You tell me what details I'm getting wrong."

"I did care about you, but I couldn't fix things. I couldn't turn back the clock and stop that wreck from happening. So I moved on and I offered you my blood like a feeder should."

There was no sobbing or heavy breathing, but tears were running down her face at this point. She wiped them away, but that didn't really help. I couldn't handle it. I just—Cleo had pain that wasn't mine to heal. She'd suffered, I wouldn't pretend she hadn't, but I also couldn't pretend that she couldn't get over it either. She was capable of anything, but she wanted to hold on to this hurt. That's why she stalked her parents. That's why she tortured me day after day. She didn't want to let go of the pain. I didn't want to be a part of it. She was on her own.

"Why do you expect me to be someone else?" I asked her. "When we got together, I told you exactly what I wanted, and as time went on and things got deeper, did I change? Did I?"

"No," Cleo replied. She took another deep breath and the tears seemed to stop.

"No. I kept right on telling you exactly what I wanted, and for some reason, you are still shocked that I stuck to my convictions. This is what I mean, Cleo. Before me, your whole life was a lie. You lied to your family. You lied to your friends. To your church. And then you meet someone who tells you the truth about who they are and what they want and how they want you to be a part of their life, and you're surprised when it was you that was expecting something else. You were expecting me to change. You wanted me to be someone else. Just like your mother."

"I was going to tell her." The pathetic volume of her claim barely reached me through the snow.

"And then what? You remember what you told me?"

Cleo remained silent.

"Now your memory is faulty. We were in your room studying and you were telling me about your mother and her relationship with white people. Remember what you said?"

Her anger spiked again. "I wasn't proud of it, and it's not like I agreed with her."

"But you remember what you said. You said, 'Mama would never approve of us. It's sick. She'd shit a chicken if I brought home a white boy in high school. Forget bringing home a white girl.' And then I told you a little about my real daddy." I could see it plain as day on her face. She did remember. "We didn't stand a chance with your family, Cleo. Not one chance. I'm a lesbian. I'm not black, and your mother would have politely kicked us both out on our asses, and for some reason, you want me to be upset that this woman, who made you hate yourself for who you are, you want me to feel bad because she's not in our life anymore."

"Jesus, Benny. She's my mom. I know what would have happened, but can't you see that I would still miss her?"

"No. I can't." That was the truth. "I don't miss my daddy at all. He treated me the same way your mama treated you and—"

"Wait, back it up. He tortured you over your weight and you're comparing that—"

"To your mother being a homophobic bigot who made you feel worthless? Yes, I'm comparing those things." It seemed Cleo had forgotten some of the other details she'd shared with me.

"I wanted to feed you. I won't lie about that. But I knew what would happen with your mother if you stayed human, and I figured if you became a demon, then you wouldn't have to say good-bye. She would have those happy memories of you and you would have those happy memories of her. If you really found the courage to do it, you'd never have to disappoint her by coming out to her with your white, very gay girlfriend. I thought you'd be happy."

"Well, I'm not happy. At all," Cleo said. "I just want—I wanted a chance. Even if she kicked me out of the family, I wanted to start *my own* family so I could come back and say 'See, Mama? I can do this.'"

"Why are you living for that woman, Cleo?" I yelled. I'd fucking had it with her delusional view of Cynthia Jones. "She wasn't living for you."

"I wanted to come back and show her my family, perfect just the way I wanted it. I wanted to marry you. I wanted us to have a baby, but what the fuck kind of parent can I be like this? I can't take my child to school. I can't take them to the park during the day. I still want those things—"

"We still can have them! Mama and Dalhem raised me for two-thirds of my life and I'm fine."

"This is fine? Being cold and closed off is fine?"

"If that's how you feel about me, then why don't you just leave me alone? Why, every time I see you, are you snarling at me? The constant comments, the constant digs. Why are you messing with people like De'Treshawn? Cold and closed off sounds a lot better than being a hyperaggressive, hypocritical bitch who welcomes leeches like Tokyo. You may hate me, Cleo, but at least I'm not cruel. At least I'm honest.

"Speaking of honesty," I went on, "how long did you wait for me to call before you started fucking Andrew? Were you still so in love with me then?"

"Fuck you, Benny. You know I had to feed. He cares about me. He's been there for me this whole time."

"Because you dumped me. So tell me again. What are we doing here?"

"Absolutely nothing," she said with a sudden calm that did scare me. And like that, Cleo vanished. The force of her emotions lingered, though. They surrounded me in the darkness as I made my way back to the car. I was shaking by the time I got inside, but it wasn't from the cold.

I turned on my car and pumped up the heat before I texted Faeth. She called me back.

"Hey. Ready to go?"

"You can send someone else if you don't want to drive, but I don't think Camila wants me to come back alone."

"Don't worry. I got you."

Faeth appeared in the driver's seat. "See."

"Hey."

"You okay?"

"Yeah," I said. Like always, I was fine.

CHAPTER SEVEN

Cleo

I hid in the trees and waited for Faeth to get Benny back on the road. One day I would learn. One day I would figure out that you can't change people, but not tonight.

I couldn't breathe.

Violently, I tore through my clothes. My arms became wings and my feet became claws. I took flight, higher, through trees and over their tops, through gusts of wind that pounded bits of snow against my face. We always felt the sun at our back, day or dead of night, so I flew west, out of the snow, away from the impending sunrise, as fast and as far as I could until I knew I had to stop.

I became human again in the rotted-out base of a massive, fallen tree. When my sister-queens found me, a whole minute later thanks to our queen bond, I was a shaking, sobbing, naked mess. The wood scratched at my legs, but all I could think of were the shitty things Benny had said. I repeated them to myself as if I needed to remember every single word. I needed my heart to finally catch up with my brain.

"Cleo," Camila said cautiously as she began to climb up the roots, but I shook her off. Whenever I was hurting, she turned into the disciplinarian. I didn't want to hear how it was all my fault for even trying to talk to Benny. Camila would probably throw in some bit about how upset Benny was now and how I'd have some explaining to do when Dalhem came around to put his foot in my ass. I didn't need a lecture. I needed to get drunk and pass out in my own puddle of suffering. But alcohol did nothing for vampires besides burn like hell going in and coming out. I'd settle for crying naked in the forest before I got another fucking lecture.

"Will all of you please—" I coughed and tried to dry my face with my hands. "Just leave me alone."

"Guys," I heard Ginger say. One by one, they vanished. First Natasha and Kina, then Tokyo, even though she didn't want to. She was in my head, trying so hard to tell me she loved me, but I didn't want to hear it. She didn't love me any more than Benny did.

I know Camila hesitated, but soon Omi and I were alone. I knew from her scent. She came closer, and all I could smell was sunshine and salt and the sand. She climbed into the tree beside me and pulled me into her arms.

Omi and I had never been close. Tokyo, Faeth, and I, and even Kina sometimes, we still lived like we were in college, but Omi seemed like she had this whole adult life outside of the house. A wife, another home. She was cool, but we just didn't kick it like that. Now, though, I let her hold me. I sobbed and sobbed with my head against her chest.

"Tell me what happened, my dear."

I told her what I could. It's hard to talk with your whole face leaking, but I think I got the gist across.

"Cleo, Cleo. She won't change because you push her. That's not how humans work. That's not how we work. I've known Benita since she was a small girl. This is her. This is her way." I hadn't expected to hear that from her, but she was right. Benny was exactly who she'd been when we met, only this time our relationship was different. "You have to let her go. She may come back. She may not, but you have to let her be. Are you hearing me?"

"Yeah."

"You have to let it out too, though. Grieve if parts are worth grieving for. You can grieve for your family too, Cleo. I don't believe you've done that." Omi was right. They were still alive and I was clinging to the idea that I would talk to Mama again. That Daddy would hold me again the way Omi was holding me, but I wouldn't be crying. I'd be smiling and Daddy would be laughing and teasing Maxwell for something silly like the low tread on his wife's tires. None of that would happen, and Benny knew it. I watched my family nearly every night because part of me believed I would come to life somehow. I'd never let my family go, because they weren't dead. I never considered grieving for them. But the truth was I had to mourn myself.

I don't know why I thought Benny would listen to me. She and her mama were close. I thought maybe if she could see just how much I missed my mama, Benny could see how much I needed her to apologize.

And that's when I saw exactly where I'd gone wrong. I'd been so angry with Benny for all this time, and rightfully so. She was glad I was dead. Who the fuck is glad for that kind of shit? I spent days analyzing how cold she was; still, I failed to see that I was looking past a major flaw in myself. I wanted Benny even though she didn't give a shit about me. I wanted her to help me in getting on with my healing.

I needed her in my life because at one point she had been the one thing that made my life bright. She had been it for me. That future we talked about, fought over, that dream was something I still wanted so badly it hurt. Standing there in the snow, I finally saw the truth. Benny was not interested in me. She was interested in the demon, and when she couldn't have it, she'd shut down. She would never see that my human still mattered to me. I was dead, but every part of my heart was still beating and it beat for her.

"Why doesn't she care?" I sobbed.

"I don't know, dear. I don't know. But you'll be okay. I swear it to you. You'll be okay."

Omi held me for a long time, sometimes rocking me and singing quiet songs I'd never heard before. When she wasn't singing, we were both quiet, listening to the sounds of the woods. Eventually, I felt the tingle of the sun.

"I don't want to go back," I told Omi.

"We don't have to." She pulled me closer and willed me to shift with her. As large coyotes, we crawled deeper into the tree base. I came to, still covered in fur, and saw the rays of the sunset breaking through the trees, Omi's equally hairy body wrapped tight next to mine. She raised her head, letting out a small whine.

I'm not ready yet, I thought. She made another small noise of agreement and went back to sleep. Around midnight, we shifted again and stretched. I sat back in the tree while Omi walked a bit. Kina came with a blanket for me. They'd found my shredded clothes and my cell phone. She didn't ask any questions, though. When she left, I slept some more.

For two nights, we sat in the tree. I thought of a lot of things. Mama and Daddy. My brothers. Benny. And stupid things like an episode of *Sex and the City* I'd made Nat watch with me. Charlotte was talking about how long it takes to get over a breakup. I wondered how you would multiply it in demon years. I thought about my old friends who were still human. Danni and Barb and Paige. Did they have this sort of drama with their demons? Probably not. This drama was something special. Even Kina with her steady stream of monogamous relationships with humans, which always ended badly, didn't bring this level of over-the-top to her breakups.

I went from overwhelmingly distraught to numb, gradually. Soon, though, I couldn't ignore my body's needs. Just as the sun set on the third day, I crawled out from under Omi's furry frame and shifted back. Omi stretched and yawned, then did the same. I stood and wrapped myself in the blanket as she put back on her dress. The whole front was stained light blue from my tears. I'd buy her a new one.

"I'm hungry," I told her. My voice sounded terrible.

"Can you vanish?"

"Yeah, I think so."

Just in case I wasn't telling the whole truth, she pulled me back into her arms and carried us through the air, back to the house.

❖

Andrew found me in Omi's shower. I'm sure Ginger let him know I was okay. He'd know if I were dead. He'd feel that. But still, he hadn't heard from me in three days. He appeared calm, but I could tell I had really freaked him out. We'd never gone more than a few hours without talking or texting. He stripped out of his clothes and got in the hot shower with me.

"Hey, honey." It felt good to have him close to me again, to smell him.

"Hey. Are you all right?"

I ran my hands over his chest and watched the water run down his stomach. "I am. I'm sorry I didn't call."

"It's okay." It wasn't.

Sliding my fingers around the back of his head, I pulled him down to me. I kissed the corner of his mouth, then his cheeks and his lips. My hunger got the best of me. "I'm sorry," I nearly growled. Watching his vein was too much. I couldn't be tender for much longer.

"It's fine. Feed."

I backed him into the wall and sank my fangs into his skin.

❖

After we dried off and dressed, Omi told us to hang out in her living room for a while. It was a welcome change from the woods. We stretched out on her white couch and Andrew gave me the rundown of the rest of his weekend. I knew he'd probably run into Benny at some point, but he didn't mention her. Listening to him reminded me of what I still had, even without her. I had amazing feeders, this one in particular, who truly cared for me, and at least one sister-queen who was willing to literally weather the elements until I reclaimed some semblance of my sanity.

When Omi came back, though, she had the cavalry with her, and all seven of them had intervention written all over their faces. I looked at my sister-queens, all seven of them beautiful and different and sick to death of me.

"Andrew, can we talk to Cleo alone?" Ginger said.

"Yeah, okay." He turned to me.

"I'll come find you," I reassured him.

"So," I said when it was finally demons only. "Let me guess. You think I'm crazy and you want to talk to me before I fly off the handle again?"

Camila answered first. "No, we think you're in love."

"Hmph." I grunted. Crazy sounded better.

"I know how you feel, though," Camila went on.

"With this shit, again." I groaned and rubbed my face. "You don't. I'm not saying you don't know the pain, but you don't know how this feels. Your families are gone. Ginger still has hers. My family is right there and there's nothing I can do about it, and the person I loved the most can't see anything beyond her own shit."

"She can, Cleo. She just—" Camila started up. Always with the infinite wisdom. I didn't want to hear it.

"Camila." Kina shook her head.

"What do you want to do?" Camila said.

"Are you kicking me out?"

"No!" Tokyo blurted out.

"No," Ginger agreed. "We just want you to be happy." She came over and sat beside me. Even though my back was up, I let Ginger hug me. "We just want to help."

"I want to stay. I don't want to pull the rug out from under Andrew like that either. But there's nothing you can do to help. I'm not over this shit with Benny." I looked up at Tokyo, who seemed to take particular offense to that confession. I looked away just as quickly. "But I need to deal with it. Like, really deal with it. I'll stay away from her and I'll keep it under control. I will."

"This is your first breakup?" Kina asked.

"Yeah."

"It's gonna suck for a while, believe me. But if you don't let it go, we might as well stake you in the sunlight right now."

"I know."

"It'll be okay, trust me. It will be okay," Omi said. She came and sat on my other side. For some reason, I believed her. Not in real terms, but her kind support gave me strength to at least try to move on.

"We love you and we want you here," Ginger said. "You'll stay and we will help you with Benny. Just promise us—"

"No more...I get it. No more all of that shit I was doing."

"And she's only here a few more months, yeah?" Faeth said. "It'll be shit for a little while, but then it'll be easier to move on once she's graduated."

I laughed. "Okay. I get it. I'll stay and I'm checking the crazy."

"I'm glad you're back," Tokyo said. "Our room is all set up for you." Translation: *I bought some new toy for you to use on me. I'm so glad you're back so we can fuck.*

"I—"

"I think you'll stay here for a little while," Omi said.

"I think that's a good idea," Camila and Ginger said at the same time.

"What about your girls?" I asked Omi. I was way too drained to cater to Tokyo's sexual desires, but she and I at least had a feed-and-fucking schedule worked out. I didn't want Omi's feeders to feel like I was putting them out.

"It's a big house," she said, squeezing my hands. Across the room, Tokyo sighed, then vanished.

Natasha rolled her eyes. "I'll go reason with her."

"Thanks."

She winked at me, then vanished after our resident crybaby.

"Rest up some more and then come talk to us," Camila said. She just had to lecture me somehow.

"So we can hang out," Ginger amended.

"I will." Ginger hugged me again then dragged Camila from the room, praise God. Faeth and Kina followed, leaving me alone with Omi.

"Are you sure about this? You've done a lot."

"If I were unsure of anything, I would tell you."

"Okay."

"In the meantime…" Omi walked over to the door. "You have some visitors."

Mel and Laura came into the room. Mel ran to me. Laura approached a little slower. I shifted to the middle of the couch, and the girls made themselves comfortable on either side. I instantly felt better with them around. They changed the whole climate of the room. In a few more months, I would lose them too.

"Are you okay?" Mel asked.

"Yes, I am. How was class today?" I asked them.

"Fine," Laura said. She'd changed her diamond nose stud back to a ruby. I brushed her white bangs out of her face.

Mel slid into my lap to get my attention. "We heard Benny was being a mega bitch."

"Mel." Laura scowled at her.

"We had a small misunderstanding, but I'm handling it," I said. "Don't worry."

"We were worried," Mel said. "We missed you."

"Is that so?"

Laura shifted to her knees on the couch cushion beside me and pulled her sweatshirt over her head. She didn't have anything on underneath.

"We missed you a lot," she whispered.

I wrapped my arm around Laura's waist and pulled her closer so Mel had to make room for her on my thighs. "You should show me how much."

As they began to kiss, I unzipped Mel's jeans and worked my hand down the back of her underwear. I watched them, squeezing her cheeks as Laura cupped her own breasts and tweaked her nipples.

Images of Benny staring back at me in the snow flickered through my mind, but I pushed them aside so I could focus on my girls.

I was their demon, after all.

I had responsibilities.

CHAPTER EIGHT

Benny

It was two nights and three days before I saw Cleo again. The drive back from Richmond had been just as awful as the ride down, with the added pain of Faeth asking me how I was every three or four minutes. Once we got home, I managed to avoid the girls for the rest of the night. I waited for Cleo to storm back some time before sunrise, pitching a fit to one of her sister-queens about how much of a bitch I was, but she didn't come back at all. Our sister-queens came and went as they pleased, but we usually saw them at least once a day. By the following night when Cleo apparently hadn't come back to the house or made an appearance across the street at the Omega Beta Alpha house, her feeders went to Camila.

When she wouldn't give them any details, beyond informing them that Cleo was alive, just not at home, they went to Tokyo. After she gave them her version of the story, Mel came and gave me a piece of her mind. Our relationship had been difficult since she and Laura volunteered to feed Cleo after she rejected me. Laura did try not to rub their sexual exploits with Cleo in my face, but after a time, Mel stopped walking carefully around me. Needless to say, we didn't talk much. She found me on my way up the stairs after I'd returned from the library.

"What did you say to her?" Mel yelled at me. I heard the shuffling of some feet over the hardwood floors, then Maddie, Ruth, Cleo's feeder Hollis, and Gwen poked their heads out of the living room. I turned my back to Mel and went up to my room. Thankfully, she didn't come after me. I had nothing to explain to Cleo's feeders. As far as I was concerned, I had nothing left to say to Cleo either. We didn't belong together, she and I, no matter how much I still loved her. She wanted me to be someone else. Someone who babied her. Someone who held back the truth to shield her feelings. I didn't consider any of those things to be a loving act, so if she wanted that type of girlfriend, she would have to look somewhere else. I was sure Tokyo would be willing to oblige her.

When no one had seen her the next day, I was a little worried. Still annoyed with her and way too emotionally drained to keep on the way we'd been behaving for so long, but worried she wasn't coming back. I started to think maybe she'd decided to nest somewhere else, but I was wrong.

Things in the house were strange when Cleo returned. I saw her in the kitchen with Faeth. They were hanging out with their feeders, like any other night. When I walked to the fridge, Faeth smiled at me. Maddie said hi. And that was it. Cleo didn't growl at me. She didn't give me the finger. She didn't even look at me. She teased Hollis for trying to bring back the side ponytail and that was it. I grabbed a soda and went back to the TV room, expecting to hear some of those telltale snickers at my expense, but that didn't happen either. Faeth went on about the eighties being a great decade for hair, and Cleo teased her some more.

The next time I saw her was in the elevator. I'd just come from feeding Camila and she was on her way back to Omi's quarters. She nodded, no smile, but a nod and kept walking. That was it. It wasn't just her behavior that was strange, though. All of her feeders started ignoring me. Soon, Omi's feeders joined in. I thought about going to Ginger. I didn't need to be best friends with every girl in the house, but I like to be acknowledged when I'm speaking to someone, especially when I'm trying to hold a chapter meeting. I decided against it when I remembered that officer elections were a few weeks away and then I wouldn't be their president to ignore anymore. It was some sisterhood.

Late one night, Cleo came to my room well after curfew, knocking softly on my door. I thought it was Jill for a moment, then thought better of it. Jill didn't usually knock, and when she did, she didn't usually wait for me to answer before she barged in, which she'd done every night recently, just to say hi or smile at me or to ask me if I was okay.

I adjusted my pajama bottoms and opened the door.

"Is it okay if I come in for a sec?" Cleo asked. She was calm, but she was a little bit upset too. Not angry, but upset and somewhat worn out. She hadn't come to start another fight.

"Yeah." I opened the door wider and gestured toward my desk. She leaned against my dresser instead. I climbed up on my bed.

"I just wanted to say that I'm sorry," she said.

"You don't have to apologize."

"I do. You were completely right. You've been very honest and forthright and I was dealing with other things and taking them out on you. I am sorry."

"Thank you." I didn't know what else to say.

Suddenly, my door opened and Tokyo poked her head in. "Hey, Benny," she said like we were besties.

"Hey."

"You almost ready?" she asked Cleo. "Andrew has the car."

"'Kay. I'll be down in a second."

"Night, Benny." Tokyo flashed a fangy smile before she slipped out again.

"Sorry about that too," Cleo said, a little embarrassed.

"It's fine." *Will you please get out of my room?*

"I talked to Mel and the girls, and they're sorry too. They didn't understand the whole story. And no, I didn't tell them all your business, but I told them that I was to blame. They won't be blowing you off anymore."

They were just following your lead. "Thanks."

"Anyway, I know it sounds lame, but I figured with Ginger and Camila being in both our lives and us living in this house together, maybe we could be friends?"

I froze for a moment. *Did Cleo just friend me?* My mouth opened, but I didn't say anything.

"Or not."

"No. Friends is fine. We can be friends. I'd like that."

Cleo came over to me. I swallowed in a deep breath to keep from inhaling her flowery scent. She playfully clenched her fists and put them on my knees. It was like our first touch all over again, when we were just friends. "I think we'll be okay, right?"

"Yeah," I replied. "Yeah. We'll be fine."

"Cool. I'll see you later."

"Yeah."

"Good night." She smiled before she left. It was the strangest smile I'd seen from her in months. It was real.

I stared at my door a full two minutes after it had closed behind her.

It had taken three years, but I finally felt it. Cleo had broken up with me.

I sat there for what felt like hours. Eventually, I changed for bed. Before I went to sleep, though, I called Mama. I thought it might be good for me to meet Paeno.

❖

The weekend arrived once again. There was another home basketball game. The Chi Thetas were throwing a party in the city. There were other plans made around the house. I fed Camila right after class, then headed home to D.C. No one but Jill would miss me during movie night or during any of the other activities.

Dinner with Paeno was to be somewhat of a formal event. I dug out a black wrap dress I had hanging in my closet, and curled my hair into a low ponytail that hung over my shoulder. It wasn't exactly a side ponytail, I thought. As I looked at myself in the mirror, I quickly pushed the sound of Cleo's teasing voice out of my head. Friends, I reminded myself. Friend. Just as I finished up my meager makeup job, Mama called me on the intercom. Gus let out a little bark at the sound of her voice.

"Yes, Mother dear," I answered.

"Come on down and see me when you're ready."

"I'm ready now."

"Well, come on down."

Mama and Daddy had two bedrooms. One on the third floor, down the hall from mine, and one in our sealed basement. Sometimes Mama liked waking up with the sun on her face. I went down the hall and found Mama sitting at her vanity. Daddy said she'd had a good couple of months, and it showed. The bones in her back were less prominent, but I still wished we could convince her to eat more. She was worth it.

"Mama?"

"Come in." When she turned around, her face lit up. "Oh, sweetie, you look beautiful."

I shrugged. "Thanks, Mama."

She chuckled at me.

"What?"

"Every time you get within two feet of me, that drawl comes right back," she teased.

"It's your potent genes."

"Come sit with me a minute." She held out her hands and led me over to the chaise by the window. "Angel," she said. "What changed your mind?"

I looked out over the backyard as I shrugged. "It's not that I changed my mind. I just thought it would be good for me to meet her so I can make a more informed decision."

"But nothing happened to push your hand?"

"Cleo and I are talking again. Sort of."

"Oh?"

"She wants to be friends."

"Oh."

"Yeah. I think she means it."

"I'm sorry, baby." Mama ran her hand over my cheek. I swallowed to stop myself from crying. "Peach. When it comes to Paeno, it's up to you. It's your decision. No matter what happened or happens with Cleo in the future."

"And I shouldn't be intimidated by Daddy's demon plans?" I replied. I didn't believe it for a second.

"No." Mama laughed. "He's just trying to help. I'll level with you, honeybee. I liked Cleo for you."

"Mama, you—"

"I know we didn't get a chance to meet face-to-face, but…" She gently cupped my cheek. "I liked how happy she made you. I hate that you two broke up the way you did, but I don't want you to be without love either. Leaving Cleo out of it, I want you to remember that your daddy would never suggest that you bind yourself to a demon he didn't think was absolutely good for you."

The fine print of what Mama was saying was, she and Daddy knew how much of a picky hardass I was. Left to my own devices, it would be another eighteen years before I tried at a relationship. My parents wanted to see me at least on my way to married after graduation, and considering who and what Daddy was, they probably thought who and what I married, now that Cleo and I were officially over, was important. If they would have some say in who I fed, they would also have some say in who I wed. They wouldn't force me into anything, but they would have some say. The whole idea sent a wave of sadness through me. It was at that moment I realized that Cleo wasn't going to come around to seeing things my way. We were just friends now, and I would have to get on with my life without her, once and for all.

"Okay," I told my mama. Then I repeated the one thing she would always tell me when I was afraid to try something new. "Open mind. Open heart."

"That's my girl." She kissed me on my cheek and smiled.

❖

Dinner was not what I expected. Faraut served Mama and me our first two courses, while Daddy and Paeno made their way through a pitcher of warm blood—they need live blood to sustain themselves, but any blood would satisfy a casual thirst for a full demon—and two full sides of raw meat. Daddy usually took more civilized meals with us as a family, but in honor of his sister, he made an exception.

Paeno was accompanied by one human, an Asian woman, who though she was very able-bodied with a bright sense of humor, was also speeding rapidly toward her seventies. Her other companion was a male demon. The young male wasn't permitted to sit at the table. Instead, he stood behind Paeno for the entire meal. The woman took her dinner in the kitchen with Faraut, where I think she was making phone calls.

Other than a polite nod of hello to Mama and me, neither Paeno nor the male spoke to us the entire time I was at the table. Paeno and Daddy spoke to each other. They had an animated conversation in their bourne language, a tongue I would never understand, and one Daddy was forbidden from teaching any human. Mama once told me it was the same language the angels speak. We weren't allowed to know.

Once, just once, Paeno looked at me. I looked back at her.

She was in her full demon form. She was a terrifying beast. Easily eight feet tall, with white horns that curved up, back, and then forward like a ram's. Instead of hands, she had three huge white talons that curved out like bent fingers and one that bent out to the side and served as her thumb. Her hair was a silky white, braided down her ridged back. Where Daddy's natural scaled skin was a deep black, Paeno's skin was dark, shimmery green, her wings edged with black and moss-colored feathers. Her teeth were the size of a lion's. Two large fangs from the top of her mouth interlocked with two large fangs from the bottom. The iris of her eyes was a bright emerald green, but her pupils were white.

A few times, I caught myself staring as she tore into her food. I couldn't imagine the physical pain she could inflict on anyone who crossed her. In further testament to her power, all six of our dogs were crowded around her feet under the table. If I hadn't been around Daddy for such a long time, his sister would have scared the shit out of me. She lacked the kind demeanor my father had. She was cold. Powerful, but cold.

I don't know what she was trying to communicate to me in the moment our eyes held contact, but I know what I felt. I responded to her power. Not so much her size and her strength, but the implications of what she could do just using her mind. My body responded. My cunt swelled and became wet. My nipples ached and I had to stop myself from touching them through the fabric of my dress. My arousal made me uncomfortable. Uncomfortable and curious.

But I wasn't sure if I could trust what I was feeling. She was more demon than I had experienced before.

When she looked away, I found myself squirming in my seat. I was sweating and my breath was short. After some sort of agreement that even more raw meat was in order, I asked Mama if I could be excused. I couldn't stay in the same room with Paeno a moment longer.

"You feeling okay, angel?" Mama asked.

"I'm fine. I'm just a little sleepy. I think I'll turn in."

"My princess is working hard at university," Daddy finally said so I could understand. Again, Paeno simply nodded as she ripped into another large chunk of meat. Blood dripped from her claws. Faraut would have to get rid of that tablecloth.

"I'll have some dessert sent up. Okay, baby?" Mama offered.

"I'd like that. Thank you." I would have kissed my parents before I left, but I would have had to walk past Paeno twice to make the rounds and make my exit. She was making me too uneasy. I settled for a quick good night and took off for my room. Surprisingly, Gus toddled after me.

❖

I was cuddled up with Gus passed out on my feet when Mama knocked on my door again. I called out for her to come in and quickly sat up when I saw she wasn't alone. Leo and Kepper beat her through the door. And Paeno lingered in the hall behind her. Her face was just visible. Our eyes held for another long moment and the calm balance my body had reclaimed in being away from her was immediately dashed. I swallowed and subtly rubbed my thighs together.

"She wants to talk to you," Mama whispered-shouted across the room as if Paeno had forgotten the battery for her hearing aid at home.

"Yeah, um, come in." I climbed out of bed and watched as Paeno ducked her huge body through the door frame.

"I'll just be…" Mama pointed down to her bedroom.

I took my eyes off Paeno long enough to nod and shoo her out the door.

Paeno took short, oddly delicate steps around my bedroom. The times Daddy was in demon form, he walked the same way when he wasn't trying to knock furniture and lamps over. I sat back on my bed with Gus and Kepper while she looked around. She clinked the glass frame over a picture of Mama and me when I was a little girl. She picked up my ABO sweatpants and sniffed the crotch. She purred with slight satisfaction. I tried not to make a face.

Eventually, she turned to me. When she spoke, the strange bass in her voice seemed to cause her words to vibrate. "Your father-bourne tried to kill me." I didn't think she would lead with that, but okay. My real father, Lamont Wilkes, was the ambassador to demons in Asia. In a horribly devised plot, he planned to murder Paeno with the help of a group of rogue vampires who were already under suspicion for feeding from unbound humans. Even though he'd dealt with Daddy many times before, Lamont Wilkes somehow forgot every single power demons have, like mind reading and the ability to teleport. Daddy had done a merciful deed by asking Paeno if he could handle Lamont's execution.

"But he failed," I replied. *And now you're in my bedroom and I'm afraid of what you might do to me*. Knowing of Paeno and being near her were such different things.

"He failed. I did not know I would want his spawn in such a way. You want me as well." So this was Daddy's match for me. Not a human or a vampire, but the most powerful bourne-demon on the planet. I wasn't sure what that suggested about my future or the ego I presented. Paeno was right, though. I was attracted to her, if attraction can describe lusting inexplicably after someone who could easily scratch my face off. I couldn't explain what was wrong with me, why I couldn't accept a normal, stable relationship with a human woman. I needed so much more than what another person could be.

"You enjoy my gifts." She reached out with a long talon and pointed over my shoulder to Gus. "He is your favorite." His ears perked up and his head cocked to the side as if he knew we were talking about him. I gave him a gentle scratch under his chin.

"Yes, he's a good dog," I said.

"You will show yourself to me." I turned back to Paeno.

"You want me to take off my clothes?"

She dipped her large head in a heavy gesture. "You will show yourself to me." Her tone had changed. It wasn't a request. Obedient as always, I started with my T-shirt and pulled it over my head. My bra was next, then my pajama pants and my underwear. I stood still with my hands at my sides. Only Cleo had seen me naked like this, but she wasn't here now.

"You will open your eyes." I hadn't closed them on purpose. When I did as she asked, she was only a foot away, towering over me.

"You are afraid."

"Yes."

"You are not in danger."

"I know."

"And you like the way I speak to you." I did and I told her that as well. She was confident in a way I'd never seen before. She would make an interesting mistress, if things ever got that far between us.

"You are healthy." She drew the smooth edge of her talon over my breast and around my nipple. Goose bumps broke out all over my body. "You please me."

"Can I see your other forms?" I asked boldly. Daddy had four basic forms: his full demon, his full human, and two forms that fell in between depending on his mood. I wanted to know exactly what else I was exposing myself to.

Paeno nodded again. "I will show you." She shrank herself by a foot. Her horns decreased in size as well, but her wings maintained their massive span. Gradually, she became more and more human. Pert breasts formed, and a slight cleft appeared between her legs. As she continued to level out, she inched closer and closer. Up close, her skin was beautiful. Her scales were a full mosaic of lighter and darker greens. She let me touch her. She was cool and smooth like a snake. Eventually, a full woman, only few inches taller than myself, stood in front of me. Green eyes with normal dark pupils sat perfectly wide in a round face with Mediterranean features. Deep brown nipples tipped deep bronze breasts, and her white hair drained to black. She smiled at me and the tips of her fangs had disappeared. She pleased me as well.

"You will be mine."

I've never been one to rush into decisions, but as I tried to think of what else the future meant for me, there was nothing. I'd work wherever I wanted, or not work at all thanks to Daddy's reign. I would drift from the girls, possibly even from Camila and Ginger, considering

I wouldn't see them as much anymore. And Cleo? There was just a painful void.

Every thought of her was overshadowed by the truth. She didn't want me anymore. She couldn't even be bothered to pick on me. It was that indifference that burned, that indifference that showed me that she had already moved on. I couldn't change who I was, and the truth remained that the real me wasn't someone Cleo wanted to be with. Paeno wanted my body and my loyalty. Maybe after time, after I learned her ways and the way she ran her nest, she would give me some bit of responsibility when it came to the other humans in her care. But for now, Paeno at least wanted me for me.

"I have conditions," I said.

"You will share them." Her human voice was sweet and melodic.

"I want to come see my mother whenever I want," I insisted.

"You will have this."

"And I want a baby."

Paeno raised an eyebrow. She seemed surprised, but intrigued by the idea. "You want a baby by birth. You want a baby bought."

"Birth. I-I want to have a baby."

"You will see your mother. You will have a baby." Her eyes narrowed slightly. She was reading me, but I didn't know what she was picking up. "There is more you desire." She stepped closer. "You wish to have your control taken from you."

I nodded. "Sometimes."

"Such an interesting child. You will have these things."

"Okay." I let out a slight breath. "Then I will be yours."

She whispered, "You will be still."

Paeno took my left wrist in her palm and turned my forearm up. The forefinger on her other hand morphed back into a talon, and with it, she set up drawing an intricate design on my arm. The sensation warmed under my skin. It didn't burn, but I did not enjoy the way it felt. It was uncomfortable. When she finished, the effect mimicked a white tattoo. My skin was raised in the pattern of the lines and swirls that resembled a flower overlapping a seven-pointed star. I'd seen the image before on a parchment Daddy had in his office. It was her mark.

"You come to me in four months' time and you will have whatever you like."

"Yes, I will," I replied. She came forward a final step and slid her arms aggressively around my waist. Her hands caressed my body as we kissed. She tasted like mint and something close to pears. She touched my butt and my back. She touched every inch that made me self-conscious, but I let her explore. This wasn't love. It was something that my body yearned to surrender to. It was possession, proved more as Paeno bit me.

I winced and pulled away, shocked at the pain her bite caused. When I tasted my own blood, I touched my fingers to the inside of my lip. They came away red.

I looked up at her. She'd backed across the room and returned to her full demon. A moment later, she vanished. When her lingering essence fully dissipated, I walked to where she had been standing. The edge of my vanity was singed.

CHAPTER NINE

Benny

I lay awake early into the next morning, thinking about the pact I had just sealed with Paeno, and thinking about the strange kiss we'd shared. I knew she would follow through on my conditions, but I was scared. Her home in China was so far away from Mama and the few people I cared about. Still, I decided eventually that I had made the right decision to move on with her. I could start over thousands of miles away from Cleo instead of an hour up the interstate. My feelings on being mated to Paeno were still a little unsettled, but I wanted to go through with it for the simple fact that my feelings for Cleo were just as unsettled.

I needed to move on. There was no debate on that fact, and with the awkward tension between me and the other girls in the house, I needed a major change after graduation. Paeno presented that opportunity for me. I thought maybe after some time we could even discuss my more specific desires in the bedroom. I knew our relationship wouldn't be traditional, but I would be her mate and her feeder, so she would want to please me sexually too. I had no doubt in her abilities, that much was true.

As the hours went by, the physical effect she had on me began to fade, but the next day when I met her and my parents down in Daddy's quarters for lunch, my body opened up for Paeno the moment she looked at me. This time the effect was more intense. She had toned down her monster a little and sat on Daddy's settee with her wings folded behind her back. I sat beside her and held still as she stroked my knee while she and Daddy talked about their feeders and various demons and humans under their control. They spoke so Mama and I could understand. Paeno told Daddy she was pleased I had accepted her proposal and she promised Mama that she would make me happy.

When it was time for me to head back to school, Paeno kissed me again, in front of my parents. She skipped the love bite. After she excused us, my parents walked me out to my car. I thought Mama would burst from excitement. It was nice to see her so happy.

"Oh, angel, you like her, don't you?"

"Yes," I told her, though I still wasn't entirely sure. Interested or maybe fascinated would describe my feelings better.

"I'm very proud of you, my princess. You have made the right decision," Daddy said.

"I think she will be good for me," I said, trying to sound more optimistic.

"She will. She will take excellent care of you." Mama beamed as she pulled me into a hug.

I was sure she would.

❖

"Does it hurt?" Ginger asked. She lightly traced her fingers over the mark on my arm.

"No," I said. "It's warm." After I dropped off my stuff, I went down to their apartment to tell Ginger and Camila about my arrangement with Paeno. The mark on my arm had held its texture and its odd temperature, but overnight the color had started to change. The fleshed-toned relief had grown a little darker with a hint of dark blue.

"I don't like this." Camila had been huffing and puffing and pacing around their living room ever since I told them the gist of the story. Though I was sure she could smell Paeno on me, I left out the part with the naked examination. And the kiss.

"I'm going to be fine, and I'm sure you can come visit."

"What are you going to do over there?" Ginger asked.

Paeno and I hadn't discussed that. I figured rearing a child was enough of a career ambition for the moment, but I wasn't ready to share that news with Ginger. "Whatever I want. Paeno has more of a fortress system under her control. It's like a vampire/feeder commune. She doesn't have direct contact with any humans who aren't under her control."

"I still don't like it," Camila grumbled. "I feel like Dalhem didn't think this through."

"He did and so did I. It'll be fine," I said again, but I couldn't help but notice the doubt had spread to Ginger's face. "What?" I asked her.

She looked at Camila briefly. "I don't really like it either. I don't want you to be so far away."

"You can vanish there in seconds. We can still see each other. I don't see what the problem is."

"Yeah, but I don't know. Something feels off about this," Ginger replied.

"It's Paeno's territory, Benny. Not Dalhem's. I'm sure she won't deny you guests whenever you like, but we can't just come and go as we please." Camila was right. Daddy and his brothers and sisters trusted unfamiliar vampires as much as they trusted unbound humans, but Camila made it seem like she and Ginger would want to see me every day, which they wouldn't. I knew things would be different and I wouldn't be around all the time, but I also wouldn't be Camila's feeder anymore. This doubt was her demon sense of possession speaking. Once our bond was broken, I doubted she would think of me much if it weren't for Ginger. Not that Camila didn't care about me, but a blood bond changes things.

"I will talk to her. You can come whenever you like, and I am sure I will learn to love fifteen-hour flights," I said with a smile. "This is for the best."

"The best for who, though?" I knew what Ginger was asking. She wanted to know if I was running. Of course I was, but she didn't need to know that. As if denying her influence had somehow conjured her up, Cleo stuck her head through the door. I scrambled to pull down my sleeve, but it was too late. I knew she'd seen the mark.

"Hey. I—sorry. I'll come back," she said as she looked at us curiously.

"No, it's fine. I should go." With an abrupt jerk, I stood, but Cleo stepped inside and tried to block me from leaving.

"What's going on?" she asked.

"Nothing. I'll see you guys later." I slid by her and out the door. She didn't follow me, but I could feel her eyes on my back as I tried to coolly power-walk to the elevator. I wasn't ready to tell her about Paeno yet. I hadn't planned on telling her at all since it wasn't any of her business, but I should have known better than to think Cleo would leave me alone after my sketchy exit, *just friends* or not.

She was waiting for me in my room.

"What is going on?" she demanded as soon as I opened my door. I knew that tone. She wasn't trying to give me a hard time. She wasn't messing with me. She wanted real answers and she wasn't leaving until she got them. I relented and pushed up the sleeve of my sweater.

She took my wrist and carefully looked over Paeno's engraving. "What is this?"

"I've been marked."

Cleo's eyes popped wide. "By who? Camila agreed to this?"

"After graduation, I'm promised to Paeno. Camila doesn't have any say in this."

Her right eyebrow flew up. "Who the fuck is that?"

"Dalhem's sister."

"What? Why!" She let go of my hand and took a step back.

"Because." I swallowed and told Cleo the truth. "You and I are over, and I thought it would be best for me if I moved on. I leave for Beijing in June."

"You're moving to China!"

"Yes," I said as calmly as I could. But my ease with the conversation didn't seem to help Cleo. Her eyes wildly searched the floor and I was positive I was about to see a vampire hyperventilate for the first time. Just as quickly, her mouth clamped shut and she looked me straight in the eye.

"No, you can't. You're not going. Break it off."

"I can't. It's too late. I'm promised to Paeno. I'm hers."

"Promised? What the fuck? Did Dalhem trade you for some cattle? Is this your choice or is he forcing you?" I wasn't surprised that she came to that conclusion.

"No one forced me to do anything. It was my choice, but you helped push things along," I told her honestly.

"Well, I'm unpushing. Tell her it's off. I don't care what I said before. I don't want you to go."

"I already told you, it's too late." I held up my forearm. "You see this? I am hers."

"The fuck you are." Cleo rushed me and pulled me into her arms. "You're mine."

I wanted to resist her. The way she'd tortured me, her constant taunting and flip-flopping, part of me hated her so much that when she wrapped me up in her scent and kissed me with everything she had, I wanted to push her away, but I couldn't.

Tears pricked my eyes as I kissed her back, and I felt even more that I should go with Paeno. I couldn't stand it if this kiss ended badly. I couldn't handle another instance of Cleo's rejection. She kissed me deeper, sliding her tongue into my mouth, and everything I missed about her came flooding back. Those few short months we'd been together had been packed with a lifetime of emotion, years of intimacy that our bickering and cold shoulders couldn't just erase. I didn't feel this way about Paeno, and I knew I never would. I would never love her the way I loved Cleo. Without a blood bond, I would never ache to be with her or yearn to have her inside me the way I did with Cleo now.

She read my need and guided me back toward the bed, her kisses traveling down my neck. Her thigh came between my legs, crushing the seam of my jeans against my clit. I must have moaned.

"I'm sorry," she purred against my skin. "Please, please. Don't go."

"Cleo—" She silenced me again with her lips on my mouth, with a kiss so tender and so sweet I lost all ability to think. Her mouth moved to my cheek, then down to my neck again. When her tongue crept out and licked my throat, I knew I was in trouble. Of course she would remember my sweet spot. Had she been a human, I would have encouraged her, but things were different now. Had I been in the right frame of mind, I would have stopped her. But like the desperate little bunny pet I used to be, I ground myself against Cleo's legs and made those pathetic, soft noises I used to make when I wanted her to take things further.

A moment too late, I remembered that I wasn't dealing with Cleo my sorority sister anymore. I was dealing with Cleo the demon who lived and fucked for blood. Her feral growl echoed through my ears.

The instant her fangs sank into my skin, I cried out, orgasming in a powerful burst that surely soaked my underwear. I reveled in the sensation for a few seconds, feeling the peaks of ecstasy as she took me. A few short seconds where Cleo and I became everything I had always wanted us to be, demon and human together.

And then everything went black.

Cleo

The second I felt Benny go slack, I pulled back from her. I stared at her in horror. Her eyes had rolled back in her head and a small amount of blood trickled from the punctures I'd made in her neck. Quickly, I sealed them, then I scooped her up and laid her on the floor. That's when she started seizing. She shook violently on the carpet, spit frothing out of her mouth.

"Fuck. Fuck. Benny." I tapped her cheek, but nothing happened. Before I could do anything else, Camila appeared. I looked up at her helplessly as she looked down at Benny. Camila dropped to her knees beside us.

She lifted Benny's head. "Shit. Benny. Benny! Wake up! Did you bite her?" she asked me.

Oh, fuck. "Yeah."

"Shit," Camila growled. She held Benny's head still and leaned close to her ear. "I release you, Benita Tarver. Listen to me, Benny. I release you."

As soon as Camila completed the vow, Benny stopped flopping around, but she didn't come to. She was turning blue.

"What happened? Why isn't she waking up?"

"Feed her," Camila said.

"Wha-what?"

"Open your fucking wrist and feed her."

"Jesus! Okay!" I unsheathed my fangs and tore a nice, gaping hole in my wrist. It hurt like hell, but blood came rushing out. Camila continued to hold Benny's head as I pressed my wrist to her mouth. Nothing happened at first. I could feel the blood just pooling in her mouth. Finally, I saw her throat move. It was only seconds, but it felt like forever. She swallowed one gulp and then another and another, moving her lips against my skin.

"That should be enough. Here." Camila tossed me the thick belt to Benny's robe. My wrist was already healing, but it would takee a few minutes for the wound to close completely.

Camila must have put out a silent call to Ginger because she appeared with wet washcloths in her hand. She had one of our ceremonial knives in the other. Quickly, Ginger locked Benny's bedroom door. Great thinking, considering the last thing we needed was Jill or Sam or Amy busting in and seeing all of this. Ginger came back over to us and passed the cloths to Camila, who started wiping the blood and Benny's spit off her mouth.

"We wait now," Camila said. "If you killed her, you're a dead woman. I hope you know that. I can't save your ass from Dalhem this time."

No shit was on the tip of my tongue, but I kept my mouth shut. I had just thrown myself into a cluster fuck of epic proportions. Hell-bound proportions. If Benny didn't wake up, Dalhem would easily have me executed and I'd be playing with his pitchfork-baring cousins in the fiery pits of eternity. Though at the moment that was the least of my worries. I was losing Benny. Not knowing what else to do, I started to pray, for my salvation and Benny's life.

I lost track of time, as if there's some way to mark progression when you're begging your Lord and savior in the most selfish of ways, full of fear that your own needs have set things in motion, things that can't be fixed. I don't know what told me to open my eyes. There was no sign, no sound, but when I did, Benny's eyes snapped open and she let out a heaving, gasping breath.

"Oh God, Benny." I reached for her, but before I could scoop her up, Camila hauled off and punched me, full force, in the arm. "Fucking shit, bitch! That hurt!" I looked down just to make sure the thing wasn't broken. It felt like I'd been hit with a tire iron.

"You deserved it." Camila took Ginger's hand and they vanished from the room. I couldn't wait for my next conversation with them.

Benny coughed and sat up on her own. "What happened?" The color was coming back to her face.

"I bit you."

"I know." She looked around at the blood-covered rags beside her and the blood on her sweater. Her eyes started to well up. Like always, she took a moment to regain her composure. "What happened after that?"

"Camila, uh, Camila released you and then I gave you my blood. That's mine," I told her as I motioned to the red stain on her top. "I think that snapped you out of it."

She started shaking. I moved closer and rubbed her shoulder. "What is it, B?"

"I think...I died."

At that exact moment, Dalhem filled my head with every bit of his essence. He was furious, enraged to the point that I had to cover my eyes. I felt like his anger was trying to bore holes through my skull.

"What's going on?" Benny asked, grabbing my hand. "Cleo?"

"Answer your phone," Dalhem said through me. Her cell phone started ringing on her nightstand. Dalhem pried my eyes open and made me stand. He took in the sight of Benny though my eyes, her ashen face and the blood on her clothes and chest. He squeezed my skull a little harder.

"Hello?" she said.

"Get yourself cleaned up and come home. Right now. Camila will drive you."

Benny turned and looked at me. Dalhem and I both stared back at her. "Yes, Daddy," she said faintly.

Before I could say a word, my body was pulled apart and dragged toward Dalhem.

❖

My parts reappeared in an unfamiliar room, somewhere between the chandelier and the floor. I say my parts because Dalhem refused to let me take form. I hung in the air, my particles conscious of everything going on around me. Dalhem was somewhere nearby, screaming at the top of his lungs. As he came closer, the chandelier started to shake.

The door slammed open all on its own. Benny came rushing into the room with a woman right behind her. And Dalhem followed.

He was in his full demon form, nude with black scaly skin. His claws were balled into tight fists and his wings seemed to twitch. Air blew from his nostrils as he kicked a coffee table out of the way. It crashed into a bookcase across the room.

The woman, I suddenly realized, was Benny's mother, Mrs. Tarver. They looked nearly identical in the face. She had an oversized men's robe wrapped around her slight body. She lightly tugged Benny's arm, begging Benny to face her. "You promise you're okay? Your daddy told me what happened."

"Yes, Mama. I'm fine. Where is she?" She turned and glared at Dalhem.

"She is here." With an invisible kick to the ribs, Dalhem let me fall to the floor. I grabbed my side as the pain quickly dissipated, my blood quickly patching what should have been a few broken bones.

Benny ran across the room and helped me up. She'd showered and changed. Dalhem must have had me in pieces for over an hour. "Are you all right?" Benny asked.

"The fuck," I groaned, rubbing my side. "Yeah, I'm okay."

"I should kill you now," Dalhem growled.

"Daddy!" Benny tried to step between us, but her presence

wouldn't do a thing once Dalhem made up his mind. He towered over us both. I looked up into his golden eyes, glowing hot with fire, a hatred he'd had for me since the first day of my demon birth. Still, I was alive for a reason, most likely two reasons named Benny and Camila. And even though I'd made a serious mistake, my blood was his.

"Do you have any idea what you have done? What you have both done?" He looked between Benny and me.

"Listen. I didn't know—" I replied.

"You will address me properly!"

"Master. My master, I didn't know what biting Benny would do."

"You did not simply bite her. You have violated my Camila's blood bond. You've forced my Camila to violate an oath she kept to me, as well as a pledge made by her Ginger. You killed my only child. We would have lost her forever if my Camila had not acted so quickly."

"But I'm fine now," Benny said, stepping closer to Dalhem. "I'm fine." She wasn't. She was practically shaking. Her skin was oddly pale and there were shadows under her eyes. But despite her distress, for once, for the first time ever, Benny was fighting for me.

"You'll have me spare her?" Dalhem asked her.

"Yes, Daddy. You know I would."

"And what of your tu'lah? What of the pledge that marks you, my Benita? Do you know what this means?"

"You and Mama said it was my choice. The tu'lah is between you and Paeno, Daddy. You will just have to choose another human for her if I—"

"If you choose to be with this one who does not value you or your love!" Dalhem shouted again. This time a crack split across the ceiling. Mrs. Tarver stepped forward and touched his trembling talon. I could tell he would have shaken off anyone else, but her touch seemed to calm him down. A little.

"And what will you do?" he said to me. "Now that you have broken these bonds? Do you even want her? Or was this another of your tantrums, and when your emotional tide turns you will toss her aside again?"

I looked at Benny. "Does he know everything? Does he know why?"

"Yes, he does. Daddy, can we just talk? Please. Just give me and Cleo some time talk to each other."

"Sweetheart, please." Mrs. Tarver looked up at him with her big blues that matched Benny's.

He sucked in a shuddering breath before glaring back at Benny and me. "You will have your talk, then, but if this is your path, my Benita, you both will see this path to be untrue. And no matter your choice, the debt will be paid," Dalhem said. And then he vanished from the room.

CHAPTER TEN

Cleo

We followed Mrs. Tarver down the hall to what turned out to be a small guest bedroom. She opened the door for us, a slight, yet earnest smile touching her lips. "You girls can stay in here for a little while. The sun will be up soon."

"Thanks, Mama." I watched at Mrs. Tarver passed Benny a long dagger with a bejeweled handle.

"Thank you, Mrs. Tarver," I said as I watched their exchange.

"We'll talk later," she replied, reminding me it wasn't just the demon father I'd have to deal with, but the human mother too.

"Yes, ma'am."

"What's that?" I asked Benny once we were alone.

She gently placed the knife on one of the night tables, then hopped up on the high four-poster bed. "It's one of our family blades."

"Oh. You're not okay, are you?" The blood I had given her had brought her back, but it wasn't enough to restore her fully.

"It's a little weird not being bound to Camila. It's making me feel strange. I think I just need to rest, but we should talk first. I'll be fine."

"Here." The skin on my wrist had already healed. This time I lightly punctured my skin as I walked across the room to her. Benny hesitated for a moment as I held out my hand, but eventually she took my arm and drank from my wrist. The color came back to her cheeks almost immediately. I could have stopped her. I let her drink a minute more. I wanted a moment to savor the connection before we went any further. I held in a deep growl as my fangs dropped in my mouth. I wanted to bite her again, and then fuck her.

Finally, she released my hand and leaned against the bedpost. "Thanks."

"No problem."

"So, we should talk."

"We should." For both of our sakes, I took a seat in a chair near the door. I couldn't be trusted near her, especially now that she no longer bore Camila's bond. I looked Benny over. My eyes settled on the mark on her arm. "I think we need to figure out what we do about that first."

Benny touched her skin. "It depends."

"On what?"

"Whether you'll actually have me, and not because of what Daddy said."

"You know exactly what I want."

"I know you don't want me to move to China, but—"

"Benny. Seriously." I laughed. "I want you. All of it. The whole deal. The way I wanted you before. That hasn't changed."

"Is that why you told me you wanted to be friends?" she said softly, like the request had been the biggest insult I'd tossed her way.

"I told you I wanted to be friends because you weren't understanding where I was coming from, and it hurt too much to love someone who wouldn't even recognize my pain whether she agreed with it or not."

"Well, I recognize it now."

"Do you?"

"When I—when I wasn't here, I couldn't feel anything. Not you, not Camila or Ginger. Mama and Daddy were gone. I've never felt that empty before. It hurt." She looked at me, her blue eyes filled with wild distress. "I died, Cleo."

"Shit, Benny." I rushed toward the bed and pulled her to me, and for the first time ever, in the whole time I had known her, Benny cried. There were moments where I had debated whether she even had tear ducts, but she was sobbing now against my neck. I felt her warm, salty tears against my skin. "I'm sorry. I shouldn't have—I'm sorry," was all I could say.

"I was here and then one second, I wasn't…I…I…didn't know that's what you felt. I didn't know that's what you'd been through. I'm sorry."

"Shh," I hushed her as I rocked her against my chest. "Shit. I'm so sorry, Benny. I'm so sorry. It was so stupid of me to do that." I let out a slightly maniacal laugh. "I guess some rules are meant to be followed." You don't bite another demon's feeders. That's all there is to it, but I had been thinking it all along. I'd even said it to Benny herself. She was mine and she always would be. My demon didn't respect her vows to any other. When it came to Benny, my demon took over. The idea of losing her to Paeno was too much.

"I screwed up, didn't I? I don't understand your attachment to your mother, but I understand how you feel now. I understand."

"B…"

"So will you have me?"

I stared at her face, still wet with tears. And then I looked down at her upturned palm. Just inches below, her pulse beat beneath her skin, tempting and taunting me. It would be so easy to accept her, no more questions asked. I loved Benny. I always would, but after the crazy-ass night we'd been through, I hadn't forgotten the days and nights leading up to this point. I hadn't forgotten who Benny was deep down inside.

"We do this my way this time. No more hiding. I don't give a shit what the girls think. I'm not going to feed from you and then pretend we aren't together. I'm not doing it."

"I know."

"And you have to let me miss them, Benny. I know you don't like my mama and you don't understand why I can't let my family go, but you have to let me miss them. I want you, but you have to give me that or else this won't work. I get your need for order and control and privacy, all that shit, but you can't control me and what I do and certainly how I feel," I said.

It sucked that I had to lay it out, but at the same time, it felt great to finally put my foot down with her. I loved her more than she would ever comprehend, and if Dalhem didn't decide to kill me anyway for putting her in danger or fucking up whatever fifth-century deal he had with Paeno, I couldn't have her by my side if she couldn't see me as more than a means to satisfy her needs. I had until the end of the world to live with myself, and I wouldn't be able to do that without my self-respect.

"Tomorrow night," she said. "We'll tell the girls and the sister-queens. I promise."

"Are you sure?" For any other couple this was no-brainer shit, but for us…well, one of us, anyway, this was a big deal.

"Yes."

"What about Paeno? Tell me what's going on there."

Benny sighed deeply, but then related the whole story of how every one hundred years Dalhem and his brothers and sisters exchanged humans, as I thought, much like cattle. Paeno had her eye fixed on Benny, and when Benny thought I was really done with her, she'd agreed to fulfill Dalhem's end of the tu'lah as a means of getting as far away from me and the remains of our relationship as possible.

"Camila was to sever our bond a month after graduation and hand me over to Paeno."

"But you're not bound to Camila anymore. *I* could refuse to give you over, but then again, she could also kill me."

"I won't let her. I won't let *Daddy* let her. I want to be with you."

I touched her cheek. It had been years since I'd touched her this way, without any anger or fear making my heart tremble. "I want to be with you too, B." I reached over and grabbed the blade and then I took her open palm in mine. "You ready?"

"Wait." I looked up into her eyes. "I have to say something before the bond changes things."

"Go ahead."

"I love you. I know it was hard for me to say it before, but I do. I love you with all my heart and I'm sorry I ever hurt you." She paused, looking at our hands between us. "I have never been more scared in my life than I was the night of your accident. I didn't know how to handle it, so I didn't. And I know I am stubborn and difficult, but I will prove it to you. I love you."

"You know you were about to be mated to your aunt?" I had to get that final crack in.

"She is not my aunt. Shut up."

"Okay, whatever. I must have driven you love-crazy if incest was looking good to you." And like that, Benny smiled. Damn, I'd missed that smile so much. I bent down and kissed her. "I love you too, and if the last few weeks haven't been proof enough, I've been going crazy without you. I'm never letting you go. Paeno can suck a dick. You're mine."

"Will you still be interested in playing with your little bunny pet?" she asked. She reached up and pulled my tank top down so the edge of my bra was showing.

"What do you think? Give me your hand." She did as she was told. "Benita Tarver, will you allow me to bind you to myself?" I skipped the sister-queens and the sorority sisters nonsense. Three more months and I was taking her out of that house.

"Yes, I will."

I kissed her again and then I whispered, "Will you let me fuck you so good you'll debate whether or not you'll be able to walk the next day? Will you bring that little bunny pet freak of yours out in the bedroom whenever I need her?"

Benny chuckled. "Yes, I will."

"Will you be my wife, my partner, my mate until we both leave this earthly plane and beyond?"

"You still want to marry me?"

"I told you," I replied. "I want all of it."

"I still want to have a baby, you know."

"I said all of it. What's your answer?"

"Will you forgive me?"

She was talking a mighty big game. Everything she was agreeing to was so far out of her comfort zone, I knew there would be a certain amount of kicking and screaming on her part, but this was something. This was a good place to start. "Yes," I told her. "I forgive you, if you'll forgive me. I think I almost broke De'Treshawn's brain, and I don't think I made a good first impression on your mama."

"De'Treshawn can suck a dick and Mama already loves you. So, yes, Cleopatra Joy Jones, I will, marry you, be with you, and bind myself to you. I love you."

"I love hearing you say that."

"Well, let's get on with this and I'll say it again." Benny held up her palm. I didn't wait. I sliced open her hand. She sucked in some air through her teeth. Benny wasn't much for certain kinds of pain, but she let me savor the taste before I sealed the wound, and boy, did she taste good. When her skin closed, I gripped the back of her head and crushed her lips to mine. She moaned into my mouth and I matched the desperate sound as our bond was made complete. I felt it through my whole body and being. We would work at putting our relationship back together fully, but now she was my feeder, my pet. She would be loyal to me and me alone. She would crave my touch and my touch only. Her pussy would weep from my bite. And I would do anything to protect her. She owned me, inside and out.

I pulled away slightly, licking her lips, then kissing every inch of her face. "You're mine now."

"Yes, Cleo." She offered me her neck, pulling her ruby necklace to the side.

"Not yet," I told her. I put the knife on her nightstand and motioned for her to scoot up the bed. It was time to test the sturdiness of the bed frame.

"Have your other appetites changed as well?" she asked as she shimmied up her comforter.

"Not at all." I kicked off my boots and my pants and climbed on top of her. I glanced up at the distance between the posts. They were too far apart for her to reach. "Do you think you can hold still?"

"Yes."

I don't know why I was shocked. I knew exactly who I was dealing with, but still, after all this time, without even being asked, Benny slipped right into her role. She bit her bottom lip and stared up at me with the most sinfully innocent look in her eye. Even the pitch of her voice changed a bit. I loved it when my little bunny pet came out to play. I leaned down and licked the seam of her mouth.

"Good. That's good to hear. We'll get to that in a minute. Lift up your arms." She did as I asked, giving me the room I needed to pull her sweater and her T-shirt over her head. After I did away with her bra, I couldn't hold in my purr of satisfaction. My clit jumped at the sight of her bare skin. Centered around hard, peach-colored nipples, her large breasts spread out under their own weight. Soft, milky-white skin covered the expanse of her stomach. It drove me crazy that she ever called herself fat. She was juicy in all the best ways.

I started at her belly button, kissing and licking my way up and across. She was ticklish, and even though she held perfectly still, her breathing grew harsher. It was a perfect distraction from where I was headed.

I reached her breasts, more than enough to fill my hands, and pushed them together. She gasped, but again kept herself from squirming. I went right for the tips. Benny arched her back and hissed through her teeth.

"Don't move or I'll stop." For now, it was an empty threat. I was way too horny to stop, but I wanted to see how she handled the command.

She swallowed and forced herself to relax. "Yes, Cleo."

I attacked her breasts with my tongue and lips again. One, then the other, sucking on the tip as she shivered beneath me, looking up the entire time as Benny's eyes squeezed shut. "Look at me," I told her. Benny's eyes opened. I barely pricked her left nipple with my fang, then soothed the spot away with more gentle sucking. Benny moaned, a loud, strained noise in the back of her throat. I knew I had her.

I sat up on my knees and went after that same nipple with just the tip of my tongue, quick, light flicks over and over. Soon, because she couldn't control it, Benny came apart, my name forced from her lips lost in the willowy canopy above. I purred in response, feeling her pleasure rush through my body like it was my own. For good measure, I dropped my hips to her stomach and coated her skin with the proof of what she had just done to me, how hot she had made me.

I covered her body with mine and again, I kissed her, long and slow. She sighed into my mouth.

"How are we doing so far?" I asked, but I captured her lips again before I let her answer.

"Good," she eventually replied. "Can I stretch a little?"

I rubbed my nose against hers. "Yes, bunny. You can." But instead of stretching, she reached up and ran her fingers under my tank top. I let her pull it off me. I let her get away with taking off my bra too. When I was completely naked, she leaned up and kissed me.

"You're gonna pay for that. So bad."

"I'll take my punishment whenever you're ready."

"For now…" I whispered as I slid my fingers into her underwear. I smiled down at her. "Come on my fingers."

"Yes, Cleo," she whispered back.

My fangs dropped further from my gums and I bit into her succulent skin. Oh, it was so much sweeter this time. She didn't pass out, for one thing. I got to enjoy the taste of her blood. I drank deep, so deep I knew I would have to give her some of my blood to keep her from feeling loopy in the morning. But I enjoyed it now. Her blood was so good, so different from my other feeders, spiked with a hint of her vanilla scent.

She came instantly, her pussy clenching around my fingers and soaking my hands. And again, I came with her.

CHAPTER ELEVEN

Cleo

Early in the morning I woke Benny up. I'd just planned to tell her we needed to talk some more. There were other things we had to straighten out, but the moment I looked down at her I changed my mind. I didn't say anything, just kissed her neck and rubbed her belly until she finally responded with a light moan. She turned in my arms, facing me so I could kiss her properly. I had no orders, no commands. I just wanted to enjoy being with her before the sun and the real world pulled us apart. It was something I would have to get used to, no doubt, but I wasn't looking forward to it. Our bond was different from what I felt for my other feeders. The unconditional affection was there. I longed to protect her and provide for her, but there was this element of lovesickness that permeated all of those other emotions.

I'd felt this way before, in the first weeks we'd been together, back when I was human. I'd think about her all day, during my classes. I would stare at her during chapter meetings, wondering if she felt the same way I did. During classes, I would text her, hoping she was alone so she could read the short love notes I'd sent her, and smile or blush without feeling like she had to explain herself. I ran to her dorm on our free afternoons, pumped out of my mind to find her waiting for me on her bed. At the time, I thought what we had was perfect, but now I looked forward to fulfilling both sides of our relationship.

I rolled onto my back and pulled her with me. She straddled my hips and went to work. In bunny mode or not, she knew what I liked. Our clits rubbed together as she ground against me. It had been so long since I had enjoyed something so simple. With Tokyo, it was always hanging from the rafters. With Andrew, well, with Andrew my clit served a whole other purpose, and with the girls, I was their sexual jungle gym. But with Benny, I could be myself. This was the part I wasn't willing to let go, even after we broke up. I hated that we kept our relationship a secret, but in every other way, she'd given me everything I needed. She knew exactly how I liked to be fucked and when I wanted to make love, and I'd learned to read her the same way.

It was that familiarity that made the lovesickness even stronger, and the taste of her blood just compounded its potency. My demon had definitely found its mate. I felt the animal inside me prowling on the fringes, ever vigilant, just waiting for some fool to try to come between us. I knew how Camila felt for Ginger now. Rodrick and Natasha's intense bond now made complete sense.

I grabbed her waist and helped thrust up to meet her every movement. She shifted against me, and just to make her desires clear, brushed her nipple over my lips. I licked and sucked her breast until she shuddered and whimpered above me, her hips grinding in a fiercer charge as she chased another orgasm and another. I joined her, calling out her name, fighting the urge to sink my fangs into her throat. My willpower wasn't enough. My demon would not be denied now that my human side had had its pleasure.

I flipped us so I was on top and rubbed my thigh between Benny's legs.

"Cleo," she whined as she offered me her neck. "Please." Benny wouldn't be denied either.

I bit her, hard and fast. Her legs clamped around my thigh in a viselike grip, and I felt her wetness cover my skin as her sweet blood rushed down my throat.

❖

I let Benny doze a while longer, but when I sensed movement around the house, I woke her up. She used the bathroom, and when she came back to bed, I pulled her back under the covers. I needed a few more minutes. She let out a sigh as she looked down at my chest for a moment as if she was considering something.

"Tell me."

"What are your plans with Andrew?"

I sighed this time as I propped my head on my arm. He had always been a major problem between us, but my feelings for him hadn't changed. "I want to keep him after graduation," I told her. "He doesn't have anyone, and he was with Moreland for too long. He trusts me, and I don't want to send him off to someone else after we built that trust."

"I'm okay with that, but…"

"You can say it. You don't want me to fuck him anymore."

"I know over time, things will happen. I understand how feedings go, and he's a natural submissive. I know how much you must like that, but for now, I was just hoping it could be us together in that way. I've heard a lot about how you fuck him, and—"

"You have?"

"Yes. For some reason, Tokyo thinks she exists in a vacuum. She goes on and on about your dick and how you fuck her and Andrew. She's said stuff in front of me plenty of times."

Note to self, punch Tokyo in the face the next time you see her.

"It's interesting, at least I think it is, but I just want to have you to myself for a while before you're that physical with him again. If I can."

Another first. Benny was asking, not just demanding. I pulled her closer and kissed her lips. "I don't have to fuck him ever again. That's not why he and I are close. It's why Tokyo and I are close, but Andrew doesn't rely on me for my cock-slinging skills."

Benny chuckled. "Cock-slinging?"

"Yes. I sling a mean cock. I would think you would remember." Benny put her head on my chest and her hand between my legs. I purred, low and deep, as she stroked my clit hard.

"I remember you slinging a strap-on pretty well, but that thing I saw in your leather pants, that was different. I don't know how skilled you are with your super clit."

"Is that what you're calling it?"

"Sure."

"Does it weird you out?" I'd taken Benny's virginity. At first, she wasn't on board with being penetrated at all even when we'd moved on to other things. But we worked up to it slowly, and after a few weeks, she was into it. Way into it.

"It scares me a little, but I have been curious."

"Well, later I'll show it to you and you can tell me how you feel about it then."

"Okay." Benny stopped moving her hand. "And what about you and Tokyo?"

"I won't sleep with her anymore," I replied.

"No, I mean, are you still going to stay with her in her quarters? I don't think I can feed you in there."

"No. I've been staying with Omi for a while."

"That's nice of her. She's a sweet lady."

"She is. What happened with the fingers? I liked what the fingers were doing."

"Oh," Benny said with a cheeky smile. "I'm sorry. You mean like this?" Her fingers started moving again between my legs.

"Yes, like that. Fuck, B."

She leaned closer and kissed me this time. "Have you met her wife, Mary?"

"No." I groaned and wrapped my fingers around her wrist, pushing her a little harder against my clit. "She doesn't talk about her much."

"See? I'm not the only person who likes their privacy."

"Yeah. I know. Don't stop. I'm really close."

"She's Mama's best friend, ya know. Mary," Benny said.

"She is?"

"Yeah. They've been really close for years. They live on our street."

"Hmm. I'd like to meet her sometime, if it's okay with Omi."

"She won't mind."

"But for now…" I moved Benny's hand and hopped off the bed. After a quick hunt, I dug up Benny's T-shirt and tossed it to her. Then I scrambled into my tank top and my underwear.

"What is it?" she asked. "I thought you were really close."

"Your mama is walking down the hall. She has breakfast."

"Oh." Benny quickly pulled on her T-shirt, then fished her underwear out of the covers just as her mama called through the door.

"You girls decent?" Being a little distracted by Dalhem's grip on my life, I had forgotten how Southern Benny's mama was. Her twang nearly slapped me in the face as she shouted through the door. It made me suddenly homesick.

"As decent as we'll be. Come on in, Mama."

Mrs. Tarver nudged her way into the room, carrying a tray loaded down with French toast and fruit. "My Lord. You two had fun last night. It smells like blood and booty in here."

Benny blushed like crazy and covered her face. "Mama." I wanted to hide under the bed, but managed just to shake my head as I sat back down next to B.

"Oh, hush, angel. You know I have to tease you. Here ya go." I leaned over the foot of the bed and took the tray from Mrs. Tarver. As I settled it over Benny's lap, her mama made herself comfortable in the chair. "Well, Cleo, darling, it's lovely to finally meet you. Though I wish we'd met under different circumstances."

"I agree, ma'am. Likewise," I said. I sounded as nervous as a teen boy with his pants around his ankles and a shotgun in his face.

"Now, none of that ma'am nonsense. You call me Leanne."

I chuckled at her admonishment. "Yes, ma'am."

"I take it the deed is done," she said.

I looked to Benny to answer that one.

"Yes, Mama. We're bound now. There's something else we have to tell you." I looked at Benny. Her voice had changed, suddenly heavy with a drawl that matched her mother's. I had never seen her this relaxed before. Even when we were alone, being honest with each other and sharing our secrets, she always seemed like she was holding back a little. She always seemed a little guarded, but when she was talking to her mama, she seemed like she was in her safe zone. She sounded really happy. I gently squeezed her thigh under the covers. She scooted closer to me. "Maybe we should tell her what else we decided last night."

"Oh, yeah." I cleared my throat and did my best not to piss my pants. "Ms. Leanne, I was wondering if I could have your permission to marry your daughter?"

She screamed so loud, Benny and I both winced and covered our ears.

"Mama. Mama. Stop yelling."

"I'm sorry. Oh my Lord! Yes, Cleo. You have my complete permission. Oh, I'm so happy. I was just telling Benny the other day I was so sad when you two split." I looked at Benny. She rolled her eyes and nodded again. "You are so welcome to be a part of our family any day, hon. Oh, I'm so happy."

"Mama, calm down."

"Thank you, Ms. Leanne. That means a lot to me. Really."

"Where is Daddy?" Benny asked. I wondered the same thing. I didn't sense him anywhere in the house. I hadn't sensed him for a few hours.

"He left during the night in a huff. He's not speaking to me now, but don't worry about him. He's just being a grumper. What I want to know is when's the wedding? Where are you two planning to live? How can I help?"

"We haven't gotten that far yet," Benny said. "Mama, what should I do about Paeno?" I looked down at the mark on Benny's arm. I traced my fingers over the intricate design. Not only was it still there, but it looked like it had gotten a little darker over the course of the night.

"Oh, who cares about your daddy and his demon sister?" Ms. Leanne said. She came over to the bed and touched Benny's cheek. "I'll talk to him and you won't have to worry a bit about Paeno."

"Are you sure? I know you are happy for us, but Daddy seemed really upset, and I know that Paeno is going to take this tu'lah very seriously."

"You're right, but I don't want you to worry. You and your daddy made a promise that I don't think was meant to be kept. You and Cleo belong together. I'm not going to let him or Paeno pull you apart. I want you to start thinking about wedding dresses."

"I think we'll only be looking for a dress for Benny," I said.

"Oh, don't worry, Cleo," Ms. Leanne said. "Benny's daddy has the best man for suits. You'll be looking so sharp. Oh, girls. I'm so happy. What time do you need to get back to school?"

"Two hours ago," Benny said. She'd already missed one of her classes.

"Eat up and I'll have Douglas go get your car. Cleo, you'll ride with her?"

I preferred to drive, but the sun was already up. I didn't have much of a choice. "Yeah. I'll shift and go back to the house with you."

"Great. Oh, you girls." Ms. Leanne tossed her hands in the air. "So happy!"

Once Miss Leanne left, Benny moved her tray and straddled my legs. I couldn't help the sudden urge I had to cry. I pulled her closer with my hands on her ass. Benny wiped my face. "I knew she would love you."

"Thank you for that," I replied. "I didn't really think I would want her approval so much, but I did."

"And you got it." Benny kissed me again and wiped the last of my tears away.

"How in the hell are you this subdued and that woman is your mama?"

"Yin and yang, baby. Yin and yang."

❖

A couple hours later, Benny and I pulled up to the house. She followed me to Omi's quarters where I shifted back from my form as a fluffy dog and changed my clothes.

"My next class isn't until two." I looked up from tying my boots. Benny had a certain glint in her eye. I definitely could have gone for another round of fucking and feeding, but there was another conversation that needed to be had. I'd left Camila in the lurch big-time.

"Let's go talk to them and then we'll find some place to have a little fun." I grabbed Benny's hand and led her down the hall.

Camila opened the door to her apartment and glared at me.

"We come in peace. I swear. Please don't punch me again."

She let us in, but did me the sweet favor of punching me in the shoulder as I came through the door. She hugged Benny.

They were watching some Shirley Temple movie on TV Land. Ginger didn't look up from the TV, but she said hey as she let out a yawn, which wasn't like her at all. Ginger was anal about the amount of sleep she and Camila got. I prayed I wasn't the reason she'd been skimping on her rest. I flopped down in their armchair and pulled Benny into my lap. She wiggled the way she used to when she was trying to distribute her weight on my thighs. But that was before I could lift a small car with no effort.

"Stop," I whispered. "You're fine."

"Sorry."

"How are you feeling?" Camila asked her. She slid onto the couch and pulled Ginger's legs across her lap.

"Fine now, but I had a really close call. Thank you for helping me," Benny said.

"You know I'd do anything for you and for you, asshole," Camila replied, nodding to me.

"I said I was sorry."

"Still angry." Camila opened her mouth to keep chewing me out, but I held up my hand.

"I know. I fucked up royally. I put her in danger. I put all three of us in the path of Dalhem's almighty vengeance. I am sorry, but you would have done the same for Ginger, and if I recall correctly, you practically did."

She did, Ginger whispered into my mind, but of course, Camila heard her too. Her anger faded as Ginger flashed her a huge smile.

"Both of you. Even you, Red." Camila bent and kissed Ginger on her lips. "You drive me fucking crazy."

"Really. I had no idea what my bite would do to her, and you know I would never intentionally steal a feeder from you."

"I know. If it were anyone but Benny I would have happily told Dalhem to kill you. But it seems like you two have really worked things out."

"Are you guys like a couple now?" Ginger asked with a mocking grin.

"Yes," Benny said.

"That's what I wanted to talk to you about," I told Camila. "Well, one of the things. After B graduates, I want to leave the house."

"What?" Benny and Ginger said at the same time.

"Are you sure?" Benny asked. "I thought you'd at least want to see Skylar and Hollis through to their senior year."

"No. You and I need to start fresh. I want to keep Andrew, but I think it would be better if I had feeders who were new to us both, didn't know our history and shit." It was a compromise for Benny. I had to feed, and I couldn't help the sexual nature of those feedings, but Benny had been through so much drama in this house, drama I had dragged her through. If we could start over with new humans who knew us as a couple and not two dysfunctional exes who couldn't seem to get their shit together, it would only help our relationship.

Benny leaned down and kissed me. "I really appreciate that."

"Aww, you two are so cute. Yay, I'm so happy you made up."

"Shut up, Ginger." I chuckled. Then I asked Camila, "So what do you think?"

"Uh, yes. I guess that makes sense. I assume you'll be joining Dalhem's nest, unless you have plans to move somewhere else." I fucking hated my soon-to-be father-in-law, but what Camila suggested made the most sense. I deferred to Benny just to make sure.

"What do you think?"

"That would be the easiest thing to do. Before my meeting with Paeno, I thought he would bind me to one of his demons near home anyway."

"What were you planning to do?" I asked her. Jesus, I had no idea what her plans for after graduation were.

"There's always a human liaison who works with the Feds in their 'paranormal' department. The man in that position is planning on retiring soon. I was going to take over for him."

"Do you still want to do that?"

Benny hesitated for a moment. She glanced up at Ginger and

Camila, and I could tell she was having a hard time really opening up in front of them, but I wanted her to feel free to speak her mind. They were on our side. After a few more moments, she shook her head. "I want to focus on us. And...our baby."

Ginger sprang all the way up then. "Wait! Did I miss something? Are you pregnant? What the hell happened last night?"

"No." Benny laughed. "I've just..." She took a breath and spat it all out. "When Cleo and I were together before, we talked about having a baby after I graduated. I still want that. We still want that."

"You ready for a kid?" Camila asked me.

"Hell no," I said honestly. I was terrified I was going to screw the kid up beyond repair. I reached up and smoothed Benny's hair off her neck. "But I want to try. I think I can figure it out with you."

"You two are rather adorable. It's disgusting. Please stop it," Camila said.

"You going to adopt or are you going to go looking for some sperm? I know a black guy." Ginger jiggled her eyebrows. Her brother Todd was indeed a very handsome black man. He had married a nice Indian woman named Tejal a couple years ago. But Tejal was a demon, and Ginger had told me Todd was only waiting a few more years before he planned to join her.

"We'll let you know, but thanks for offering up his gonads for us," I replied.

"Hey. No problem." Ginger yawned again.

"Have I been keeping you up?" I asked her.

She shook her head and yawned again. "No. Jill and Sam are."

"Oh."

"Don't worry about it," Ginger said, waving me off.

"So this means you're breaking off your engagement to your aunt?" Camila asked Benny.

"Yeah." Ginger sat up again. "About that. Isn't Paeno your aunt? That's so gross."

"No. She's not," Benny replied.

"I'm joking. She's right, Red." Camila snickered. "Abrah was Dalhem's only blood-bourne sibling. Paeno is no more his sister than Natasha and I are blood related. It's just a familial term they use."

"See," Benny said, nudging my shoulder.

"Whatever. It's still gross," I replied before I kissed her again, feeling that lovesickness swirl through me.

"Eww. Stop," Ginger said.

Much to my disappointment, Benny pulled away. "Excuse me. All the times I had to watch you two make out good-bye. Make out hello. Make out it's Tuesday."

"For real, though. You two define get a room. Come here, baby." I grabbed Benny's cheeks and playfully shoved my tongue into her mouth.

"Okay. We get it." Camila chuckled.

"You're really going to leave?" Ginger asked me.

"Yeah," I said, unable to mask the sadness in my voice. "I'll miss you dickheads, but it's time to go. Plus I think I need to get away from Tokyo for good."

"Ha. Good luck with that. She's gonna go postal when you tell her she's not getting any more—what did she call it that one time?" Ginger asked Camila.

"Your sweet dark chocolate cock."

I closed my eyes and shuddered. Out of one mess and still left to clean up another. "She'll have to get over it. But I don't think she'll be my biggest problem."

"You worried about Dalhem?" Ginger asked.

"You should be," Camila added.

"No, actually." And I wasn't. I knew for a fact that Benny had him wrapped around her finger. I'd follow his orders, sometimes, but I wasn't afraid to tell him what I thought and how I felt for his daughter. If he really wanted to keep us apart, I think dealing with Benny and her mother would be more of a pain in the ass than it was worth. I had other things on my mind. "But that's the other thing I wanted to talk to you about. Do you know anything about Paeno?"

"No. I've never met any of Dalhem's brothers and sisters, save Abrah," Camila said. "But she orchestrated their escape. She brokered the deal with God. She's extremely powerful."

"I was afraid you'd say something like that." I flopped back in the chair and prayed that Paeno was as forgiving as she was persuasive. Something told me she wouldn't be. "Do you know anything about the tu'lah?"

"Not much," Camila replied. "I know of them, but I'm not that old. I wasn't around for their last exchange." I wanted to be annoyed with Camila's lack of knowledge, but it wasn't her fault that she was nearly the most powerful vampire in this hemisphere and also one of the youngest.

"Natasha and Kina were, though," Benny said.

"It's worth a shot." I shrugged.

"I'm on it." Ginger closed her eyes and made a show of wiggling her nose. A few moments later Kina and Natasha appeared. Kina was covered to her elbows in paint. Natasha was half-dressed in a loose T-shirt, and she smelled strongly of blood and other bodily fluids.

"Oh sorry." Ginger, grimaced as she caught sight of what Natasha was wearing and the way she smelled.

"No matter at all, my queen. This feeding was simply recreational."

"I was painting something for you," Kina said to Camila. "I'm sure you won't mind if the paint dries all fucked up."

"I'll double your commission," Camila said.

"What's up?" Kina took a seat on the other end of the couch and Natasha joined her on the armrest.

"Do you know anything about tu'lahs?" I asked them.

Natasha basically froze. Kina stopped picking the paint out from under her fingernails. "Why?"

"I have been marked for exchange to Dalhem's sister Paeno." Benny pulled up the sleeve of her sweater and showed them Paeno's mark. "But I'm bound to Cleo and I want to keep it that way. We're gonna get married."

"Uh. Well…" Kina glanced at Natasha, who cleared her throat and sat forward on the couch.

She cleared her throat again. "Technically, Dalhem has to answer for the tu'lah."

"But I'll be honest, Benny. I've never heard of a tu'lah being broken. Like ever," Kina said.

"So what does that mean?" I asked.

"That could mean anything. If you refuse to leave Cleo, then Dalhem will have to give Paeno something or someone she wants even more," Kina replied. "But there is a chance that Paeno might let you call it off. Just because it hasn't happened before doesn't mean it can't. I guess it just depends on why she wants you in the first place."

"Well, she wasn't exactly clear on that. You know how they talk all strange."

"Yup," Ginger said.

"She made it sound like she wanted me just because I was linked to Dalhem. The rest of it seemed a little carnal and cryptic."

"Shit," I muttered.

"I'll call Daddy tonight. I want to be with you," Benny said.

"I know. I won't let her take you. I promise." I prayed to God it was a promise I could keep.

❖

After our talk with my sister-queens, and a few minutes with my fangs in Benny's neck and my fingers between her legs, she had to take off and get ready for class. I had no idea what I was going to do about the shitty situation with Paeno. I understood the seriousness of the tu'lah. Dalhem and his demon family didn't take any pledges lightly, but I refused to believe that Dalhem would just ship Benny off against her wishes. He hated me, but he loved Benny and her mama more than anything. I just had to hope that his anger with me didn't tear Benny and me apart in some other way.

From what Benny told me, we had three and a half months to figure shit out with Paeno. In the meantime, we had a few more issues to deal with in the house, like shuffling a few of the girls around, and I knew Hollis and Skylar would throw a Class A temper tantrum when I told them I was leaving, but once they were bound to Camila, they'd be fine. I had to talk to Andrew, though.

I called Rodrick.

"Hey, can I use your basement common room?" I asked. Rodrick was two hundred years older than me, wiser and more even-tempered than I could ever wish to be. He was so cool to me, and he always understood when I needed special time with my boy in his house. Rodrick made my relationship with Andrew so much easier.

"Of course, my sister-queen. I will call Andrew down."

"Thanks, man." I hung up the phone and vanished across the street. After I took a seat on one of their couches, I wondered how often Rodrick had them reupholstered. I couldn't imagine the size of the cum stains after their movie nights. A few minutes later, Andrew came through the open archway with their house dog, Motherfucker, at his feet. The puppy ran over to me and licked my hand.

"He stop shitting on the rug yet?" I patted the couch beside me. Motherfucker thought I was talking to him and jumped up on the cushion. Andrew sat on the arm of the couch instead.

"When the freshmen remember to walk him, yeah. What's up? We never meet down here."

"Benny and I are getting married and I think we're moving to D.C.

at the end of the semester," I said almost in one breath. "And I want you to come with us."

Andrew blinked, then looked to the side. "Uh, so you're marrying Benny, but you want to keep me as a feeder?"

"Yes."

"I'm happy for you. I know how you feel about her, but she hates me."

"No, she was mad at me. She and I already talked about it. We want you to stay with us. If you want to."

"We or you? I'm not trying to be a dick, Cleo. She really doesn't like me. She was really pissed that you were sleeping with a guy."

"Well, that's part of it."

"Right, like I said."

"See, I didn't want to do this to you. I have to be a wife to her, ya know, and I...I sound so selfish."

Andrew just stretched his neck and huffed out a deep breath through his nose. He was really upset.

"Listen. I love you and I just want you to be happy. I want you to do whatever you're comfortable with, and if you're not comfortable with being with Benny and me together, I understand."

"No. You're my only family. That's all. I just don't want to come with you and then Benny decides I can't even talk to you anymore."

"That won't happen. I promise."

"Can I think about it?" he asked.

"Yeah, sure. But *know* that I want you around. I want to keep feeding from you. I want you to be in my life. We just have to cut it with the sex."

"I get it. Man, you fuck me really good, though." He laughed a little. "You're the best mistress I've ever had."

"I know, honey. We'll work something out. And maybe we'll find someone just as good to keep you satisfied in that way. While you're thinking it over, there is one more part for you to consider."

"What?"

"How would you feel about being an uncle?"

I chuckled at Andrew's reaction. His whole face lit up.

CHAPTER TWELVE

Benny

On my way to class, I texted Sam, Anna-Jade, and Amy and told them to meet me for dinner down in the food court in the student union. The prices for meals were murder on your meal plan, but a bunch of our sorority sisters and frat brothers would be in the cafeteria, and I wanted to talk to them alone. I ran into Jill by the library, and even though I felt like a jerk, I lied and told her I was having dinner with some of the seniors to plan something special for the rest of the girls while we were away on spring break. I'd come up with an actual treat so Jill wouldn't have a lot of questions for me later. She was hesitant. Luckily, Micah passed by on his way to the café and dragged Jill with him. When I thanked him, he just told me to come by and see that puppy, and we'd call it even. I'd have to come up with something special for him too.

I paid for the girls' food, and once we found a table, Amy pounced on me.

"Okay," Amy said. She propped her elbows on the table and clasped her hands together. "This has to be big. You never—I mean, B. Come on. You never ask for girl time with us. Ever."

"She's right," Sam said. "What gives?"

I took a deep breath and told them about my new relationship status. Amy freaked. A.J. clapped and told me how happy she was for us. Samantha sulked. Amy nudged her under on the table. "Do you have anything to say?"

"What?" Sam shrugged and twirled her fork in the middle of her plate. "I'm happy for you. Congrats."

I don't know what I expected from her, but I tried to explain why things were changing and why I was telling them. "Sam, Cleo and I—"

"No. It's cool. I figured it was only a matter of time. You two are fucking psycho for each other. You belonged together."

"Fucking psycho? Is that how you see it?" I wasn't mad, but this was exactly why I didn't like talking to people about my private life. Someone always had a negative opinion. I glanced at Amy and A.J. to gauge whose side of this conversation they were about to take. Amy had my back. A.J. was just uncomfortable.

"I mean, yeah. You've been so fucking weird with each other for three fucking years and then you're engaged all of a sudden? Doesn't sound too healthy to me, but whatever. We all know how my last relationship ended. I'll be right back." She didn't even give me a chance to respond. She just walked away toward the bathroom. I looked after her, feeling the frustration gripping my throat.

"Hey," Amy said, pulling my attention back. "We're happy for you. I'm sure Ginger and Camila are too."

"They are," I replied, still irritated.

"Sam's just having a bad semester. There's all this stuff going on with her mom. And you were her last single friend. I don't think she's in the mood to be happy for anyone."

"Have you and Cleo done it yet?" A.J. giggled.

I swallowed and pulled my sweater down over my fist. I could almost feel Paeno's mark taunting me. "Yes. We have."

"Oh," A.J. said. She looked confused.

"What?"

"Nothing. I just thought you were celibate." Rumors. Precisely why I loved them.

"Well, I'm not. Amy just likes to make things up."

"Sorry," Anna-Jade said bashfully, which made me feel terrible. She was the last person I should have snapped at.

"I'm sorry, A.J. I'm not angry with you. I'm pissed at Amy and her big mouth."

"You should be pissed at Sam for ruining this lovely dinner we were having," Amy said. "And speak of the devil." I turned around to see Samantha walking back toward us. She sat down and immediately hugged me.

"I'm a huge bitch and you know it. I love you, and if Cleo makes you happy enough to call a special dinner, then you must be making the right choice."

"Thanks, Sam," I said.

"Now I just have to find another bed to sleep in for the rest of the semester. You and Cleo are going to mess up my rotation."

"There's always Jill's bed," I suggested.

"No, thanks. She won't shut up long enough for me to get any sleep. Plus, those braces have to come out first before she's of any real use to me. I'm not letting her go down on me with that much metal in her mouth."

A.J. tried to hide her snicker. She was too sweet to laugh full-out at a sister's expense.

"So," Amy said, "did you guys have the best pent-up make-up sex ever?"

"Yes," I said as I brushed my jeans in my lap. "And that's all I'm saying."

"You really thought she would give you details," Sam said.

"It's okay, Benny. A lady has to have her secrets." A.J. smiled.

"Oh, whatever. For such a little girl you are fucking loud. I've heard Micah working you out from across the street," Sam said.

"Oh my gosh." A.J. turned bright red. "No, you haven't."

"Oh yes, we have," Amy said. Samantha held her hand out and gave her a low five.

"You guys stink." A.J. giggled.

As we finished dinner, we continued to give A.J. a hard time and they teased me a little too, mostly about Jill, but it felt good to know that they were happy for me, even if Samantha's initial response had been a little cold.

On our way back to the house, Amy hooked her arm through mine. "I'm really glad you told us, B."

"I am too."

"So, a night wedding?" she asked.

"If we want to get married anywhere other than my mama's living room, yes."

"Have you picked a maid of honor yet?"

"It's me, you bitch," Sam said.

"I'll let you two fight it out with Ginger."

"Fuck that," Sam said. "She can have it."

❖

Sometimes in life you find yourself in situations you'd hoped you'd never repeat. I looked around at my sorority sisters, and the glances I got back proved that Amy really couldn't keep her mouth shut. I hadn't expected her to, but a bunch of the girls now knew why we were having this special chapter meeting. Part of me wished our sister-queens had held their own private meetings with their feeders. Camila needed to replace me in her meal schedule, and we had a stern policy of taking volunteers. We could have done it by secret ballot, slipped under each girl's door, but Cleo had asked me to be open about us, and she was right. Telling three of my friends would still allow me to pretend Cleo and I were a secret to the other girls. None of them expected me to own up to anything even if rumors were flying around the house. I tried not to notice the way everyone was looking at us, but gave up when Cleo pulled my hand into her lap just before the meeting started. I wanted to take my hand back. PDA was a foreign concept for me, but I also wanted to do this for Cleo. I *knew* I should do it for myself.

Ginger got everyone's attention and the room quieted down. "I can't believe we're doing this again," she said under her breath. "Okay. We're gonna mix things about a little bit here, girls. Who wants to feed Camila?"

"What's going on?" one of Natasha's sophomores asked.

"Does this have anything to do with our new lovebirds over there?" Amy said, winking at me. I appreciated her putting a positive spin on things before we faced the firing squad of public opinion.

"Why yes, Amy. It does," Ginger said.

I swallowed, then took the first of many steps. I didn't want Ginger to have to speak for us. "Cleo and I have some history and we've decided to give our relationship another try."

The reactions around the room were mixed. The seniors who knew us from the beginning seemed to be on board, even Laura and Mel, who were ready to push me off the library roof the week before. The younger girls were just confused. They'd heard all the insanity that had been going on between Cleo and me, especially in recent weeks, but they hadn't realized we were in this type of territory. Jill, though... I looked at her from across the room as her whole face fell. Another second and she would start to cry.

Before Ginger could call the room to order again, Mel raised her hand. "If Cleo is getting another feeder, then shouldn't she lose one?"

"Speak for yourself," Hollis said.

"I am, *puta*," Mel said with a little snarl. "Ginger, I'll do it."

"You sure?"

Mel looked at Cleo. "We're done with the, ya know?"

"Yeah." Cleo nodded.

"Yeah, I'll do it."

"Thank you, Mel. That's twice for you." The first time being when Cleo herself became a demon—Mel had cut her bond with Tokyo to feed Cleo.

"Okay. That's it," Ginger said. "Meeting adjourned."

Jill jumped up and bolted from the room.

I turned to Cleo. "I have to talk to her."

She nodded up the stairs. "Go."

I took off for the freshman and sophomore floor, but Cleo grabbed my hand before I made it two steps. "Hey. Come right back here when you're done."

I hesitated for a moment before I answered. There was something different about her tone. Something commanding. "Yes, Cleo."

The wink she gave me sent a tingle through my stomach. "That's a good bunny."

I cursed Jill for delaying whatever Cleo had planned and chased her up the stairs. I found her in her room, which she shared with another freshman, Portia. We matched them together because no one wanted to live with Jill, and Portia spent most of her time with her boyfriend, who lived off campus. And here I was about to tell Jill, once again, that someone else wasn't interested in her.

I knocked and cracked her door open a little. "Can I come in?"

Jill was weeping. Not crying, but curled up on herself on her bed, sobbing her eyes out. I sat beside her. I didn't know what to say. Nothing would appease her. I just sat with her and let her cry for a while. Eventually, she asked me to hand her a tissue. I grabbed the whole box from Portia's desk. She took some time to clean her face and then we got our chance to talk.

"Is that what you were talking about at dinner? Is that why you didn't want me there, because you wanted to talk about getting back together with Cleo?" she asked.

I couldn't lie to her. For once, Jill was breaking my heart.

"Yeah. I—" I almost said I wanted to tell my friends first; a horrible choice of words. "I just didn't know how to tell you."

Jill fell apart all over again. "You can't be with her. She was so mean to you, Benny. Don't you remember? I've seen the way she looks at you and I've heard the things her feeders said about you. You're so nice and you deserve someone who will love you the right way."

It was just great to have a freshman making me sound like a main character in the movie of the week. I just kept going back. But this was different. Cleo and I had both made mistakes, but at the end of the day, or the end of the night, we belonged together.

"Jill…" I couldn't say I loved Cleo, because that would only hurt her more. I couldn't tell her that she never had a chance with me, because that would just make her feel more rejected. I had no idea what to do.

In the next moment, Jill and I weren't alone. Ginger appeared by the foot of the bed. I'd noticed during the meeting what Cleo had noticed that morning. Despite her chipper mood downstairs, Ginger was exhausted.

"Hey," I said, a bit confused.

"I can feel this." She motioned toward Jill. Fantastic, I was making Jill so miserable Ginger could sense her pain. Absolutely fabulous. "Trust me. When she's in a good mood, it's like I'm on crank." Ginger slid onto the bed on Jill's other side and pulled her into her arms. "I got her. You take off."

"Are you sure?"

"Yeah. Beat it."

I reached out and rubbed Jill's shoulder. "I'm gonna go. I'll see you tomorrow?"

Jill sniffled. "Okay."

After thanking Ginger again, I walked to the door, careful not to look back. I hated what I had just done to Jill, and Ginger, and Camila by default, but before I closed Jill out of my life for good, she called after me.

I turned around just as she slammed into my body with a hug. I hugged her back.

"Can we still be friends?" she asked quietly.

"Sure we can. Like I said, I'll see you tomorrow." Jill finally let me go.

"Come back here, Jilly Bean," I heard Ginger say. Jill didn't complain about the nickname for once as she let go and walked back to the bed. I knew she was in the right hands.

❖

When I came back down to the TV room, Cleo was watching a rerun of some *Real Housewives* show with Faeth, Ruth, and Maddie. A few juniors were in the corner pretending to study, but they were watching television too. Faeth made room for me on the couch. I sat between her and Cleo. The moment Cleo put her arm around my waist and pulled me closer, I forgot all about Jill. I made myself more comfortable with my hand on her thigh.

On the TV screen, two women with horrible addictions to Botox and prescription drugs were arguing about the dress one had worn to a charity event. Maddie and Ruth had a lot of opinions on who was right and who was more medicated, but my focus was on Cleo's fingers moving up and down my side. My whole body was keyed into her. I could hear myself breathing and I was hot all over. All I could think about was her taking those simple caresses to another level. I held particularly still, trying not to draw attention to my own arousal. Every part of me sparked with the knowledge of what Cleo was capable of. Every nerve ending and sensitive bit seemed to stand at attention, just waiting for her to make some sort of move. Maybe we would just watch TV with the girls, then head to bed. Cleo was after a little normalcy these days. Or maybe we would go for a walk in the cold and she would feed from me out in the open.

Or maybe she'd decided on my punishment. I had diverted from the script the night before.

The housewives ended their hour. I looked at Cleo as she glanced past me to her sister-queen.

"Hey, Faeth."

Faeth stood and made a show of dusting off her pants. "All right, kids, let's go."

"But a new episode is about to start," Maddie whined.

"You have a TV in your room," Faeth replied.

"But I don't want to walk up the stairs."

"I'll carry you. Let's go."

"Okay!" Maddie handed Ruth her book bag, then hopped on Faeth's back.

Begrudgingly, the study group in the corner broke up their slack efforts and followed Faeth upstairs. I knew they would be annoyed with Cleo or possibly me for kicking them out, but again my focus was elsewhere.

Cleo was quiet for a few minutes. We watched a brief recap of the train wreck we had just seen, then the start of a new sixty-minute mess.

Soon Cleo's fingers found their way into my hair. "How was class today?" she asked quietly.

I looked at her gorgeous face, her amazing full lips, and her light brown eyes. She would be this young forever, always this beautiful. "It was fine."

"Come here." She wrapped her fingers deeper into my hair and pulled me into her lap. I straddled her and we were kissing. Weeks' and months' worth of kissing. Her lips were so much softer than before, her technique more masterful, which I didn't think was possible. She'd been an amazing kisser as a human.

"Fuck, I missed you," she whispered against my mouth.

"I missed you too." I knew we were both talking about more than our afternoon apart.

"Go turn off the lights," she said.

I calmly climbed off her lap and flicked the switch on the overhead lights by the door. The lights from the hallway and the kitchen would still come through the curtains on the French doors that separated those rooms from the TV room. I moved to close the doors to the hallway.

"Uh-uh," Cleo said. I looked at her over my shoulder. "I didn't say anything about the doors. Leave those open and come back over here." I didn't like that idea at all, but I followed her orders and went back to the couch.

"Right here." Cleo indicated for me to stand between her legs. When I was in position, she reached under the pillow beside her and pulled out a roll of red bondage tape.

"What do you have on under that sweater?" she asked.

"A camisole and a bra."

"Take off your sweater. I don't want you to get too hot."

I pulled the cashmere over my head and placed it in Cleo's outstretched hand. She draped it over the back of the couch.

"Wrists together. Hands out." I looked down at her soft fingers as she traced Paeno's mark.

"I talked to Mama. She told me Daddy is working on Paeno." We'd had a quick chat before the chapter meetings. Daddy was still in a horrible mood, but she insisted that I focus on Cleo and our relationship. I wasn't foolish enough to think we were scot-free, but I didn't want another demon to ruin this moment.

"That's good," she replied. It was obvious that she didn't want anyone else to ruin the mood either. Effortlessly, she bound my wrists together. She remembered that I liked the tape better than the handcuffs we'd toyed with before we did some proper investigation. The cool plastic stuck to itself and not my skin. Cleo wrapped it pretty tight, but not uncomfortably so. Still, my heart was racing.

"How does it feel?" she asked.

"Fine, Cleo."

"Good." She sat forward and undid the button on my jeans, then pulled down my zipper. "I want you across my lap. Do you need help?"

I sized up the couch cushions. "I think I can manage."

"Okay. Kneel here." I maneuvered myself onto my knees beside her. She gripped my jeans and my underwear and pulled them down to the middle of my thighs. I swallowed anxiously as the air in the room hit the now-damp spot between my legs. "Lean forward. I got you." I did as she asked, and after a few adjustments, I was across Cleo's lap with a pillow supporting my head and neck, and my ass in the air. My arms were stretched out in front of me, just touching the other end of the couch.

"We're going be here for a little while. Are you comfortable?"

I moved my knee a little bit then settled into place. "Yes, Cleo."

"That's a good bunny."

I took deep, measured breaths as I waited for Cleo's next move. She flipped through the channels and found a block of *Sex and the City* reruns, but she turned the volume down low. I closed my eyes and continued to wait. The sound of the TV almost faded completely after some time and all I could hear were the little noises there on the couch. The slight movements Cleo made, her breath and mine. I thought I could hear my heart beating too, louder and louder as the moments went by. I focused on the heat between our bodies. I knew I would start to sweat soon. Where my skin touched her leather pants, I could feel the temperature rising higher and higher. My pussy was swollen, the most eager part of me, impatient to be touched. I couldn't tell how wet I was, but I felt the moisture growing thicker with every minute that passed.

Cleo began on my right butt cheek. She stroked it and then petted my skin very gently before she grabbed a rough handful. She released it with a thick pinch and then slapped the cheek. I jerked but didn't cry out. She repeated the motions again: a gentle stroke, a grab, and a slap.

With every grab, she pulled my cheeks apart, and as they bounced back together, they split again under the weight of the smack. Every impact sent shocks to my clit.

I bit my lip.

"I want to hear you. You don't have to scream, but I want to hear you."

I exhaled sharply as she ran her thumb lightly up my crack and finally moaned as she delivered another slap. "Yes, Cleo."

The spanking lasted a long time. Cleo switched to the other cheek, and by the end, my ass was burning, pleasantly, but still tender and hot. My pussy was on fire. Knowing I couldn't take any more, she parted my lips. I said her name again, begged in a desperate moan. I would die if I didn't come soon.

She found my clit and toyed with it between her two fingers and then her hand was gone. I heard the smacking of her lips. "Mmm," she said. "My bunny's sweet." I shuddered, rolling my head on my shoulders, just picturing my juices in her mouth.

She replaced her fingers again and touched every tender inch. She played with my lips and spread them again to get to my clit. She brought me to a peak and backed off just in time. I writhed against her thighs, chasing the friction to get me there, but Cleo quickly reminded me who was in charge. Another firm smack on my ass and I settled. I would come when she was ready.

Her arm came around my back and under my leg and she stroked my clit fully this time as two fingers tunneled inside me. The groan I let out was greedy and pathetic.

"Fuck yourself," Cleo said, her voice threaded with a deep growl. "Fuck yourself on my hand." I thrust back against her palm, back and forth, rubbing my clit back and forth between her fingers. I came in a tight explosion, my whole body focused and coiled where Cleo claimed me in her grip. I muffled my own screams with my face in the pillow. I shuddered and came again as I heard her growl above me. I needed her bite.

Cleo pulled her fingers out of my pussy abruptly and left me twitching and still aching for another go. She rubbed my ass, trying to soothe me, but it only riled me even more. I looked up just as she cut my hands loose with her knife. I wiggled my fingers before Cleo helped sit me up. When I was standing between her legs again, she pulled up my pants and underwear and zipped me up. She was breathing hard and her fangs had dropped completely. She wasn't done with me.

She swallowed and pointed toward the floor. I eased to my knees and looked up at her. She took my chin in her hand.

"What were you thinking about while I was spanking you? Think carefully," she said. My body tingled at the husky sound of her voice. She was barely holding her demon off.

"I was thinking about coming," I replied.

"And what were you thinking about while I was fucking you?"

"I was thinking about you making me come."

"Were you thinking about the girls?"

"No," I told her honestly.

"Did you want me to stop just in case Florencia walked in?"

"No. I was thinking about how you were making me feel."

She leaned forward and lightly kissed me on the lips. "That's what I want you to remember. You don't have to care about what other people think when we're alone together. You don't have to worry about other people at all when you're with me. I'm going to take care of you. Do you believe me?"

"Yes, Cleo."

"Do you trust me?"

"Yes." This was exactly what I needed to hear. This spanking right out in the open was something I needed for us to move forward. It wasn't enough that we were blood bound. Our relationship needed more care and more attention; I needed to learn to really trust her. I blinked a sudden assault of tears away. Cleo kissed me again.

"We're going to work on your fears. I will never embarrass you. I will never hurt you. I want you to see this"—she motioned between us—"is all that matters."

I nodded. "I understand."

"Good. Can you walk?"

"Yeah." My legs were a little rubbery, but I'd make it up the stairs.

"Good. Finish your homework and then I'll let you finger me while I feed."

CHAPTER THIRTEEN

Benny

When I woke up, I saw Cleo had sent me a text. She'd offered to let me sleep down in Omi's apartment, but I felt weird imposing. Our night together had been amazing. My whole body was still humming after her spanking lesson, but somehow I managed to finish a paper for my international media class after Cleo delivered on another promise.

I knew I'd been missing out on certain intimate aspects of the demon/feeder relationship by sticking to my strict code of requirements. Even when Ginger and Camila became more open with their marriage and began to occasionally incorporate their other feeders into their sexual escapades, my friendship with Ginger made it impossible for me to engage Camila in that way even if Ginger wasn't in the room. I wanted the intrinsically sexual aspects that came with a blood bond. They almost defined the reason I wanted to feed from Cleo the moment we got together. It was true that I had made some mistakes, but in a few short days, Cleo had shown I'd been right in those desires.

When I finished my homework, she lay me down on my bed and stripped me bare. She climbed on top of me with a few simple instructions. "Give me your fingers. I want you to feel what your blood does to me." I had held out my hand and let her guide me between her legs. I slid a finger inside her tight wetness and then another. It was the first time she'd let me touch her that way since her change. She felt amazing. "I'm gonna ride you." She'd gently dropped her hips on the weight of my fingers before pulling herself back up. "Just like that. Okay?" I nodded weakly and shoved the fingers of my other hand into her thick curly hair when she finally leaned down to kiss me. Our relationship had been fun and passionate before, but now with her demon calling the shots and her human heart driving her motivations, every kiss and every touch packed more love, more meaning. More heat.

She'd ridden my hand for just a few more moments before she bit me, and even though her hips all but stilled, I could feel her muscles tightening and spasming around my fingers. I could feel her pussy soaking more and more as my own nerve endings shot fireworks of pleasure over every inch of my body. She'd licked my vein closed and quickly slipped lower on the bed. She got me off twice more with her mouth on my clit and her fingers thrusting away. That wasn't the end of our play for the night. We kissed and touched for what felt like hours until I couldn't stay awake any longer. I hated that she wasn't there, or couldn't be there in the morning. I was able to admit to myself that there were some downsides to being with a demon.

I reached for my phone on my nightstand. "Call me," her text read. I dialed her right away.

"Good morning, bunny," she purred into the phone.

"Good morning. What time did you leave?"

"Five-ish. You were drooling."

I glanced at my pillow. "No, I wasn't."

"Go into the bathroom. I left a few things in there for you."

"Okay, hold on." I walked into the bathroom and found an enema kit on the sink counter. I picked it up and examined the box. The same one I had at home, stashed under my bed with the remains of our previous relationship. "Before class?" I asked. I picked up the lube beside the box, a little something to grease the way.

"Yeah. Come on down to Omi's before you go. I have something for you."

"You mean something for my butt."

"You and your butt," she clarified.

"Okay. I'll be down in a little while." I hung up my phone, then turned on the warm water.

❖

I knocked on Omi's door a little while later. Cleo let me in. "Is she home?" I asked as I let her take my hand and lead me toward the couch. She sat on the arm and pulled me between her legs.

"Nah. Damn shame too, 'cause we could've crashed down here last night."

I let out a slight laugh. "I don't know. I would have felt bad doing what we did in Omi's bed."

"I can always get her new sheets."

"That's very sweet of you. Uh, before you start sticking things in my butt, there was something I wanted to ask you."

Cleo tilted her head up and licked my neck. "What's that, baby?"

"I was thinking I should talk to Andrew," I said when I stopped shaking.

Her eyebrows shot up as she sat back. "You want to?"

"Yeah. I've been a bitch to him." A huge bitch. Cleo had no idea. I never spoke to him. I'd leave the room if I could whenever he came around. I'd suddenly be full at dinner if he joined our table in the cafeteria. I'd been rude and cold. I had a few things to make up to him. "I want him to be comfortable. I don't want him to feel like I'm pushing him all the way out. He might like Daddy's nest too. There are a lot of good feeders and demons. Who knows? He might meet a guy he likes. A guy his age."

"That's a good call. Moreland's place wasn't ideal for him, but this hasn't been much better. Even if I'm glad he's gotten his education back on track."

"But he's creeping up on thirty and living in a frat house."

"He's not that old." Cleo laughed. "But he's older than I am, in literal human terms, and even I feel like I've grown out of this place."

"It's supposed to be a pit stop. Not forever."

"Thank you, baby. I think you and Andrew talking alone is a good idea."

"I know."

"You know what else?" Cleo stood and wrapped me in her arms.

"What?"

"I love you," she said with a smile.

"I love you too. I'm sorry. The fangs are sexy on you."

"I bet you said the same thing about Camila."

I shook my head. "I didn't even notice she had teeth."

"That's nice, B. Really." Cleo sighed, then roughly palmed my ass. "So. Let's talk about your butt. I thought we needed to rebuild our stockpile. This way, please."

I followed Cleo over to Omi's small kitchenette. She had a few anal plugs out on the table. She held up the smallest one, a skinny red plug with a rectangular base. It couldn't have been any thicker than my finger. "How about this one?"

"To wear to class?" I knew I'd made a face.

"Yeah. What's wrong?"

"It's so little." I took it from Cleo and looked it over more carefully. If Cleo was trying to open me up to anything bigger than a pencil, this wasn't going to work.

"Whoa-ho, excuse me. How about this one?" She grabbed a larger plug and held it for me to examine. It was bigger than the red one, with more of a bulbous shape, but still small enough that I wouldn't regret wearing it around.

"It's purple," I said, smiling.

"You think I forgot your favorite color?"

"I like that one."

"I got this one for you too, but it's too pretty to hide in your jeans all day." She let me try the weight of a third plug. I turned the stainless steel around in my hand. A large purple gem was anchored in the base.

"Later, I want you to pick out a new tail," Cleo said as she took the plug back and placed it on the table.

"I still have the old one. It's at home."

"You kept it?"

"Yeah." Along with some other things I couldn't bear to part with.

"Well, let's get you a new one anyway."

"On purpose this time?"

"Exactly. I also want a list. It's been a while, so I want a numbered list of everything you want to do, especially if it's something we haven't tried before. I don't care how simple or complicated. You can include things that have sparked your interest, but you're nervous to try. And I want a list of things that are off-limits. Can you do that for me?"

"Yes, Cleo." She knew the things I wasn't willing to try, no matter what the circumstance, but there were a few new things I would like to have a go at, with her.

"Good. Drop your pants, bunny." I made a face for sure that time, but unzipped my jeans and pulled them down. Cleo grabbed a bottle of lube. After she poured a generous amount in her palm, she started coating her two fingers. She scrunched her nose and exposed her fang in what would have been a very menacing sneer if it were a vampire other than Cleo, sneering at me while moving her hands like she was jerking off a carrot.

"Can you please not make that face?" I laughed.

"I can't help it. It's my lubing face."

"Should I just throw out all of my pants? It would make things a lot easier."

"It's up to you, bunny-girl. You do have some sexy gams." I had to agree. My legs were the only part of my body that didn't drive me crazy. "Lift up your shirt and the bra." I did as she asked and exposed my breasts. Cleo immediately started kissing my stomach. She was the only one who got away with that sort of thing.

"Stop. That tickles. Ah, God." She hushed my whining by slowly, very slowly inserting her finger behind me. She added to my pleasure by licking the undersides of my breasts and my nipples as she stretched me. I moaned as she moved to my other nipple. She slowly added another finger and, when I was ready, added the plug.

"How does that feel?"

I stood still for a few moments and let my body adjust to the pleasant intrusion. The inner walls of my vagina quivered and pushed back against the plug. It would be an interesting walk across campus. "It feels good, but now I don't want to go to class."

Cleo lightly pinched my butt. "Bend over and let me see." I did and Cleo spread my cheeks a little farther. "Oh that's pretty, baby. The metal one will look better, though." She tapped my hip and motioned for me to turn around. She stood as I put my clothes back in order. I caught her staring down at me as I pulled up my zipper, her purr growing louder and louder.

"I know you're not hungry."

Her growl rumbled between us as she brushed my hair off my shoulder. "Oh, but I am."

I rolled my eyes and gave her my neck.

❖

Considering they were our brother fraternity and their house was right across the street, I spent very little free time with the boys in Omega Beta Alpha. I'd been avoiding Andrew. Micah was extremely fun to be around. Though I wasn't all that cuddly with them, Tim and Jim were like big teddy bears you couldn't help but like. I'd been avoiding Andrew for three years, and unless we were thrust together for chapter functions, I avoided the majority of the chapter members because of him. Micah was their president, but Andrew was their God. They just thought I was shy, but I'm sure Andrew knew the truth.

After class, I walked over to the OBA house to talk to him.

Surprisingly, Micah answered the door. They usually had the freshmen tend to those types of menial tasks.

"Hey! You came to see Motherfucker."

"If that's what you're calling Andrew," I said as I stepped inside. They had the same cleaning crew we did, but their house had this underlying smell of boy and beer.

"Oh, well, you're getting a twofer. That dog fucking loves him." I scooted out of the way just as Tim and a sophomore they called Fart (his named was Derek) came barreling down the stairs.

"Hey, Benny," Derck said as he head-butted Micah in the arm.

"Hey, guys."

"'Sup, Ben." Tim picked up my hand and manually high-fived me. They bolted into the kitchen, probably to share a whole side of beef between them.

"Come on. I'll show you to his room." We walked up to the third floor and Micah led me to the presidential suite in the center of the hall. He pounded on the door.

"Hey, man! There's some hot chick here to see you."

"One sec," Andrew yelled back. I knew that tone. He had someone in there.

"I'm sure he'll be right out. Later." Micah patted me hard on the back and strode down the hall. I had no idea how he didn't break Anna-Jade's tiny body in half.

Andrew's door opened halfway. He only wore boxers, the onyx dog tag that labeled him as Cleo's, and this oddly dreamy, slightly confused smile. If I were straight...

"Hi. I didn't mean to drop in on you like this." I nodded toward his lack of clothes.

"Not a problem. Want to come in?"

"Sure." I stepped inside and saw my assumptions were correct. He wasn't alone. Van, a very sweet freshman, was asleep in his bed with Motherfucker.

"He's still a little homesick," Andrew said with a shrug. He walked over to the bed and rubbed Van's shoulder. "Hey, Van. Wake up, buddy."

"What?" Van's eyes flickered open. "Oh, hi, Benny."

"Hi, Van."

"We're gonna talk a sec. Why don't you go see what the guys are watching downstairs?" It took a few moments, but Van eventually got up. I turned around so he could get dressed. Walking over to the window, I was reminded that Andrew had a direct view of my window across the street. When the door opened and closed, I faced Andrew. He'd put on some lacrosse shorts.

"So what's up?" Andrew leaned against his desk with his arms folded across his chest, covering his nipple rings. "Cleo ask you to talk to me?" On the bed, Motherfucker yawned and stretched. He looked at Andrew and me both and decided our conversation didn't need his input.

"No. I asked her if I could come talk to you."

"Have a seat."

I wanted to, but I was ready to take this plug out. "I'll stand."

Andrew smiled. "Cleo up to her same old tricks?"

"That's it."

"I'll level with you, Benny. I—"

"Let me say this. I can't share her like that right now. I know how that sounds."

"I don't blame you. She's the closest thing I've ever had to a best friend, or a sister, or even a mother. But I'm not in love with her, so I'm sort of at a loss as to what to do here. I think you feel threatened by me, but you shouldn't be. I'm not trying to *be* with her."

"I understand that, so here's what I propose. You stay with us. You're trying to teach kindergarten, right?"

"Yeah."

"Come to D.C. with us, and if you want, you can live with us or I'll have my father set you up with your own place. Your pick of schools. I think you need something different from this, different from what you had with Moreland, and we want to help with that."

"Why? If you want her to yourself."

I'd asked myself the same question, but I had to stop thinking about myself and think about the bigger picture. What Cleo needed. What Andrew needed. I wouldn't be happy if they were both miserable.

"I'm working on some things," I said. "What I need from her for a while is a normal relationship, but none of this is normal. You know I have a plug in my ass." Andrew laughed but nodded as I kept talking. "You and I have similar needs. It's a part of both of us, and I know Cleo is the best person for you in that way. I don't want you to have to go looking somewhere else for good." I glanced at the floor, considering what really needed to be said. "I owe you. You kept her sane when I couldn't. You stuck with her when I lacked the sensitivity to be there for her properly. She didn't do certain things because of you, and I'm not sure you know how much that helped her. Thank you."

"You don't have to thank me, and I don't think you have to be so hard on yourself either. You lost someone close to you in a lot of ways when she changed. You have to remember, though, I know Cleo too. I know how she can be. She's stubborn and hardheaded, but she missed you a lot. I'm not sure if she'll ever admit how much."

I shrugged. "You may be right. We both screwed up and we've called it even for now. But what happened between Cleo and me doesn't change how you and Cleo relate to each other. What if we found someone else for you, a demon? You wouldn't have to feed them, but just someone to help with your other needs?"

"Someone to handle the pain slut inside me?"

I'd never considered what Andrew was into, but… "Yeah."

"That would be cool, I guess. I just want to be in her life. She means a lot to me."

"And you will be."

"Well, we'll play it by ear."

"Okay. Good." I walked over to the bed and gave in to the need to sit down. The knowledge of the plug made me a little squirmy with every movement. I made sure I sat on top of the comforter, at the foot of Andrew's bed, and gave the Rottweiler puppy a few strokes down his back.

"So this is Motherfucker?"

"That's him."

At the sound of his name, Motherfucker lumbered over and crawled halfway into my lap. He didn't waste any time before he started licking my hand.

"Cleo was your only domme?" Andrew asked. I focused on the dog as I answered. It was easier to tell the truth if I didn't have to look Andrew in the eye.

"Yes. We learned a lot, but it was hard to find the time. Can I ask you something?" I looked back down at the puppy. He had on a black and red collar complete with a dog license that featured his lovely name.

"Sure."

"Did Cleo ever flog you?" I asked hesitantly. I'd never had another person I could talk to about this stuff, and I never had anyone I could talk to about Cleo in the same context. My curiosity outweighed my jealousy.

"Sure. A bunch of times. The flogger is one of my favorite implements." I was quiet for a few moments, debating whether I was curious enough to ask my follow-up question. "Do you want me to tell you about it?" Andrew said.

I looked up into his dark brown eyes. There was no judgment, just understanding.

"Yes," I said, suddenly relieved. "Would you?"

CHAPTER FOURTEEN

Benny

I sat on the edge of my bed, considering my pajamas. We'd made it through the week with no trouble. Camila had helped me explain away Paeno's mark. Portia had caught a glimpse of it one day in the kitchen. Camila came to my rescue, telling the freshman that the mark was Daddy's nest insignia, a design I'd gotten at her tattoo shop in preparation for graduation. Portia accepted that story and wasted no time spreading that news around. All the girls wanted to see it, of course, but none of them questioned it. Amy thought it looked cool. Not having to hide it made things a little easier, even though I was still waiting for a definitive response from Daddy. Mama claimed he was still taking care of things, but he hadn't spoken with Paeno yet. They communicated differently, I knew that. I just had to be patient.

I went to class and studied. I handed over my list. Cleo fed from me and we fucked as often as we could. I didn't feel comfortable sleeping in Omi's apartment, so I woke up most mornings alone, but still, for the first time in years, I was happy. I held my sister counseling sessions, and even though most girls came by to ask me about Cleo, those sessions weren't so bad. I found if I just told the boring details, the girls who didn't really know me that well lost interest. They didn't think I had anything juicy to keep hidden. It made sitting through those sessions with one of Cleo's plugs inside me that much more interesting.

It only took two brief conversations with our sister-queens, but Cleo was able to find a replacement for Andrew. Rodrick. It turns out we weren't the only ones involved in our own kind of kink. Rodrick and Natasha had participated in several BDSM scenes in their lifetime. Rodrick had even run an exclusive dungeon at one point before moving to America. He and Natasha had just recently considered starting up again with one of their adult feeders outside of the house. Rodrick was more than willing to take Andrew on, and due to her general fondness for Rodrick, Cleo had no problem accepting their offer. Andrew was very happy with the idea. He and Rodrick were close and Andrew had had a slight attraction to him ever since they'd taken him into the OBA house. On the terms that Cleo was his primary demon, Rodrick made arrangements to take care of Andrew's submissive needs at least twice a week. More if they both desired.

I was thrilled with this decision, though I kept my exuberance under control. It was a load off Cleo and me both. Still, other challenges remained. As we neared the weekend, I realized I wasn't ready for movie night. Cleo had asked me to come, and all day I'd kept replaying her words to me in my head.

"You need to get used to me feeding, B. It will be a part of our lives forever, and I need you to accept that," she'd said. I told her that I understood, but she was still skeptical and rightfully so. Though I'd claimed I was, I wasn't comfortable with Cleo feeding from other people. I'd never witnessed it because it would traumatize me for life, but I knew Mama and Daddy had a similar relationship. They were married, and Daddy claimed Mama as his mate. His feeders knew exactly where they stood with him, but the totality of those relationships couldn't be avoided.

Mama had to deal with sharing Daddy with other people in certain ways. Mama didn't seem to mind, though. I could chalk that up to her understanding nature or the fact that Daddy treated her so well she was willing to put those feelings aside. I wanted to ask her, but if it was the latter I didn't want to make her feel bad. In the interim, I had to suck it up. It was just another downside to being insanely possessive and sharing your life with a vampire. Unless I wanted to change myself, which I didn't, or unless I was okay with Cleo draining me in a few short days, which I wasn't, I would have to come to terms with sharing Cleo with Laura, Skylar, Andrew, and Hollis for the rest of the semester. And I might as well get used to it now. Twenty minutes before movie time, and I couldn't back out now. I'd never made it through a whole movie night, so I had no idea what to expect.

I changed and brushed my teeth. I put my hair up and stared at myself for a long time in the mirror. I'd been eating less, but for me that wasn't saying a whole lot. It wasn't like it showed. I changed into a looser shirt, then sat on my bed.

With no minutes to spare, Amy knocked on my door. "You ready to round up the troops?"

"Yeah," I said even though I really wanted to hide out in my room. Amy and I went around, door to door. We were really conducting our nine o'clock curfew check. All the girls were accounted for. By assigned sister-queen, they headed to the lower floor on the elevator. I used to ride in the second group with Camila's other feeders;, now I rode third with Cleo's other girls. Laura and I listened to Hollis and Skylar gab about some boy Hollis thought was cheating off her in her biology class. Neither of us had any idea who she was talking about.

When we stepped off the elevator, Cleo was waiting for us. She kissed each girl on the cheek, then slung her arm over my shoulder.

"Just relax," she said as we walked down the hall to the common room. Camila and Ginger always took the couches and cushions closest to the door. Cleo and Tokyo usually set up shop on the farthest side of the room, the farthest from me, but this time we sat near Ginger and Camila and their girls. Tokyo, who'd been acting like a baby all week, went back to her usual spot, so our other four sister-queens and their feeders sat between us. I could still feel her sideways stare from where I was. Cleo seemed to be ignoring her.

Skylar and Hollis made themselves comfortable on the cushions on the floor. Cleo sat near the center of the couch and I sat beside her with my legs balled up to my chest and leaned against the arm of the couch. Laura sat on Cleo's other side. I tried not to notice that she was casually starting to undress.

"Come closer. I want you to see," Cleo said. I sat up straighter so my arm was draped behind Cleo's back and my knee was resting on her thigh. "That's better, bunny. I promise it'll be okay." I kept silent and focused on my breathing.

"What are we watching?" Faeth yelled.

"A Madonna classic," Natasha said "An eighties classic, if you will. *Who's That Girl?*"

"Madonna was in movies?" Portia asked as she tossed her shirt on Kina's head. She slid to her knees and started unbuttoning Kina's jeans.

"Yes," Natasha replied.

"Were any of them any good?" Omi called back across the room.

"No," Camila, Faeth, and Tokyo said in unison.

"I've never seen this one," Cleo said.

"It's fantastic," Natasha replied. She smiled at me as she slid into the DVD room behind us.

"Fire it up, Tash. I have no beatdowns to dole out this week," Ginger said as she petted Samantha playfully. Movie night was the night we dealt with anyone who'd stepped out of line during the week. Missing curfew, trying to sneak a boy into the house, committing some major academic no-no or other stupid mistake that our sister-queens had to clean up. Samantha had the record in the house, five brutal spankings, but I had a feeling she enjoyed them much like I did.

"Wait. Before we start, I have an announcement," Ruth said. I looked at Maddie as Ruth extracted her hand from hers and walked to the center of the room. "As you all know, I applied early to law school at the University of Miami because I never want to see snow ever again. But today I got my acceptance to Georgetown." I looked at Maddie again as her hands flew over her mouth in surprise.

"Oh my God, baby. Does this mean we can stay?" Maddie said, scooting to the edge of the couch.

"It looks that way. I might have to commute a little, though."

Maddie launched herself at Ruth and showered her with kisses as we all clapped and cheered for them. When they finally unsuctioned themselves from each other, tears of joy dotted Maddie's cheeks.

"Faeth, if you have any crusty old feeders on their way out, we'll both be sticking around a little longer," Ruth said.

"Well, none about to kick the bucket anytime soon." Faeth laughed. "But if you want to stick with me after graduation, I'll talk to our master. See what he has to say about it, yeah?"

"I'll put in a good word too," I offered. Though their bickering had been a thorn in my ass for months, I was happy to see Maddie and Ruth getting answers to their frustrations.

"Thanks, you guys," Maddie said. "Baby, I'm so happy. You don't even know. The humidity in Miami would have screwed up my hair so bad."

"Okay. Okay. Sit down. You can make out and be giddy on the couch," Ginger said. Maddie dragged Ruth back to their spot by Faeth.

Then the lights went dim. I glanced around the room as soon as the old-school FBI warning lit up the screen. I heard Ginger mumble something to Samantha, and on our other side, Portia looked up at Kina, anxiously awaiting some sort of cue. At our feet, Skylar and

Hollis were entertaining themselves, kissing and slowly taking off each other's clothes. I finally looked back at Cleo. Laura was naked beside her. She had a beautiful body that contrasted well with her two-toned hair and her piercings. She was paler than me with small, light pink nipples and much slimmer everything.

"You okay?" Cleo asked.

"Yeah," I said, though my voice was shaking a little.

"Laura asked to go first."

"The sooner you can have her all to yourself," Laura said with a smile.

"Okay." I swallowed and tried to make myself more comfortable. It didn't work.

Cleo patted her thighs and I caught on just in time to move my leg as Laura straddled her. At the last second, I almost asked Cleo to take from Laura's wrist, but that would have been a major mistake. To ask Laura to give Cleo her wrist after she'd been feeding her for almost four years would be a major slap in the face to Laura and a blatant declaration on my part that I didn't respect the intimacy in their blood bond.

Instead, I bit my lips and held my breath as Cleo laced her fingers into Laura's hair to keep her in place. She tilted Laura's head toward me so I could look Cleo in the eye. She stared up at me as her tongue traced Laura's skin, trying to locate the perfect point on the vein. Then her fangs sliced into Laura's neck.

Laura moaned immediately, her body jerking in a sudden motion. I could tell she was trying to keep her hips still, but she failed. The emotions warred inside me as I watched. I wanted to be angry, and at the same time I couldn't help being aroused. I could smell Laura, the smell of her wet pussy and the tangy, copper scent of her blood as it covered Cleo's tongue.

Out of nowhere, Laura grabbed my hand and shoved it between her legs. At first, I tried to yank it away, but she held it there. I clamped my mouth shut and met Cleo's eyes again. I could see just how turned on she was. I left my fingers where they were and let Laura masturbate herself on my hand as Cleo continued to claim her blood.

Since it was part of their weekly ritual and not for Cleo's health, their feeding was shorter than usual. When Cleo finished and she sealed Laura's neck, Laura took my fingers and licked her juices off. My pussy twitched. She kissed me on the cheek and then hopped off the couch.

Having fulfilled her duties, she went over to Camila's couch and started making out with Mel.

I turned back to Cleo. "They're just used to each other," she said. Her voice sounded like more of a purr.

Skylar was next. Not wanting to be left out, though it was a little surprising to me, Hollis nudged my legs down and sat in my lap so we could watch Cleo feed together. At no point in the day did I think I would end up with a naked freshman in my lap, but she was perfectly content, and after a few moments, I found she helped me relax.

When it was her turn, they switched places and Skylar plopped down on top of me. She lay slack against my shoulder, breath heaving from the round of orgasms Cleo had just put her through. I could smell her too, rich and potent. Soon, Cleo sealed her bites and then held Hollis back at arm's length.

"Let me see your teeth."

She was still shaking a little, but Hollis said "ah" and let Cleo look in her mouth.

"Lay off the sugar, kid. You have like three cavities."

"Fine," Hollis whined.

"Don't fine me. I'm gonna get the first case of vampire diabetes if I keep fucking with you."

Hollis started to argue, but Cleo slapped her butt and pushed her gently onto the other side of the couch. Skylar scurried off my lap and pounced on the other girl. It seemed Cleo and I were far from their minds.

Now it was my turn.

Cleo slid closer and tucked a loose piece of hair behind my ear. "Talk to me," she whispered. In front of us, Madonna was talking in a horribly nasal voice. Around us, naked sorority girls were preoccupied with their vampires and one another.

I thought carefully before I answered. "I expected it to be worse."

Cleo stood and started peeling out of her clothes in front of me. I looked around frantically, as if she were undressing me. When she was done, she leaned down and gently took my chin in her hand.

"You see how strong I am? How healthy?" she said in hushed tones. I nodded. "Their blood does that for me. It gives me the strength I need for you. The power I'll need to take care of you." She leaned closer and kissed me. "And our family. This…" She took my hand and placed it between her legs. She was so wet. "This is for you and no one else. You understand?"

"Yes, Cleo."

"You see how no one is focused on us?"

I glanced around. She was right. Even Tokyo had taken a break from her glaring and was fingers and fangs deep in one of her girls. "Yes."

"Just remember that." Cleo straddled me and in almost the same motion bent my head to the side and took my neck. My eyes slammed shut as I came, again and again, until she stopped and closed the bites.

I was too weak to stop her as she slid to her knees and pulled down my pants. She went at my pussy with her mouth, attacked my clit with firm strokes of her tongue, and teased me with light nips from her fangs. I held on to the thick roots of her hair and did the only thing I could do: I let her have control.

I nearly screamed as I came with a violent, blinding shudder.

When I opened my eyes, I saw that Cleo was right again. No one seemed to notice.

CHAPTER FIFTEEN

Benny

We flew out of Baltimore the following Thursday morning. When we left, it was forty-eight degrees. I wore extra layers because, depending on the environment, my body temperature bounced between normal and that of a woman streaking through menopause. Despite my thinking ahead, I was still uncomfortable on the plane, freezing or burning up. Luckily, I was sitting in a row with Amy and Sam and they didn't seem to mind my fidgeting, an added bonus to not being seated next to a stranger while dealing with the size of the seat. It was not made for someone of my carriage.

Mama and I always flew first class when we traveled, but to get our whole sorority and the OBA boys on the same flight, we were all in coach. I would have been mortified if I were trying to hold myself in place in between two strangers, always terrified that some part of my body was touching theirs. Amy gave me the window while she took the aisle. Sam sat between us and used me as a human pillow.

Many long hours later, we landed in St. Martin, or as they call it on the Dutch side of the island, Sint Maarten. It was seventy-eight degrees out. Amy took my coat and my sweater from me as soon as we got off the plane and shoved them into her carry-on for me. She had extra room for presents for her mom and Danni.

"God, I need a nap," Sam said as she stretched.

"You slept *and* snored the whole flight." Amy laughed.

"I'm in vacation mode now. That's at least fifteen hours of sleep. Don't give me that look," she said to Amy. Amy's face said what I'd been thinking. Sam would sleep like that all the time. Being on vacation had nothing to do with it.

We grabbed our luggage and waited in line for the shuttles that Florencia had arranged for us. She'd be down in a few days to check on us, but she definitely was not in housemother mode. Three local feeders who belonged to a friend of Omi's wife had been assigned to be available to us during the day. We were usually pretty well behaved, but you never knew with college kids. Our demon chaperones would be arriving that night. Cleo had plans for us, but she hadn't clued me in to what they were. She had only told me to wear a dress and nothing else.

I watched the gorgeous town creep by as we made our way to the house in bumper-to-bumper traffic. Our chapter owned a house, and Omega Beta Alpha owned a large one next door. We shared the beach property in the rear, but every day, a group would take off for the French side of the island to hit the nude beaches. I always skipped those field trips. When we got to the house, we let the freshmen down and told them they'd have to share rooms on vacation too, four to a room. I was bunking with Amy, though I hoped most of the nine nights we were on the island I would be busy someplace else.

We unpacked, and after a shower and a few minutes of nagging, I changed into my swimsuit and joined the girls out by the pool. I thought having a beach and pool was a little redundant, but it came with the house. It was a gorgeous day out and the breeze from the ocean made the heat mostly enjoyable. Laura and Mel were putting on quite a topless show in the pool, and from the looks of things, Gwen and Ashley were fixing to join them. Still, I needed a distraction. I tightened my sarong, parked myself on a lounge chair between Samantha and Amy, and opened my book.

"Ugh, why are you reading?" Amy asked.

"Why? You want to talk about politics? Complex genetic engineering? Boys?"

"Duh. I fucking love boys."

"Seriously," Sam said dryly. "Don't even get her started. It'll be boy, boys, cock, cock, cock all afternoon."

"You know me." Amy sighed and rolled over onto her stomach. "So are you just bursting with excitement waiting for Cleo to get here?"

"You know me. Always bursting."

"You'll have fun, though. First vacation together." Cleo had chaperoned every year, but each trip had been a nightmare for me. Watching Cleo flirt with her feeders everywhere we went. And worse, watching her with Tokyo. This year, Tokyo would be back, but things would be different.

I was anxious for Cleo to arrive and just as anxious for the sun to go down. Our sister-queens hated making the trip. Their quarters in the house on St. Martin were a fraction of the size of their apartments at school. To compound the discomfort, their only escape during the day meant they would have to shift. I would love to spend the day with Cleo, walking down the beach or checking out the shops, but with Cleo in her human form, not Cleo the tropical bird on my shoulder or Cleo the dog who defied leash laws. The days here would be much harder. Avoiding the snow was much easier than avoiding sunshine and tropical breezes.

"Who's coming with her?" Sam asked.

"Tokyo, Kina, and Faeth."

"They lose a bet?" Sam asked.

"They volunteered."

"Still sucks they have to babysit like this."

"Whatever." Amy yawned and then she smiled. "They have Christmas and summer break all to themselves."

I gave up trying to read and stared out across the pool. A few of the OBA boys were already starting up some shenanigans on the beach. Anna-Jade, Ruth, and Maddie ran out to meet them. Sam yawned on my other side, and suddenly, I was sleepy.

"Just nap with me, B," Sam said, caressing my arm. I tried not to shiver as she grazed the mark. "You know you want to."

"I'll stay awake to keep you from roasting."

"That works too."

I picked up my book again and did my best not to think about Cleo. It didn't work.

The afternoon went by slowly, to a painful degree. Florencia had food sent over for us. We finally went down to the beach. I dipped my toes in the water while the others played touch football with the boys. I saw that as an ankle sprain just waiting to happen and decided to watch. Jill kept me company. She talked incessantly, but she seemed to finally understand that I was seeing someone else now. She just talked about class and how Hollis and Skylar were becoming her new best friends.

For the most part, I enjoyed myself, but the minute the sun set, I found myself waiting by the front door. Shortly after the sky went from a deep blue to a pure black, I saw their headlights approaching the house. A black SUV pulled up, and as soon as Cleo shut off the engine,

Tokyo, Kina, and Faeth hopped out and started unloading their bags. Once they headed into the house, Cleo lagged behind. The moment our eyes met, I regretted letting Amy put together my outfit. I had a handful of dresses, but in a pathetically insecure moment, I couldn't find anything I wanted to wear. Amy hushed me, found one of my longer, less see-through sarongs, and wrapped it up in a cute style that tied behind my neck. I was covered down to my knees, and the color and fabric helped disguise the fact that my boobs were also hanging down to my knees.

Cleo scooped me up with one arm behind my back. I was still getting used to how easy it was for her to pick me up. Our bodies pressed together, and I was suddenly aware of every inch of her body. Her loose jeans and her tight T-shirt, her crisp white sneakers. Her breasts touching mine. She didn't seem to notice the dress. She was staring at my mouth. "Did you miss me?" she asked, just before she kissed me on my lips. She smelled so good.

"Did you miss me?"

"Of course I did." I knew she had made plans for us, but as soon as she put her bags away, I planned to tackle her on the nearest flat surface. She wasn't in my mind, but I think she could read my intentions all over my face. She put me down and kissed me another time, but longer and sweeter. I felt that she missed me. I felt that she wanted me too.

"We were just gonna talk to the girls right quick," she said, touching my cheek. "And then I'm all yours."

"Okay."

"Come on."

Ten minutes later, I found myself sitting with the other girls in the main lounge while Cleo gave us the rundown of the rules, mostly for the freshmen. She'd changed and now stood in front of us in a black bikini top, black linen pants, and sandals. She looked so good, I was having a hard time focusing on anything she was saying.

"Stop messing with it. You look great," Amy whispered as I readjusted her makeshift dress over my knee.

"Check in with your partners every few hours. If you are separated, you know who to call. Do not go off anywhere with strangers. Do not bring any strangers back here. If I see a man in this house who is not wearing an OBA dog tag, or even a mildly attractive local woman, your ass is mine and not in a good way. You are on vacation. If you meet the love of your life, they should be perfectly fine with your e-mail and a promise to Skype with them once you get home. You've all checked with your vampires and worked out a drinking schedule?"

"Yes," the girls all whined. We knew the drill. No drinking before you fed your demon.

"Good. I don't think anyone wants to hear that their blood tastes like rat poison. Any questions?"

"No."

"Good. Use the shuttles. If you want to leave some place early, call us and we'll come pick you up. No cabs. Okay? Okay. Go have fun."

The girls dispersed. Most of them were going to Coco Bananas, the club we'd been frequenting the last two years. The place was usually packed, the crowd was younger, and the music was always good. I wasn't the slightest bit disappointed to be missing it. Cleo had a few last words with Kina and Faeth, then came over and took my hand.

"You ready?"

I nodded and let her lead me outside. The night was perfect. The temperature had dropped and the moon was starting to rise.

"Where are we going?" I asked.

"For a walk."

We walked a few blocks, and I told her about the flight and our day. I also reminded her how much I'd missed her. Eventually, we stopped at a smaller house, white with a beige tile roof. The garage took up the floor at street level. I kept quiet as we walked up the stairs to the front door, but when Cleo pulled out a gold key, I had to know.

"Whose house is this?"

She guided me inside with a hand on my ass. The lights were already on and I could hear music coming from another room. "I don't know, but it'll be a while before they're reported missing."

"Cleo."

"I'm kidding. I'm renting it for us while we're here."

Pausing in the entryway, I looked up at her in surprise. "You're amazing."

"Come this way." We walked down a short hall into a great room that combined the living room with the kitchen and a dining area. The table was made up with a spread of Caribbean dishes and candles and flowers.

"I'll cook tomorrow night," Cleo said. "I just have to go send someone to the market."

"I'm not really that hungry," I told her honestly. I appreciated the spread, it smelled delicious, but I'd been waiting all day to be alone with her. Between the relief of finally being together and a late lunch, food could wait till tomorrow.

"Okay. We'll heat it up later." She quickly replaced the covers on the dishes of rice and chicken, then took me out to the back.

The house was built into the low rock ledges of the beach below. Stairs carved into the rock led down to the sand. There was a large daybed by a fire pit that was already piled high with burning wood. There was a hammock on the opposite site of the deck. This house skipped over the pool and went right for the hot tub. I walked over to it and knelt to test the water. The whirlpool was lined with synthetic stones that hid the jets, and if blue lights weren't illuminating the tub from the inside, the rock motif would give the illusion that you were stepping into a natural hot spring of some sort. There were two ledges inside that led to the deepest point in the middle.

"I had it cleaned this morning. No spring break cooties are lurking in that thing."

"I trust you." I stood back up and stepped into Cleo's arms. She smiled down at me, then kissed the tip of my nose.

"I just wanted to give you a taste of what our honeymoon will be like."

I almost sighed. Instead, I shivered as Cleo's hands slid over my bare shoulders and down my back. "You want to go someplace tropical?" I asked her.

"I want to go any place that will make my bunny happy."

"Hmm, okay." I let my forehead drop to Cleo's chest and started to undo the drawstring on her pants. "No leather?"

"It's too hot for those fucking things."

"Well, these look good too." I slid my hand down the front of the linen and was pleased to find she wasn't wearing any underwear.

Her voice dropped to a rumbling purr as her fingers tangled with the knot of fabric at the back of my neck. "I like this," she said. With a flick of her hand, the knot came undone and the sarong started to slip from my body. I caught it with one hand on my chest.

"Amy made it."

"Points for Amy. You should wear something like this tomorrow night when we go out." Cleo's tongue swept over the tips of her fangs. "Move your hand."

I let the fabric drop to my feet.

"Get in." Cleo leaned over and turned off the jets. Soon, all I could hear was the small crackling of the fire, and the ocean below. "I want to look at you." I slid into the hot tub and turned to face her once I'd swum to the other side. It was wider than it looked. When I looked up at Cleo, her eyes were starting to glow.

"What do you see?" I asked.

"Your big ole tits that I love too much." I looked down. Nearly all I ever saw was my own breasts when I looked in that direction.

Cleo undid her top and dropped it with her pants next to my sarong. She stepped down into the water, but sat on the edge. I treaded back to where Cleo reclined with her hands supporting her, and raised myself out of the water. Slowly, I licked her left nipple and then her right. Her ankles rubbed against my thighs as I settled my knees on the rock ledge inside the tub.

"You sure you want to get the beast all riled up?" she purred. "It's early still."

"You're the one who suggested we get all buck-naked. Besides…" I moved up to her neck and gave her a gentle bite. "I think I want to see it now." I leaned back to gauge her reaction.

"What? Oh! You mean my monster demon cock."

"Well, not when you put it that way," I said dryly. It had been on my mind for a while, ever since I first heard Tokyo talk about it. I wanted to see what Cleo could do with her body.

"I'll show you. I just don't want to freak you out. Once it's seen, Benita, it can't be unseen."

"Show me."

"Okay. Move back. I don't want to put your eye out."

"I'm sure it's not that big."

"I don't know. Andrew had three eyes when I met him."

"Just show me." I lightly jabbed her stomach, but then I sank back into the water on my knees to give her a few extra inches to work. When she reached down and spread her lips, I'll admit I leaned a little closer. I was curious.

Cleo rubbed her clit a few times and my own started to tingle between my legs. She drew her hand down lower and fucked herself with a single finger. She was watching me. When she knew I couldn't wait any longer, she withdrew her finger. I opened my mouth and sucked it clean.

"I thought you said you weren't hungry."

"For food."

"Let me give you something else you can put between those lips."

I watched closely as her clit started to grow.

All demon powers became stronger the more you used them, but vampires had to be careful with those powers. A demon who learned how to enter people's minds and did so frequently might one day find himself slipping into people's thoughts involuntarily. A demon who shifted all the time could lose her true shape. Cleo seemed to be well in control of all her powers. Shifting separate body parts was a difficult skill.

I exhaled as her clit grew large enough for her to grasp with her fingers. I'd never seen a penis in real life before, but I knew this was something different. No foreskin, of course, no circumcised head. The shaft was the same deep brown as the rest of her perfect body. The tip was rounded and smooth. I wanted to touch the length, but I didn't. I braced myself on her thighs and leaned a little closer.

"Did Kina teach you this?" I asked.

"Not exactly. Something like this just sort of happened the first night, but Kina taught me how to control it with more finesse."

I looked closer. It was so strange to see the opening to her vagina was still there. I reached down and stroked her there. She purred a little louder. "Can you make this disappear?"

"I can, but I don't like to. Making my clit bigger feels good. Closing my pussy off feels weird."

I tilted my head the other way. Though I probably looked foolish, I wanted to come at this from somewhat of a scientific angle. The longer I looked at it and the more questions I asked, the more comfortable I felt with this aspect of Cleo's abilities. "Can you make it bigger than this?"

She laughed as she drew her thumb gently down my cheek. "First my plugs are too small, now my magic demon cock."

I ignored her joking for a moment. "That night we had the meeting, before that game when you sat with me. How big was it then?"

Cleo cocked her head to the side for a moment and let the length extend down her thigh. The size around almost tripled. "About there."

"Oh." I swallowed and sat back a little on my heels. "That's big."

"It doesn't have to be."

"No, leave it," I said when her distended clit started to shrink. Cleo chuckled and let her flesh fill back out. It was really big.

"Can I touch it?"

"Yes. You can touch me wherever you want."

I stared at it a while longer, not moving my hands. "Remember, it's just my clit," she reassured me.

I took a deep breath and went for it, wrapping my hand around the base and giving the shaft a gentle stroke up. Cleo's head rolled back on her shoulders and she moaned. "How does that feel?" I asked.

"Lord Jesus. It feels like you're stroking my clit with your whole hand."

"Did you want to have a penis when you were human?"

Cleo scowled and shook her head. "No. Why?"

"I just wondered. You seem so comfortable with this." She reached forward and ran her fingers through my hair as I continued to stroke her. Her clit felt nice. A little slick from how wet her pussy had been before she caused the length to grow, and harder than I expected. But the skin was so smooth.

"I am. It's a part of me and it's much handier than carrying around a suitcase of leather and plastic. Plus, you ever try shifting with a harness on?" I bit my lip and looked at my fingers moving up and down. The contrast between her skin and mine was remarkable. And beautiful.

"Does it still weird you out that I do this?" she asked after I was quiet for a while.

"No. What you said makes sense. I was just wondering." My inquisitive nature took control. I bent over her lap and licked the tip. I did it again and took more of her in my mouth.

"Benny." I gazed up at Cleo. "I was kidding. You don't have to do that."

"Trust me, I know. I just want to see how it feels for you." I lowered my head and went at it with a little more enthusiasm. The shaft was way too long for me to take the whole thing, but I liked the way the smooth surface felt in my mouth. I liked the way sucking her made me feel. A little dirty, in a good way. Cleo's fingers gripped my hair. I let her guide my head up and down. That turned me on even more. "Like that?" I asked, panting slightly. Her purring grew louder and more rhythmic.

I kept sucking her clit as she answered. "Yes. Jesus. I'm two whole seconds away from bending you over the edge of this tub."

"Hey, Cleo—Oh, I'm sorry."

Cleo whipped her head around just as I peered around her side to see Tokyo standing on the back deck. I shrank down into the water and closer to Cleo to hide my naked body from Tokyo's view.

"The fuck, Tokyo!" Cleo yelled. She wrapped her arm around me to shield me even more. "What do you want?"

"I just wanted to tell you that Faeth is staying with the girls at Coco Bananas so we can find a strip club, but I'll tell Kina you're busy," she said, all smiles and amusement. I could feel the anger coming off Cleo. It was like the temperature in the hot tub went up.

"Leave," Cleo growled.

"Okay, geez. Sorry. Later, Benny." Tokyo smiled at me, then vanished.

I was so upset, I started trembling. Cleo kept her hold on me as she slipped down into the hot tub. She wrapped me in her arms and nuzzled my neck, trying to calm me down. I closed my eyes and focused on her touch and the pattern of my breath. I listened for the crackling sound of the fire and the ocean waves behind me. A beautiful night with the perfect person, and all I could see was that heinous grin on Tokyo's face just before she disappeared.

"She did that on purpose," I said.

"I know."

I leaned back so I could look Cleo in the eye. "Have you talked to her?"

"There's nothing to talk about. She knows you and I are together."

"Are you sure? Because she doesn't act like it."

"She's just being a cunt 'cause she's not getting her way. But I'll say something to her tomorrow."

"Whatever." I turned around and sat in her lap. She was still for a few moments, probably considering whether or not I was angry with her. I was annoyed, mostly with Tokyo, but I was a little irritated with Cleo. I had dealt with Jill the best way I could. But I had a feeling she had never planned to have any real conversation with Tokyo. I didn't want her to pop up like that again.

Soon, though, I did start to cool off. I had two choices: I could turn this into a full fight with Cleo, or I could accept that even though Tokyo was almost one hundred and fifty years old, she wasn't above acting like a jealous teenager. The second choice involved pushing her out of my mind and enjoying my first evening on this gorgeous island with the woman I loved. I decided that choice was better. I'd trust Cleo to speak with her, and if she didn't and Tokyo thought she could continue to behave that way, I'd have some words with her myself. Tokyo was one demon who didn't scare me.

Cleo must have felt my body start to relax. Her arms came around my waist and she pulled me snug against her lap.

"Did that ruin the mood?" she whispered into my ear. Her clit had shrunk, but I could still feel its hard tip poking my ass.

I smiled and wiggled my hips a little. "I see it didn't ruin yours."

"Not even Tokyo barging in could keep me from wanting you," she replied. I let my head fall back on her shoulder as her hands started to caress my breasts. Her lips found my throat just as my eyes closed again. She kissed the most sensitive spots, nipped at me gently.

"I'm sorry she did that, baby," Cleo whispered. She traced my vein with the tip of her tongue. She was teasing me, but I didn't mind at all.

"It's not your fault," I rasped out. I turned my head so she could kiss me properly. I eagerly took her hand between my legs as our tongues met and my whimpers began to match her growls and purr.

"Put it inside me," I begged.

Cleo stilled and looked me in the eyes. "Are you sure?"

"Uh-huh."

"Okay, baby," she said. "I'm gonna go small. I don't want to hurt you." I started to move to give Cleo a little room to work with, but she grabbed my hips. "Nah. Just let me." With a strong grip under my thigh, Cleo lifted my leg over the bend in her arm. I let the water help with her efforts and rested my back against her chest. Without a single shift in her hips, I felt the tip of her clit nudging the opening of my pussy. I was so wet it had no problem working its way inside me. Once she was in as far as she could go, she pulled back, then thrust back in. With every push and retreat, I could feel her growing thicker. No toy we'd ever played with before could do that.

She grabbed my other thigh and bounced me in her lap, sloshing the water against the sides of the hot tub. She didn't have to tell me to vocalize the way she was making me feel. I couldn't keep myself quiet.

❖

We spent the whole night out on the deck. After we made love in the hot tub, Cleo brought the food out to me and we shared dinner on the daybed. We made love there in that same spot once we were finished. In the morning, I woke up wrapped in my sarong, but I wasn't alone. A brown tabby cat was snoozing on my chest. My hand in her fur woke her. When she looked up, I saw Cleo's eyes gazing back at me. I laughed when she lowered her head and started nudging and kneading my boobs. I hated that she had to change, but at least we were together. The fire pit was doused and the hot tub was covered. Cleo hopped off the daybed while I straightened my wrap, then she followed me inside as I went to clean up the remains of our dinner. Quickly, though, I saw that she'd already put everything away. I found her clothes folded neatly on the counter next to the keys and a note.

Leftovers are in the fridge if you're hungry. I love you.

I looked down as Cleo rubbed herself against my calf. "You want to spend the day with me?" I asked. I could easily carry her back to the house and get her to the sealed quarters below, but I thought I'd ask. I wasn't in the mood to be apart from her. She paused a moment and seemed to nod. I gathered her clothes and locked up the house as Cleo trotted down the front steps.

A few girls were up and about, eating breakfast and getting their early morning UV blast. Maddie and Ruth passed us on our way in, all dressed and going for a run. Clearly, they were only on a partial vacation. I grabbed some juice and went back to my room to find Amy and Sam passed out in Amy's bed. I showered and lay back down to sleep some more. Cleo joined me, purring softly in my arms until I fell asleep.

A few hours later, even though she'd probably drunk herself silly the night before, Amy was up and ready to go. We peeled Sam out of bed and gathered up a small group to go out to breakfast. Cleo took the form of a beautiful tropical bird and took the walk with us into town on my shoulder. Luckily, we found a nice outdoor café that was bird-friendly. After food and a little shopping, the heat and the walking started to take their toll on me. Sam and I headed back to the house and spent the rest of the day under an umbrella by the pool with Cleo beside me in her cat form. It wasn't ideal, but again, at least we were together.

Chapter Sixteen

Benny

That night, I went to Coco Bananas with the girls. This time, Cleo had precise instructions for me. She told me what to wear and told me exactly what I was to do when I saw her. There was no possible way for me to go out dancing with no bra on. With some quick Googling, Amy whipped up another wrap creation that allowed me to wear the one strapless bra I'd brought with me. It did its job of supporting the girls, but just barely. Per Cleo's orders, I didn't wear any underwear.

We'd been out for at least an hour, and Cleo hadn't showed yet. Coco Bananas was once a warehouse. They added more patron-friendly restrooms, some furniture, and three bars. We'd never been there on a "slow night," and tonight was no different. With the OBA boys, we took up a whole elevated VIP section. The music was great, and Sam made sure that everyone who was drinking had plenty to keep them nice and loose. But I was glued to the railing, scanning the crowd below.

Finally, I saw her. It seemed like the sea of people parted and Cleo emerged with Faeth and Kina at her sides. The three of them looked amazing, but Cleo looked the best. Her hair was pulled back in what she liked to call her puff ponytail, and she had on a tight, white muscle tee. The muscles of her arms looked downright lickable. Dark jeans hung off her hips. I could imagine how good her ass looked. Tokyo was a few steps behind them. She was pouting, which led me to believe Cleo had finally had a talk with her.

Amy stepped up beside me and grabbed my arm. "Hey, let's— Holy shit. Is that Cleo?"

"Yeah." I remained calm, but inside, I was screaming like a preteen at her first pop concert.

"Okay. I love Danni, but seriously, B. I am so jealous right now. And damn, Kina looks good too." She did. "That is like a three-way of mighty butch fineness." They kept moving through the crowd and headed to the bar. Faeth said something to Tokyo. She ditched them with a dramatic gesture and seemed to be heading toward where we had set up camp. Cleo didn't look back to watch her storm off.

"Let's go dance." I took Amy's hand and towed her toward a section of the dance floor in the opposite direction.

"What? Are you joking? Forget about me. Go hump her."

"No. Let's dance," I said. Amy held firm and refused to budge.

"Is this some kinky thing? I've heard what Cleo likes to get up to," she yelled over the music, squinting at me.

"Yeah, very kinky," I replied. At this point, I was completely indifferent to her opinion on the matter. "Let's go."

The DJ did a great job of mixing club-jumping hits with hip-grinding reggae and reggaeton. I didn't do it very often, but I wasn't a bad dancer. I think I shocked Amy with my moves. She was laughing and having a grand time shimmying up on me. I was doing my best to remain calm while I waited for Cleo. She was moving around the enormous room, but I could feel her eyes on me from every corner. A few times, I caught her gaze, but if I looked away, if I even blinked, she would be in a different spot.

I felt like a small animal being stalked in the wild. Though I wanted to be caught.

In the midst of a deft move I executed, a little wiggle and spin away from Amy, I heard her let out a pleasant screech. I turned around just in time to see Kina dragging Amy away with an arm around her waist. "Good-bye, Benny," she yelled. "I've always loved you."

"Farewell!" I called back.

"Do you mind if I step in?" My stomach jumped up into my chest as I started in shock. I spun around and almost bumped right into Cleo. She stared down at me like she was deciding which part to eat first. I'd followed her first few instructions. I was wearing the dress. I ditched the panties. I'd let her watch me dance. Now to see the rest through.

"Is it considered stepping in if you've already scared away my date?" I said defiantly.

"I'm sorry. I can have my friend bring her back."

I laughed and turned back around. Quickly, my hips found the beat of the music and I started moving again on my own. Cleo stepped closer behind me, but I didn't give her my attention.

"Is she your type?" Cleo didn't have to raise her voice. I heard it clearly through the booming bass.

"I'm not sure I have a type," I replied. "But I usually get what I want."

"I bet you do."

I closed my eyes and moved a little farther away from Cleo. An older gentleman whose attention I'd apparently captured mushed his way up in front of me. He was handsome in a greasy rent-a-bandleader sort of way and completely indicative of the type of men I attracted, men I wouldn't be attracted to even if I were straight. He did not blend in with the barely legal crowd that filled the room. Keeping a safe distance from his pelvis, I humored his over-punctuated moves. He smiled at me. I did my best not to laugh. Behind me, I heard Cleo growl. I glanced over my shoulder to see her staring us down. The man took that as an opportunity to spin me around and grind his very small, but erect, penis into my ass.

I looked back at Cleo, biting my lip, still trying hard not to laugh hysterically, knowing my face told her everything. The fierce look of concentration dropped from her face, but just as her lip nearly twitched into a smile, she regained her focus.

"Come here," she mouthed. I slithered out of Dr. Mambo's grip. Luckily, he knew our love affair wasn't meant to last. He slithered his way up to the girl dancing right beside us.

I approached Cleo slowly, taking my time dancing my way over to her. She stood there, her muscles straining impatiently. I caught a glimpse of the points of her fangs. She was enjoying this little game she'd thought up, and so was I.

I stopped inches away from her, but she didn't touch me.

"You're doing a lot of standing around for someone who wanted to cut in."

"I was trying to be polite."

"Sometimes polite doesn't work for some girls," I said as I looked her up and down. "Let me know when you're done watching." I took a few steps back and kept dancing. By all appearances, I was in my own world, dancing hard, enjoying the rhythm, the heat and pressure of the other bodies around me, the feeling of being alive. But even though we were in a packed club, my every movement was for Cleo's eyes only. She stood there watching me for a full song before she made her move. The DJ switched tracks to a song even more suitable to two bodies making contact. I stayed where I was and let Cleo come to me.

She approached me like a stranger would, dancing close behind, but keeping her hands in seemingly respectable places, like my hips or just barely on my waist. I ground my ass into her crotch. Her rumbling purr told me she approved. I kept my back to her, switching my speed and the direction my hips would sway every now and then. Soon I was soaking wet. I could only imagine how I was making her feel.

We danced for a long time, and after several songs, I realized why she wanted to play this particular game. We'd never been out like this together before. We'd never danced together. All the parties we'd been to together on the row, I'd always been afraid to. I'd known I couldn't keep a platonic face if she touched me like this in public. Later, I'd have to commend her for the creative thinking.

Eventually, I turned around. "I'm thirsty."

"Can I buy you a drink?"

I licked my lips. "Since you asked nicely." As I made my way to the bar, I could feel Cleo pushing through the crowd right behind me. It took a little shouldering, but I finally got the bartender's attention and ordered two bottles of water. I was tempted to order something strong, just to see what Cleo would say if she really thought I'd make her go twenty-four hours without a drop of my blood, but I didn't want to tease her that way. I opened my bottle while she paid and moved to watch the people on the dance floor. Kina and Faeth were out there with their feeders. Amy and Sam were with them too, entertaining each other. I smiled when I saw Jill dancing with Hollis. I caught a glimpse of the lights bouncing off her braces as she laughed.

"So. Do you want to tell me about yourself?"

I looked at Cleo out of the corner of my eye before I took another swig of water. "Not really."

She boldly let her hand rest on my shoulder. Her fingers lazily passed over my skin. I looked down at her fingers, pretending to be frozen at the forwardness, then I glanced up at her face. "What do you want to tell me?" she said.

"I'm going to walk over there. You can follow me if you want to." I grabbed my water without hearing her answer and walked over to the farthest side of the club. When I found a good spot, I leaned against the wall and waited for Cleo to make her way to me.

She braced her arms on either side of my shoulders and leaned down to whisper in my ear. "What are we doing over here?" I turned my head and did my best not to shudder when she nipped my ear. I unbuttoned her jeans and slid my hand down the front of her pants.

"We're dancing."

We looked into each other's eyes while I stroked her wet slit with my fingers. Her breath came in deep, harsh pants through her nose as she fought off her climax, but I knew exactly what I was doing. Even her demon could only resist me for so long. Her eyes squeezed shut and her fangs shot down from her gums as she growled out her orgasm. I reached up with my other hand and pinched her nipple through her shirt just to help things along.

The next thing I knew, I was pressed flush between Cleo and the wall. I hadn't even blinked and she'd pulled my hand from her pants and was leaning into me. She bit hard but so quickly that by the time I really started coming, she was on her knees in front of me. I didn't stop her as she hiked my skirt up around my thighs and buried her face between my legs. A few strangers heard my gasps of pleasure and turned to glance and then gawk at what Cleo was doing to me. It might have been the fact that I was still fairly covered, Cleo's head and the bunching of my dress hid my private parts from view, or possibly the fact these people had no idea who I was, but I found their voyeurism turned me on.

I clenched my teeth and rubbed myself against Cleo's face, my eyes sliding closed as I came in a room sparsely littered with my sorority sisters, but mostly full of strangers.

❖

Our time in St. Martin went by too quickly. I did spend a few days down under the house with Cleo in the dark, but for most of our trip, Cleo slipped into some animal form and stayed with me and the girls during our adventures around the island. Most of the adventures involved shopping. We found plenty of time to make love, and we played the way we liked to best. She bound me in the rental house several times and spanked me properly, had me service her on my knees. One night we even went over to the OBA beach house and watched Rodrick flagellate a blindfolded and bound Andrew.

Jill became less and less annoying as the days went by, to the point where I didn't mind when she tagged along with us almost everywhere we went—during the day. Tokyo kept a respectful distance, but she seemed like she was waiting for some weakness in our relationship to make itself evident so she could butt back in between us. So sad for her that that opportunity never presented itself.

The last night on the island we joined the girls out for dinner, but when they decided to hit the Gold Coast, a slightly fancier nightclub, we opted to head back to the rental house. I begged for another spanking, which Cleo gave me, with gusto, but she didn't let me come. Instead she lubed up my ass and filled me with the weighted steel plug. Then she led me outside to look at the stars from the privacy of the hammock.

We were silent for some time, just holding each other, listening to the crackle from the fire pit. It took a great deal of effort to forget about my slightly tender ass cheeks or the plug nestled between them, but eventually, my mind was able to focus on other things. I was not easily amazed, but it was stunning to see how much my relationship with Cleo had changed. I'd thought I was in love with her before, but now I felt that love and its intensity was matched with this deep infatuation. I wanted to be with her always, where before I felt I had to measure and space our time out together. I was afraid of a number of things, but it was this all-consuming feeling I was hiding from.

I thought if I could control every aspect of our situation I could control my emotions toward her too. I was wrong. When she had her accident, I realized that I had no control over anything and that led to my horrible reaction. My fear and unease led to me showing Cleo a side of myself I wasn't proud of, the side of myself that forced us apart.

Recently, though, I'd begun to think about Cleo differently. When I was younger, I was particularly selfish, and I was honest about that fact. My mind was made up about Cleo's family and her life with her parents and her church. I thought I knew what was best for her and the best solution for the future of our family, but now that we were together and Cleo was no longer a human, after spending this time with her and seeing how her demon nature changed simple things like kissing, I was able to see Cleo. Nothing about her, as a human, had changed.

Same sense of humor. Same gentle authority. Same sense of selflessness that was masked by the humor and the confidence. When she wasn't fighting with me, she was kind to everyone, even Jill. She was vigilant in her concern for the girls' safety, and not just her feeders, but the whole sorority. That concern was genuine, but she had been the same way when she was a member of Alpha Beta Omega. During initiation, it was clear that I was terrified of meeting a new group of girls. Not to mention I knew in advance what the initiation ceremony would entail. It was Cleo who promised to look out for me before bid day even rolled around. I could have told Daddy I didn't want to go through with joining ABO, but Cleo had made me want to go through it. Cleo had made everything okay.

And I'd never heard her complain. She joked, sure, but she never asked why she should care about us. She never challenged Ginger and Camila's orders, except when it came to me, of course. Part of me wanted to know why and then part of me just wanted to know Cleo better. Now that the dust had settled, I wanted to know what was on her mind and how she felt about her own life and us moving forward. I had a bunch of questions, but one that I think caught us both a little off guard came out of my mouth first.

"How are you feeling about your faith? After all of this."

"I don't know." It felt like a long time before she went on, but I stayed quiet, rubbing my hand on her stomach under her shirt. "The same. A little better. The faith part has kind of been stripped." She chuckled, her voice sounding a little tight. "The stuff with my mama wasn't about that, you know."

"I know. I knew that when you were human."

"It feels strange because I know that bad things still happen. I know evil exists for sure."

"That's how I feel." Mama had raised me in the church, and my experience had been a good one, but things changed when I met Daddy. When I knew exactly what he was, his positive presence in our lives changed my views on a lot of things, particularly with my faith.

"But I *know* good exists too," Cleo said.

"Feeding you wasn't the only reason I wanted you to change."

"Hmm?"

I looked up into her eyes, then back down to where my fingers raised bumps in the fabric of her shirt. "Did Camila tell you anything about ascension?"

"No."

"She might not know about it. Daddy told me…sometimes, maybe once every hundred years, a demon like you is offered ascension."

"Into heaven?"

I nodded against her shoulder. "You get your wings."

"Hmm." Cleo let out a thoughtful sigh. "I've thought about that."

"Being an angel?"

"Not myself, but just what it must be like. Kina said she's met one, once, but it was four hundred years ago or some shit and she never saw an angel again."

"They do things much differently. And when I say that, I mean I have no idea what they really do," I said.

"I imagine it's not much different from what we do now, minus the blood drinking."

"What do you mean?"

"I've always thought of angels like employees to God, just like Dalhem would have been on the payroll to evil."

"I like this business model you've thought up," I said, chuckling softly.

"I know. It's brilliant, but I don't know. I just thought if I live like this for hundreds of years, and then I finally die and I've passed my interview into heaven, I don't know that I want to go back to work. I always imagined the real afterlife to be somewhere I can relax. Doing evil seems so easy, but doing good for eternity would be much harder."

"Daddy said the same thing to me once. I mean, he expressed the same idea. He's under contract to God now. Forever. He knows he's done enough to never earn those wings, but in the end he will still be under his 'employ,' as you phrased it."

"I was talking to Ginger about her parents, you know, since her brother wants to change. I asked her what they'd planned to do, and her dad said he was so tired that they had no interest in living forever. He just wanted to do the most good that he could in his given tim,e then take Ginger's mother and go."

"I will change with you, eventually," I said. "I'll probably be sixty or seventy by then, but I will."

"It's cool. I like old bitches."

"You're so sweet. But, no. I think that will give us enough time to get a couple kids off on their own."

I looked up as Cleo looked down at me. "A couple?"

"We can start with one and see how it goes," I replied.

"Mmm-hmm. You want to have like seventeen kids, just admit it."

"No, I don't. I…" I dropped my head back down on Cleo's chest and reconsidered what I wanted to say. Complete disclosure was a new thing for me.

"What is it?" Cleo asked softly.

"I've been sort of fixated on one, actually."

"Me too."

"Really?" I looked up again in shock.

"Yeah. I told you, I never stopped thinking about us being together and having a family."

"I—God, I sound so crazy." I buried my face in Cleo's shirt. I wasn't sure if I could say this part of what I'd been holding in.

"Bunny, tell me."

"I've had this image of this baby in my mind for a long time," I confessed. It wasn't an exaggeration either. When most girls were thinking about senior prom, I was thinking about baby names. Before Cleo, I'd never told anyone how badly I wanted to be a mother.

"Tell me about it," she asked. "Or him. Or her."

"It's a girl. I've always wanted a girl."

"Dalhem can't control that sort of thing, can he?" Cleo laughed.

"I don't think so. I hope not. That would be too weird. I'm sure boys are fun, but I've just had such a clear picture of a girl in my head. With the best of both our features. Your hair and your lips—"

"I think a baby would look strange with this sexy butt," she said as she grabbed a handful of my ass. I groaned and wiggled against the pressure of the plug.

"You never stop, do you?" I asked.

Suddenly, Cleo was quiet. When I glanced at her I was surprised to see tears lining her eyes. "I'm sorry I can't give that to you," she said.

"Sweetie, we can't change the science of making a baby, but don't worry. You'll have hours and hours of diaper duty ahead of you," I said trying to make her laugh. "You'll get to parent your ass off."

"Is that why you want me? Round-the-clock child care from someone who rarely needs to sleep."

"No." I leaned up and kissed her bottom lip. "I want you because of who you are. Any child you help raise will be the luckiest child in the world."

"You know what I'm looking forward to?"

"What's that?"

Cleo grabbed another handful of my E cup. "I'm looking forward to these getting even bigger."

I shook my head as I laughed. "You're going to have to share them, you know."

"I know. But not tonight." Cleo's hand trailed from my breast to my arm. She touched the raised edges on my forearm. I'd give anything to scratch the mark clean off.

"Paeno offered me a baby." I confessed. "She said I could have whatever I wanted."

"You can have whatever you want with me."

"I know."

"Always the princess."

"Always."

"What if Dalhem can't fix this?" she asked.

"I don't know. I have this feeling she won't want me if I don't want her, though. The blood bond wouldn't change the way I feel about you. I'm not sure she'd want to deal with that."

"That's a good point."

"I'm sorry. I shouldn't have brought her up. You were saying something about my boobs and my butt."

"You're right. I was." With skilled hands, Cleo easily exposed my breast. I whimpered against the feel of her tongue sliding across my nipple. I wiggled closer and started to beg, but it was a while still before she let me come. The delay didn't bother me at all.

CHAPTER SEVENTEEN

Cleo

The girls slipped right back into their regular schedule the day after we returned from St. Martin. That Friday, though, we skipped out on movie night and headed to D.C. I felt bad leaving the girls behind, but once they had the honest truth, that I was going to spend more time with my soon-to-be in-laws, time where Dalhem wasn't kicking me around, they were completely on board with me dipping out for the weekend.

In my head, Dalhem kept Benny and her mama in a sealed fortress under the White House. He fed off the First Family in their sleep and probably replaced the First Pets he chewed on on a daily basis. The truth was, the Tarvers lived in an extravagant colonial town house in Georgetown.

An hour and a half after sundown, I was standing on the Tarvers' stoop with Benny, waiting for their butler or some similar servant to answer the door. It was nice to see the place from the outside. It was even nice to have been invited this time by Ms. Leanne instead of being ordered by an enraged master. Benny had been chewing on her bottom lip since we left the house. Now she was wiggling her foot. She rang the doorbell again.

"Shouldn't I be nervous? I'm having a formal dinner with your mother."

"No. Mama loves you and you hate Daddy. It all works out."

"It'll be fine." I wrapped my arm around her neck and pulled her closer. I kissed her hard on the top of her head, but that didn't stop her erratic twitching. Not that it would. Benny didn't have many friends in high school, and the majority of those she did have weren't the come-over slumber-party types. She confided in me that she'd never had any friends over after they moved. Her need for privacy kept the rest away. The night I'd first met Ms. Leanne, Benny had been overwhelmed by the whole almost dying and trying to keep Dalhem from killing me aspect of the evening. Now she was on edge because for the first time I was seeing a different part of her world. My being there under these new circumstances was shooting her anxiety through the roof.

She rang the doorbell one more time. Just as I thought to question the work ethic of this butler, the heavy, dark blue door swung open and light flooded the steps.

"Angel!" Ms. Leanne screamed and yanked Benny into her arms. I noticed something right away. Ms. Leanne was unnaturally skinny. It had only been three weeks since I'd last seen her, and she'd been pretty small then. It seemed like all of the available weight had just dropped off her frame. Her face, gleaming with Benny's same blue eyes, looked pale and gaunt. But she was just as vibrant as before, her smile just as wide. Her thin arms crossed around Benny's back. I tried not to stare, but I was fucking surprised. So much so that I almost missed the sandy brown dog shoving his head in my crotch.

"Hey, boy," I mumbled, but my eyes were still glued on Benny's mother.

Ms. Leanne caught me with my mouth popped slightly open, and I'm sure my eyes opened in shock. Benny caught Ms. Leanne just in time see what she was looking at. I quickly fixed my face. Thank God, Ms. Leanne went right on screeching, "Come here, girl!" And then it was my turn to be corralled into a hug. She may have been slight, but the woman had a mean squeeze. Benny grabbed the dog by its collar and extracted him from the middle of our embrace.

"Hi." I laughed. "Thank you for having me."

"Oh, Cleo. You know we'd have you over any time." She held me back at arm's length, and I did my best to forget that I could've counted her ribs through her blouse.

"Come in! It's freezing out there. Come on, Kepper." The dog barked and led the charge into the house. As we followed Ms. Leanne inside, I grabbed Benny's hand. She gripped my hand back.

I'd only seen Dalhem's study and the one guest room. Benny decided I needed to see the rest of the house like a proper guest. The first floor of their house was exactly how I pictured it. Old paintings, mahogany sideboards, stiff chairs, yellow painted walls, crown molding. I felt like there was a butler lurking somewhere. Ms. Leanne led us to a library where she, for real, touched the head of an iron jockey next to the fireplace, and the bookcase slid open revealing a hidden set of stairs. The dog, Kepper, took off down into the depths.

I glared sideways at Benny as we walked down to the lower level of the house. "Really?"

"Wait till you see the underground moat," she said. I was glad to hear her voice had lost some of its strain, but she still had my hand in a tight grip.

"Oh, don't listen to her. We don't have a moat," Ms. Leanne said.

"And the ogre. You have to see the ogre," Benny went on.

"Well, we have one of those." Ms. Leanne looked over her shoulder and winked at me. "Benny calls him her daddy, but you already knew that."

We passed several doors, then stopped at a well-furnished guest room. A blue pastoral theme decorated the toile wallpaper. A large four-poster bed took up the bulk of one side of the room. On the other side was a sitting area with two blue chairs and a low coffee table. A small desk sat where a window would be if we weren't below ground. The door leading to a large bathroom was open. I felt like I was in a proper bed-and-breakfast.

"You'll stay down here," Ms. Leanne said. "But show Cleo around some more. Introduce her to Faraut and Douglas. Oh, and Mary and Omi are coming."

"They are?" Benny asked. I looked at Ms. Leanne with the same surprise. It was movie night, after all.

"You bet. Mary's been wanting to meet Cleo forever. I just can't shut up about you two. I'll call you down when dinner is ready." With a wave and an air-kiss, Benny's mama left us on our own. The dog followed her.

I dropped our bag at the foot of the bed and looked around the room some more. There were no personal touches around the room, no signs of family, but there were little trinkets like candles, and in the bathroom a few seashells that probably told a fuller story of Ms. Leanne, or even Benny, for anyone who cared to dig deeper. The room we'd been in before was pretty bare.

"Are you ready for the grand tour?" Benny asked as I stepped back into the bedroom.

"Yeah." Benny took me around the entire lower level of the house, which I'm pretty sure extended beyond the floor plan of the stories above. I saw the outer sitting room to Dalhem's office, another library, a few more bedrooms, one that did have more of a personal feel to it, and the room where we'd spent our first night as a bound couple. Along the way, we collected two more dogs, Leo and Keel. Same breed, different color. When we reached a kitchen built to handle the population of an elementary school, a fluffy, blue-gray dog sprinted full speed for Benny.

"Gus-Gus." She fell to her knees and let the dog kiss her all over her face. I'd heard a lot about Gus. This was her true puppy love. I knelt beside them and was slavered with Gus's affection. Leo and Keel took this as an opportunity to smell and lick me on a more personal level. "This is my baby," Benny cooed in Gus's face.

"Aren't there two more?" I asked, leaning away from an overeager Leo.

"Yeah. Boomer and Sandwich are in Daddy's office."

"Sandwich?"

"Daddy named him. Don't ask."

"Who goes there?" a booming voice called from around the corner.

"It's just me," Benny replied. We stood, and the dogs bumped our sides as we made our way over to two gentlemen by an industrial stove. One, a demon with a barrel chest, a bald head, and a black handlebar mustache, had just thrown some chopped onions into a sauté pan. A gray-haired human sat on a stool beside him, flipping through the *New York Times*. He wasn't as wide as the man on supper detail, but he was in shape. He lowered his paper and gave us both a good looking over.

"This is our chef, Faraut, and our driver, Douglas. They're boyfriends," Benny joked. I could tell then just how close she was with the two men. It was rare for her to be so at ease.

"No. We cannot stand each other," Faraut said, reaching out to shake my hand. His French accent was thick. "It is our love for this darling girl that keeps us together."

Douglas smiled and nodded politely, but didn't stand. He was in full chill mode. "It's a pleasure to meet you. You are the new mistress of the house?"

"Sort of." I smiled back at him.

"Here. I have braised the beef to perfection." Faraut grabbed a chunk of meat from a nearby pot and held out a piece for me and then one for Benny. My mouth started watering before it even hit my tongue.

"Damn. That's good," I said with my mouth half-full.

"A perfect assessment. There is a mousse for dessert," he replied. He pinched Benny's cheek for added effect.

"Thank you," she said. "We'll be back."

After we said our see-you-soons, I, along with Gus and Kepper, followed Benny to the upper floors.

"I should have guessed you'd have a chef and a driver. At least they aren't black," I teased her as we walked.

"Shut up. Douglas is Mama's driver. He's ex-military, so Daddy feels comfortable when he escorts Mama out during the day. What are you thinking?" Benny asked when I didn't have a snappy comment.

"I'm wondering if he has a buddy."

She took my hand this time and said, "I'm perfectly fine going out by myself during the day. Douglas attracts more attention than he deflects."

"I'm not worried about you. I'd feel bad for whoever decided to kidnap your ass."

"Hey!" Benny almost hip-checked me into the wall. I pulled her in front of me before she got a good knock in and draped my arms over her shoulders.

"I was thinking about you and the baby."

Benny laughed but wrapped her hands around my wrists and led me down another hallway. "You say that like I'm already pregnant."

"You are. I knocked you up in St. Martin. Sorry. But seriously. It is something to think about."

Benny stopped at the bottom of a flight of stairs and turned around. "We'll worry about it when the time comes. I want to show you my room."

We walked up to the third floor and Benny took me down a bright, white carpeted corridor to her bedroom. I shook my head in disbelief at the sign hanging on the door. "Princess Benita's Palace." I didn't give her a hard time about it, though.

My brothers and I had destroyed every piece of furniture my parents held dear. My name could still be found scrawled in bright red crayon under Daddy's TV stand. Benny's room held the only evidence that a young person had ever lived in this house. Her bedroom was easily triple the size of the bedroom I'd had growing up. Another king-sized canopy bed took up one corner of the room, the other side extending out to accommodate the needs of a princess: a vanity, a chaise lounge, a window seat that had been constructed sometime after the house was built.

There were cloth tack boards on the walls filled with pictures of Benny and the girls. Stuffed animals and ABO trinkets were on various surfaces.

My attention was snagged by a corner of the room that housed an enormous array of beauty pageant crowns, sashes, and trophies. I made right for them, in awe that Benny hadn't mentioned this part of her life at all.

"These aren't yours, are they?"

"These are mine." Benny pointed out a now-obvious division in the collection to a shelf topped with tiaras and little trophies. "These are Mama's. Miss South Carolina." I glanced at the most elaborate crown in the bunch, but not the largest, then back at the smaller cluster of prizes that belonged to my bunny. I had a shitload of questions, but let them drop the moment I spotted a glamour shot of little Benny in her pageant finest.

I picked up the frame for a closer look. No five-year-old should wear that much makeup. "Oh my God. Look at those cheeks." Benny was suddenly still. I put the picture frame down, freaked out that I had really embarrassed her. "What's wrong, baby?"

"Cleo, I didn't tell you the whole story about my real father."

This was exactly what I didn't want. We'd come a long way, and I didn't need her to dig up any painful memories to justify these new parts of her life that she was sharing with me. "B, you don't have to."

"Yes, I do, because I know you're wondering about Mama, and I'd rather you know the truth than have you come to the wrong conclusion."

"I won't—" Benny stopped me with her I-can-see-right-through-your-bullshit face. "Okay."

"A year after she won this crown, she was at a function at my granddaddy's country club. My real father had been courting her for a while, but..." Benny always got to the point, and I could tell she was deciding what information was absolutely necessary.

"Once her year as Miss South Carolina was over, she knew he'd propose. But he didn't. He said something like he wanted to finish law school before he settled down, but that night he attacked her on the golf course. That's how she ended up pregnant with me. She wasn't going to say anything, but when she missed her period twice, she figured she had to come clean. She was scared to tell my grandparents, so she told her best friend Stevie, thinking Stevie would give her some advice.

Instead, Stevie told the whole town that Mama willingly had sex with my real father and she'd made up the rape because she didn't want to get in trouble. After my granddaddy found out, he forced Lamont to marry Mama the next day."

"Benny."

"People knew. Everyone knew, but people still treated Mama like she had done something wrong. Granddaddy made things even worse by paying for Lamont's law school like he owed him something."

"How did he end up working for Dalhem?" We didn't get along, but I couldn't believe that Dalhem would knowingly let a dirt bag like that into his nest.

"Granddaddy kept pulling strings for him, and eventually, he was bound to this demon named Karl."

"That's a good vampire name."

"I know. We should have known he was up to no good. Karl was executed too after their plan failed."

"What did they try to do exactly?" I knew there had been some serious foul play involved, but again, Benny never really talked about it.

"They tried to kill Paeno."

"Great." I couldn't seem to shake this demon.

"But even before he died, Mama and I were all each other had. I was the little brat who ruined his life, and Mama was the tainted beauty queen he had to put up with. When I started getting heavier, he became even more disgusted with me, but Mama would always stick up for me. It was the only time she ever stood up to him."

"She wasn't standing up for herself," I realized.

"No. When I was old enough to understand the names he was calling me, I started eating more to make him angry, but Mama was eating less. She's gotten help, but it comes and goes. She'll be nearing a healthy weight and maintaining it for a couple months and then she stops. And of course Daddy gives her his blood, so things that would usually be affected, his blood fixes that."

"But he can't fix what's going on inside her mind."

Benny shook her head. "He would have to wipe her mind completely and give her another existence, except that doesn't work. It would just leave her crazy with parts of her memory trying to resurface. When we first started dating, I wasn't ready to expose you to that."

"You thought I would judge her? That's what you meant?" I could hear Benny's words that night in the churchyard loud and clear. I was mixed up now. I knew why she'd left this part of her history out, but maybe if she'd told me… I let the what-ifs go and urged her to finish.

"And maybe you would judge me too. I thought you would see how we were and you wouldn't want to deal with it. I didn't want you to think she was a bad mother for not taking care of herself and for letting me get this way."

"Benny, every family has problems and secrets. Remember, you so nicely pointed out mine." I took her face in my hands and kissed her softly on the lips. "I am not judging you or your mama. I am judging your piece-of-shit father for the way he treated you both, but I'm not judging you."

I kissed her again, and this time she stepped closer to me and claimed my lips with hers. She was still hurting inside and I could feel it at every point where our bodies touched.

"I love you, no matter what you look like. I don't care what size you are. But if you're eating to hurt yourself, then I do want to know."

Benny started to turn away from me. "I don't know anymore."

"Come here." I walked her over to the window seat and pulled her into my lap. She sighed and finally leaned against me.

"I lost the weight I did walking around campus so much, but I try not to think about it. That was one of the reasons I loved you. I knew you didn't care how fat I was."

"You are not fat. I want you to be happy and healthy, whatever size jeans that comes in." I didn't know what else to say. Benny's weight had never been a problem for me. I knew she was self-conscious about it sometimes, but I never knew it ran this deep.

"I passed my last physical with flying colors," she said quietly.

"That's good to know, but if you want to talk about it, I'm here, okay? If something is bothering you, tell me."

"I will."

"I love you," I said, kissing her neck. She let me hold her for a while, and soon the clouds over her mood started to lift. I hoped she remembered how much she meant to me. I hoped she understood that I would never let anyone hurt her the way her father had ever again.

"There's something else I wanted to show you," she said. I followed her over to her bed and sat beside her on the floor. Benny shuffled to all fours and started digging for something deep underneath the bed frame. I didn't resist giving her butt an affectionate pat. She emerged with a wooden chest, complete with gold hinges.

"Ooh, Benny's secret box."

She shrugged dismissively, then flipped the lid. She pushed it toward me for inspection. The first thing I pulled out was her old bunny tail, a white ball of fake fur attached to a pretty sizable black plug. Beneath a few of our other toys, I found the remains of our previous relationship. Cheap jewelry, pictures, so many pictures I'd thought I'd lost. Three of my favorites, Polaroids of us kissing from the night of some random toga party. Benny had pressed them into a frame with a small bouquet of violets I'd given her the same day. Some of the keepsakes had been in my room and I thought were now lost to Mama and Daddy's storage shed.

"Jesus, B. You kept everything. I was wondering where this stuff went."

"Barb and Paige grabbed a few things out of your room."

I pulled out my monogrammed ABO hoodie and ran my fingers over my name stitched into the sleeve. I remembered the day I gave it to her. She wanted it, as a piece of me, but she'd been embarrassed that it wouldn't fit. It did. "You kept this too?"

"Yeah," Benny said, her voice suddenly shy. "I would sleep in it when I came home on vacation."

"For how long?" How long had she been carrying me with her like that?

"I never really stopped. Christmas morning, this year. I had it on."

I rested my hand on the side of her neck and begged her to look my way. "Why didn't you tell me?"

"Because I thought you hated me."

"I never hated you. I just hated your reactions to certain things. We should have just talked."

"We're talking now, though."

"We are."

"Tell me about your family. I know you miss them." Benny slid closer and pulled my hand into her lap. "Tell me about them."

My sister-queens knew what I'd been doing all along. Andrew knew that I went home nearly every night, but it was nothing I could really talk about. What could I say? My parents were struggling through, but my brothers were living, getting on just fine without me, and it killed me inside. But I needed to talk about them. I needed to grieve losing them in my life, and Benny was the only person who could help me with that.

"My brothers are doing well. Stephen moved to Charlotte. He's a chef now."

"That's great," Benny said with a genuine smile.

"Yeah, he could always cook better than me. Better than Daddy."

"What about Maxwell and Nathaniel?"

"Max and Tina have two kids now. Max Jr. is two and Angelica is five months. And I've never held them. Never talked to them." Benny reached up and touch my face. When she pulled away I could see the tips of her fingers moist with my blue tears. My next words just flowed. "I miss Nat the most. I miss Mama and Daddy like crazy, but Nat…"

"He was your best friend." I nodded after Benny wiped another tear away. "I remember you saying that. You know he misses you too."

"He does. He's getting along better these days, but in the beginning I would sit on the roof every night and listen to him cry. He would talk to me and I couldn't answer him back."

"I'm sorry I wasn't there for you."

"It's…Daddy's drinking now, and Mama's pretending he's not. Nathaniel wants out, but Mama keeps insisting he needs to live at home a while longer. I know part of it is me. She doesn't want to feel like she's losing another kid. I think she just needs a distraction from Daddy. She wants to pretend like nothing's wrong."

"I know a little something about that." Benny jumped up and grabbed a box of tissues, then joined me back on the floor. I wiped my face, glad that I was done with the tears for now.

"Nat's been coming home later and later, and Mama's been ignoring Daddy more and more. And there's nothing I can do."

"I can't change things with my family and you can't change things with yours," Benny said. "So let's be our own family. You and me."

"I like that idea, bunny."

"So do I." Benny moved a little closer and cupped my cheek. Her thumb grazed over my lips.

Because my demon seemed to suddenly have something to prove, I shoved Benny's keepsake box aside and tackled her to the floor. I kissed her hard, my lips pushed at her, my tongue sliding into her mouth the moment she opened to me. She kissed me back just as fiercely, grabbing at my sides as she shifted her legs to fit perfectly on either side of mine. That keyed into my demon's more animalistic needs, and before I knew it, I was wrapping her winter boots around my back and grinding her hips into the carpet.

When she broke away from my lips and let out the sexiest, breathy moan I'd ever heard, I just happened to glance up at her bedroom door. I chuckled, wondering if it was locked.

"What are you laughing at?" Benny gasped.

"This is the first time I'd have to worry about someone's parents walking in when I'm trying to get my freak on."

"She always knocks." Benny grabbed my chin and brought our lips back together. I growled into her mouth, letting my fangs drop a little more in anticipation of what was sure to happen next. Dry-humping always made me hungry.

And then Ms. Leanne knocked on the door. "Girls?"

"What did I tell you?" Benny sat up and gently nudged me off her. As she stood up and straightened her clothes, I closed my eyes and counted to five to get my dental boners under control. I flashed to my feet the moment Ms. Leanne poked her head in.

"Did I interrupt something?" she asked with a knowing smile.

"No, Mama."

"Good. I wanted to show you girls something before we eat."

CHAPTER EIGHTEEN

Cleo

"We own this whole block," Ms. Leanne explained as we hustled across the street. "Well, we own it for other demons. Every building is linked by underground tunnels. Omi and Mary are down there at the end." She pointed to a yellow town house similar to theirs with black shutters.

"But this is what I wanted you girls to see." She climbed the few steps to a brick home directly across the street. She opened the front door with a gold key and ushered us inside. When she flicked the lights, I saw that a massive remodeling was under way. The floors in the front parlor had been stripped and drop cloths lined the entrance hallway. It smelled of paint and new wood.

As we walked through, Ms. Leanne flicked on lights in various rooms. Covered furniture was centered in the middle of what might have been another living room area. Another room was home to a baby grand piano. New shelves had been installed in an office/library space.

"What do you think?" she said as we made our way past a couple bedrooms on the second floor.

"It's nice. Who is it for?" Benny asked.

"You two, silly."

"Mama."

"Ms. Leanne." Benny and I blurted out at the same time. Dinner and a cozy room underground was the perfect way to say welcome to town, but a house? I knew we'd live nearby. Still, I was expecting us to choose a place together, and my only requirement was a comfy basement and off-street parking for the Range Rover. This was too much.

"I'm not hearing any arguments. Now, there's room for your friend Andrew here, but if he wants his own place he can have the one next door."

My mind flashed to the equally large town house right beside this one. "That place is huge for one person."

"Plenty of room to stretch out," Ms. Leanne said, scrunching her nose up with her smile. "There are bedrooms upstairs, of course, and you'll have your master bed and bath upstairs and down, just like your daddy and I do, but this is what I wanted to show you."

On the third floor, we stopped in the master bedroom. I saw that Ms. Leanne really did have a thing for canopy beds, but that's not what she wanted to show us. On the far side of the room she opened a set of double doors. She flicked on a light switch and revealed the start of a nursery.

Benny's hand flew to her mouth. "Mama."

I stared at the infant furniture. The crib and the changing table were the same mahogany cut as the bed frame behind us. "Ms. Leanne, you didn't have to do this."

"Oh yes, I did. Your daddy is still all bent out of shape, but he knows what you girls want. When he told me, I knew this was exactly what I needed to do." She looked at Benny and me like we were crazy. "I want my grandbaby close, and what's closer than right across the street? Well, under the same roof is pretty close, but I'll know you'll want your privacy. So I just want to know when."

"When what?" Benny asked. Her confusion mirrored mine.

"When am I going to see this grandbaby?"

"You are the only woman I've ever met who wants to be a grandma." I laughed.

"Sure do. So?"

"Mama, we haven't even really thought about our wedding yet, let alone a sperm donor or—"

"Oh nonsense. It'll take your daddy no time at all to find someone. Just tell him what you're looking for."

"And I should graduate first," Benny added. I was waiting for her to put her hand to her mama's forehead, just to check the temperature on her sanity.

"Summertime sounds great."

"Mama."

"Oh stop. You two have nothing to worry about."

"Except raising a baby," I muttered. I knew everything would be okay, but I was still terrified. Dalhem hadn't raised Benny from infancy. Even if her father was a lousy piece-of-shit bum, she had time to adjust to the world of humans like any normal child. How do you explain to a toddler that one of her mommies can't go outside during the day? I feared enough for her having to deal with a world that wasn't all that into her having two mommies in the first place.

Sensing my panic, Benny's mama put her hand on my forearm. Her fingers were freezing, but still I felt comforted. "I'll be here to help you every step of the way."

"Thank you, Ms. Leanne," I was able to squeeze out.

"It's Mama to you."

❖

We almost made it all the way to the dining room when Dalhem appeared out of nowhere and stood in our way. He was mostly human, but his horns and wings were out, as were his obnoxiously large fangs. Ms. Leanne embraced him and stood on her tiptoes to kiss his chin. Clearly, they'd made up. Instantly, he was in my consciousness, letting his strength and authority be known, not that I cared.

See, here was my problem with Dalhem. The man-demon, whatever he was, had all this infinite wisdom, all this power. He had thousands of humans and vampires in his service. Having lived for thousands of years on earth and in hell, he understood the human condition better than most, but just because Benny and I had gotten into it, he treated me like shit. I thought of all the insane shit I'd heard my demon brothers and sisters getting up to, but when it came to me, Dalhem behaved just as human as the next. The overprotective father in him reared its ugly head. It worked out great for Benny, but hours after my change, I had to deal with the fact that the being who was essentially the father of our kind, the master of our race, was not there to support me when I needed him the most. He showered Ginger with attention and respect, but he damn near hissed and growled at me every time we were in the same room.

I did respect his authority and I would never go against him in any major way that would jeopardize his control or put the girls in danger, but when it came to his pissy attitude with me, well, he could kiss my ass. I let all of that roll around in my head in the split second before he addressed Benny and Ms. Leanne.

"I will speak to your Cleopatra alone." I was so tempted to just throw myself on the floor while groaning, "Lord Jesus," but I kept the drama between Dalhem and me.

Benny turned to me, frowning nervously. I stroked her cheek softly and said, "I'm pretty sure he won't kill me." I didn't think he would.

"Daddy. Be nice," she said. He didn't respond, just mentally asserted that I should follow him. We ended up in his study. This time I actually looked around. It was decorated in golds and creams and dark woods. He stood beside his desk and I made myself very comfortable on his couch. I stopped short of putting my boots up on his coffee table. I wasn't *trying* to start a fight with him.

"I see that you still have no use for respect. Do you, Cleopatra?"

I winced at him using my full name. "No?"

"You've broken a vow that was not yours to break, and now you wish to mate my Benita, to join my nest, though you have not asked my permission."

"I have to know. What were *you* getting out of the tu'lah?"

"You do not question me!" he roared. I think it pissed him off even more that I didn't jump with fear or wet my pants.

"Okay, whatever. I don't know what you expect me to say. You know exactly what I'm thinking. You're in my head. You and I never talk. Ever. I asked Ms. Leanne and she said yes, but you know Benny would marry me without approval from either of you, if that's what she really wanted. She suggested we join your nest, and your wife seems more than happy with the idea. I think you know that too, unless she's managed to keep those renovations across the street a secret from you. It seems like I'm not the only one who can get on just fine without your approval."

The temperature in the room cranked up a bit. "I know you have no respect for the plans of greater beings." Dalhem growled.

"This isn't about respect. Bottom line, do you care what Benny wants?" It wasn't a question he intended to answer. "I love her and you *know* I have loved her this whole time, but if you want to call her in here and ask if she wants to be with Paeno instead of me, go for it. I won't argue. But I'm pretty sure Benny made her choice."

"You are not right for her."

"That's a lie. You don't like me. I made things difficult for you with your sister, but really, that's not my fault. You presented Benny with an extreme choice and all it did was drive us back together." I leaned forward and looked him square in his golden eyes. "I'm sorry if that screws up your plans, but I love Benny and I'm not letting her go."

Dalhem's mind was closed off to me, but he was so easy to read. He would never hurt Benny. End of story. And hurting me would tear her apart. As he stared me down, he and I both knew there was nothing more to talk about. Benny and I were getting married. We would have our family, and Dalhem would just have to deal with this demon pact with his sister on his own. He could be pissed at me all day long. Still, his emotions wouldn't drive Benny and me apart.

"Someday, your actions will have repercussions, Cleopatra."

I rolled my eyes. "Master, I—" Dalhem disappeared before I could finish.

❖

I found my way to the dining room and smiled at the look of relief on Benny's face when she saw I was still in one piece. I was also happy to see my sister-queen.

Omi came around the table and gave me a firm hug. A woman who I guessed was her wife, Mary, stood beside her. Mary was beautiful. Though her skin was near a buttery white, she was unmistakably black. Her thick, curly hair, a deep shade of auburn, was tied back on the top of her head in a full bun, and dark brown freckles were spattered across her nose. She and Omi were dressed alike, both wearing dark blazers over light sweaters with tight jeans under knee-high boots. They were a perfect pair.

Omi introduced us and Mary hugged me as well. She was fairly powerful, though less so than Omi and myself, but Mary had a very positive energy about her, and I could tell that her kindness was genuine.

"I trust you are okay?" Omi asked. She looked me over like she was checking for bruises.

"Yeah, I'm fine. He just wanted to bitch at me some more," I replied. "What are you doing here?"

"We're here for dinner. I wanted to meet you," Mary said.

"I fed from the girls and set them on each other. They barely even notice when I'm gone." Omi pulled me closer and lowered her voice.

"This next change in your life will be big, and we want to be there for you."

Mary reached out and squeezed my hand.

They wanted me to cry. I could feel it. Instead, I squeezed Mary's hand back. "Thanks."

Dalhem appeared and took a loud, huffy seat at the head of the table. Benny and Mary did their best to cover their snickers at his brattiness. We took his arrival as the official start to the meal and took our seats around the table.

As Faraut served dinner, Mary and Ms. Leanne jumped right into their conversation about some feeders Mary had to take from a demon who was losing his grip on reality.

"I'm what we call an eraser," she explained to me. "Most demons are good at concealing themselves and wiping the minds of unbound humans, but sometimes there are mistakes or a wipe isn't complete so I track down the humans and give them a slight reprogramming."

"It's nothing drastic," Benny asserted, though I didn't think it was.

"I'll do something simple like alter the details to a demon they saw to make them think they were dealing with another human."

"You might need to teach me that trick," I said. Camila had taught me how to conduct complete wipes, but I could see where that might leave a human feeling a little confused, and nothing caused problems like a confused human. I thought of De'Treshawn and how he'd probably had nightmares for a few days after I'd dealt with him.

Dalhem growled from the end of the table as the thought passed through my mind. Ms. Leanne hushed him with a light pat on the back of his massive palm. Mary went on with her story like he wasn't even there.

"I was telling Leanne about this particular demon who wasn't wiping humans properly, so we took away a few of his feeders to give him some time to think."

"Do you think he'll come around?" I asked.

"He will." Mary smiled.

"How did you two meet?" I asked Omi. Mary was an interesting woman, very different from our other sister-queens.

"We were born on the same plantation," Omi replied. I almost choked on my beef.

"My forbear owned a sugar plantation on Barbados. He owned a large number of people as well," Mary said. I knew they would tell me the whole story if I asked, but I could only imagine what their early lives had been like. I held off my curiosity for another time.

Faraut stepped in the room with a tray full of desserts, and coffee for Ms. Leanne. "Let's take dessert by the fire," she suggested.

"I will leave, my ladies." Dalhem stood with another grunt and vanished.

❖

One a.m. came and went, and the three of us demons were just settling into our night. Ms. Leanne excused herself to bed and Benny excused herself to change into her pajamas. Once we were alone, Omi's mood became a little somber.

"How often do you visit your family?" she asked me.

"Lately, not that often, but usually…every night."

"We understand your loss, but—" Omi started.

But Mary finished for her. "It has to stop, Cleo. Holding on to the past and holding on to things you can't control will only drive you mad."

"More so because you are getting nothing in return," Omi added.

"We understand that you and Benny plan to have a family."

"Yes. That's the plan," I replied.

"You need to live for them. Not for your past, or you will turn around one day and find that you are missing things in the present," Omi said.

"I get it." I saw how my death had affected Daddy. How would my marriage to Benny be if I slipped out every night to check on them? How would my child feel if I kept this part of my life from them?

Mary perked up in her seat and offered me another one of her true smiles. "We have a proposition for you. Two propositions, actually."

I laughed at the way she nearly bounced on the cushions. It couldn't be a bad proposal. "I'm listening."

"With you and Benny leaving the sorority, we thought you could come work for me," Mary said.

"As an eraser?"

"Yes. We all have our responsibilities in this nest. Omi says you are wonderful with the girls, and I think you should keep dealing with humans in a way that strengthens your powers."

"I'd love that." Raising a child would be work enough, but when it came to being immortal, I knew there would come a time when I would want and need more to do with myself. Training and working with Mary seemed like a good fit for me. "What's the other part of the proposition?"

"We meant what we said," Omi replied. "We want to be here for you."

"We thought that perhaps we could be your surrogate family," Mary said.

Omi clarified. "Your relationship with a Camila is like a sister bond. She is your friend, but you two have a certain dynamic."

"She treats me like a child?"

Omi laughed this time. "Yes, she treats you like a friend and sometimes like a child. I see how that has made it hard for you to confide in her sometimes. She cares, but you are the first vampire she helped create. She doesn't know how to work with you from time to time. Benny has her support here, and not that they won't support you, they will. Leanne is lovely, but Dalhem will always be Dalhem."

"And in-laws are still in-laws," I said, getting her meaning.

"We want you to feel like you have someone to turn to as well. You and Andrew."

I got a little choked up, okay. I wiped my eyes against the onslaught of emotion beating against my chest. Omi had been watching all along. She seemed to know exactly how I felt, about Camila, about Benny. Ms. Leanne was amazing, but that didn't change the fact that I'd lost my mama, that I still longed for a little something of my own.

"I would really like that, you guys. Really."

Mary whipped out a dark blue handkerchief and handed it to me. "If there is anything you need from us, it doesn't matter how small, you may come to us."

"Well, there is one thing," I said.

"What is that, my dear?" Omi asked.

"Would you like to help me pick out a ring?"

CHAPTER NINETEEN

Benny

Cleo stayed up all night with Omi and Mary. Though I could have stayed in bed with her all day, my biological clock and my growling stomach woke me up at nine in the morning. I left her sleeping and went to have breakfast with Mama. Cleo was still asleep when I came back. Leo and Boomer were snoozing at her side. I watched her for a few seconds. She'd fallen asleep on her back, fully dressed. Her legs were crossed at her ankles, and her arms, folded over her stomach. I was sure she thought she'd lie down beside me for just a few minutes, but even demons need their sleep. There was no need to disturb her, so I took some time to finish my German assignment. I would have finished much sooner if I hadn't been fantasizing about Cleo the whole time, the thought of dropping out becoming more and more tempting every minute. I couldn't wait until we could just be together.

When I checked on Cleo again, her eyes peeked open when I poked my head in the doorway. I stepped inside and closed the door with my butt.

"Did you have a good nap?" I asked, walking slowly to the foot of the bed. She eyed me warily as I moved.

"I did. It would have been nice to sleep with you, though."

"I just had to take care of a few things."

"Oh yeah?" Her eyes narrowed as she noticed my hands were still behind my back.

"Yeah. I have a wonderful date planned for us tonight, but Daddy is pretty much in hibernation mode for a few hours and Mama is out for the day. I thought we could play for a little while." I showed Cleo the new tail and the bottle of lube I'd been hiding.

"Where did you get that?" She sat forward.

"I ordered it right when we got back from St. Martin. I wanted to surprise you."

"Well, I am surprised. Let me see that right quick." I came around to her side of the bed and handed her the brown-black tail, plug end first. "Hmm. I like this. It's much softer."

"I did my research." It took several hours, actually. White seemed to be the preferred color for a bunny tail, but eventually I stumbled across a site that made custom animal tails plugs with faux fur. No animals needed to be harmed for our play time. Cleo shifted to the edge of the bed and wrapped her legs around my waist.

"Do you have anything in particular in mind?" she asked. This was the first time she'd asked.

I thought for a moment, going over my list in my mind. "Um, can we do number two and number seven? And anything else that tickles your fancy." She hadn't tied me up properly yet, and I was still craving a certain kind of spanking.

"I like number seven a lot. But thinking that I would be spending the weekend at your mama's house, I didn't bring any of our playthings with us. Do I need to swing back to the house so we can pull off number two?"

I rummaged through our bag and pulled out the bit of silk rope I'd hidden in the leg of a pair of jeans and roll of bondage tape, just in case.

"Ooh, baby. Extra points for planning ahead. I might have to throw in a number five for good measure."

"I'm okay with that."

"I'm gonna put this in." She held up my bunny tail. "We're going to talk for a little while, though, after we get down to business. Okay?"

"Okay."

She lay back down and crossed her arms behind her head, then she nodded, gesturing up and down my body. "Everything but the bra."

"Yes, Cleo."

Knowing she wanted a good show, I took my time. I slipped out of my boots, then pulled my oversized sweater over my head. "Eyes here, bunny," she said just as I hooked my thumbs in the waistband of my leggings. I looked her straight in her light brown eyes, then, unintentionally, at her mouth as her lips parted slightly. The sight of her fangs had become an instant turn-on. My T-shirt came off next and then my underwear. I thought I'd be completely naked by this point, but just in case, I'd worn one of Cleo's favorite bras. She licked her teeth as she took in my cleavage.

"You are so fucking beautiful. Turn around." I did as she asked and showed her my backside. I could have sworn I heard her lips smacking. "Bend over. All the way. Grab your ankles." I did as she asked and found myself panting as my ponytail dragged over the carpet. I remained still and in that position as I heard the bed creak slightly under the movement of her weight. Soon I saw her socked feet meet the floor behind me. Then I felt the heat from her body.

I closed my eyes against the shivers that racked my spine as she ran her palm up and down the length of my back.

"Are you ready?" she purred.

"Yes, Cleo."

"Up."

I straightened myself into a better position and then took a deep breath. Cleo knew exactly what she was doing, and to help matters along, I'd taken some time stretching myself before I'd joined her. I was more than ready. She slowly slid my tail in, but with ease. I groaned helplessly as it settled into place. The whole area was sparking with sensation, the feeling of fullness and the slight, yet soft tickle of the fur brushing my cheeks. My clit throbbed, aching for tender attention. The walls of my pussy contracted, needing the same.

"You want to see how it looks?" she asked quietly.

I swallowed and was able to find my voice through my arousal, though my eyes did close. "Yes, Cleo."

"Hand me my phone. Don't worry. I'll delete it." I walked across the room, my every step reminding me exactly who I belonged to. I found her cell in the front pocket of our bag and handed it to her. She directed me in several positions and snapped a shot of each pose. We looked at the pictures together. A few with her hand gripping my ass cheek, one with the indentations of her fingers leaving delicious pink marks on my skin that I knew would fade quickly.

"Do you see how fucking sexy you are?"

I hesitated to answer. I felt unbelievably sexy with Cleo, but... Well, there was always a but. She still wanted an answer. I ignored how much I hated my back and focused on my ass and the tail. Cleo's hand covered my breast and I fought the urge to close my eyes and lean against her.

She licked the curve of my ear.

"Do you know what I see?"

"No, Cleo."

"I see a gorgeous round ass that some women would kill for. And you know what? I'm gonna enjoy fucking that ass. You know what else I see? Your beautiful, smooth skin and that sexy-as-hell birthmark right there on your thigh." I'd caught a glimpse of the brown spot plenty of times over the years, but I never knew Cleo took much notice of it. Her hand moved lower, over my stomach, which twitched at the unwanted attention, and between my legs. I moaned, my eyes finally slipping shut as she ran a single finger between my lips.

"I see the bunny I am very proud to own." She threw her phone on the bed and turned me in her arms. "You know what would make this look complete? Bunny ears." I bit my lip and eyed the bag. I loved the smile that spread out over Cleo's lips. "Bring 'em here." I laughed and hustled back to the bag. I had shoved some stuff into little hidden spaces. Cleo's eyes lit up when I produced the matching floppy ears. When we played with my first tail, we were both aware of the ridiculous nature of me in a complete bunny outfit, but now?

"When I saw these on the site, I couldn't resist," I explained as Cleo slipped them onto my head. She took a few seconds to readjust my hair and then an even bigger smile broke out on her face.

"Oh, bunny. You have to hop for me."

Through my giggling I did as she asked and hopped around the room a little, feeling my ass and my breasts jiggle with every bounce, flicking my head back every time one of the ears flopped down in my face. Cleo broke out in a laughing fit, and by the time I made it back over to her we were both in hysterics. "Oh fuck, babe. You look so cute. These were a must. Excellent call." She kissed me, then straightened the ears again.

"Okay. Get up here." She slid off the bed and stood while I climbed up and sat back with my heels under my butt. The plug did an excellent job of reminding me it was still there. "I'll be back in a little bit. Take a few minutes to really get your head together."

"Yes, Cleo."

Cleo left me alone for almost twenty minutes. It was the perfect amount of time. I was able to relax and think about my body. Not about the little things I hated about it, but the way Cleo would soon be touching it. I thought about how good it felt to put my control in her hands and how well she took care of me. I thought of her biting me and how hard I was sure to come. By the time she returned, my whole mind and body were completely primed for her. I wanted to be petted and spanked. I wanted to be tied down and dominated and fucked. It was something amazing to know that she would do those things for me, to know that I was completely safe and loved in her hands.

Cleo slid through the door silently and purposefully did not make eye contact with me. In her hand was a silk scarf and one of our vibrators. I didn't question where she'd gotten those particular items. She didn't hesitate before she blindfolded me. Knowing I had to give up even trying to see, I closed my eyes behind the silk and focused on the sound of her body and mine. She kissed me as she moved around the bed; on my shoulder, between my breasts. On my lips. I jumped a little when she placed a little nibble on my butt. In a few minutes, she had me on my knees on the bed with my wrists tied to the two posts at the foot of the bed, my legs spread wide enough for her liking.

She was in front of me moments later. Her lips lightly brushed over mine. "We are going to try this, but you need to tell me if I need to stop. Do you understand?"

"Yes, Cleo."

"And I want to hear you, bunny. Don't hold it in."

"Yes, Cleo."

She kissed me fully this time and finished me off with a slow swipe of her tongue along the seam of my mouth. Holding on to her taste as long as I could, I imagined the look on her face as she pulled away. I thought of how she must be looking at my breasts or the ruby that hung between them. Another symbol of our bond. Careful, slow breaths, I told myself.

Her fingers touched me first. My mind was seconds behind each motion, trying to predict where she was going next. Her fingers were there one moment and gone the next. Back one moment, then slipped inside me the next. I moaned like she asked me to, letting her know exactly how it felt to have her fingers pumping in and out of me. I groaned helplessly as she cupped me, massaging my lips and my clit all at once. I listened to her purring and my cries, and suddenly I wanted her to let me down. I wanted to touch her. But that wasn't part of the deal.

The first strike between my legs came from nowhere. She smacked me hard right on the height of my slit. My lips were parted and my hard clit exposed. I couldn't have guessed how amazing it would feel. The impact sent shock waves through my pelvis. I shuddered and sucked in a breath. "Shit," slipped from my lips as my legs seized up. The plug fired back as my muscles clenched.

Before I could recover, another smack landed on its target. She didn't soothe me with her palm the way she normally did. A moment after she made contact, I realized it was her mouth covering me. She sucked my tender skin gently, running her tongue slowly over me. She taunted me with the tips of her fangs. I wanted to drop my hips lower to ride her mouth more thoroughly, but the hold the rope had on my arms made it impossible. Instead, I moved my pelvis forward. That's when she pulled away.

"Nah nah, bunny," she said. "Only when I say."

She spanked my pussy until I couldn't take any more, bringing me to a point of painful need and reining me in when I thought I would go over the edge. She must have used her powers to appear behind me because out of nowhere I felt her jeans brushing the backs of my thighs. She slid my tail out of me, and as I was adjusting to the loss, I heard the sound of her zipper. It became useless to try to track her with my senses. She was inside me—I assumed it could only be her clit replacing the plug—slim at first, then longer and fuller with every thrust. Her hands were on my sides. She filled my ass to my limit and pumped slowly in and out until I found myself begging.

"Harder," I panted, my voice sounding less like my own. "Cleo. Please. Harder."

She stopped. But she didn't pull out. I could have sworn that even though she'd reached her maximum girth, she was tunneling deeper. But her hips were still.

My confusion didn't last long. I heard the whirling buzz of the vibrator. She pushed the smooth, rattling length inside my cunt. "Just like you wanted, baby." We'd never done this before, but it was on my list. She reached up with her other hand and pulled down the cup of my bra. Her strong fingers pinched my already hard nipple and I honestly thought I might drool. My whole body shook simply at the thought of what we were doing, how good it felt. I started to orgasm, my pussy and my ass both spasming wildly, gripping at their perfect intrusions, and it was a long time before I stopped.

Cleo took me down and cleaned me up, then she gave my arms, shoulders, and thighs a good massage. After, she didn't ask me to dress. I was still wet and I knew she enjoyed the smell. We lay in bed instead, me still bare with my head on her chest and our legs intertwined. Mama would be out for a little while longer.

"I was thinking about what Ms. Leanne said," Cleo told me. There was still a slight rumble to her voice. It matched nicely with the way my crotch continued to tingle. I'd be pretty sensitive for a while.

"You don't feel comfortable calling her Mama, do you?"

"No, I don't."

"Okay," I said lightly. I didn't think she would. Sometimes Mama comes on a little strong. "I think Ms. Leanne sounds just as endearing."

Cleo went on. "Let's talk, baby." I knew we had to. I was feeling this odd pressure to come to some sort of decision. "I know your mama is pretty eager for us to get the ball rolling, but I don't want you to feel pressured."

I laughed and rubbed my face against her chest. "I was just thinking that."

"Ya know?"

"Do you feel like we need to get on this baby making, like now?"

"Yes, but not in the way you think. I want Ms. Leanne's help, and I know Dalhem will do whatever you ask him to do, but I want us to take our time. I want these decisions to be ours."

"Do you want to live somewhere else?" I asked cautiously. Cleo was never one to look a gift horse in the mouth, but even I was shocked that Mama had set aside not one, but two houses for us to use. I wouldn't be surprised if that sort of thing put Cleo off a little.

"No. No. Hell, I will definitely take an eager babysitter right across the street. Believe that. I just want to make sure you and I are making these decisions together. I know what it's like to get lost in a whirlwind of making other people happy."

"I talked to Mama about it this morning, and she said you should be able to tell when I'm ovulating."

"I can." She muzzled the top of my head. "I'm sensitive to all your bits." It was something I should have guessed. Daddy could tell when you were going to sneeze ten minutes before the dust even hit your nose. I just never thought about Cleo being that in tune to my body.

"Here's what I want, or how I feel, rather. I do want to get the ball rolling now. Realistically, I'm not going on to any form of higher education, and when you and Daddy figure out what your new responsibilities will be, it's not like you'll be clocking in a nine-to-five.

And my gut is pretty much in line with that thinking. What I want is to leave school now."

Cleo's eyebrows quirked down. "I didn't expect you to say that."

"Why?"

"Because you're thorough. You always see things through, even if it's the last thing you want to do."

"Precisely why I want to get on with my life with you. Knowing what you know about my life now, can you imagine how pointless college felt for me?"

Cleo laughed. "Yes, I've thought about that a lot, actually."

I sat up so I could see her face. "I almost dropped out after we broke up."

"I almost asked Camila if I could be assigned to another nest."

"I'm ready now. Ready to be your wife, ready to be a mom. Being with you makes me so happy. The idea of more German classes, and chapter elections, and spring formal, and graduation, I am over all of it," I said as I reached up and played with her curls on the pillow. "But I do think it would be pretty cruel to the girls and Andrew if we just picked up immediately and left. Even if Andrew decides to follow us eventually."

"I think he will. So we wait?"

Her fingers trailed over my hip. The topic of conversation and her touch made me sigh. "I think we wait. In the meantime, though, we should definitely think baby. Daddy has his special doctors, and if your nose is pretty keyed into when will be the right time, we'll just…have to decide on where we want to get this sperm. What do you think?"

"Do we hold auditions?"

"To see how far they can shoot it?" I said dryly.

Cleo cracked up. "That's disgusting."

"Do you want it bluntly?"

"Of course. I love it blunt from you," Cleo replied.

"We need a black guy."

"It sounds terrible when you put it that way. God, Benny. You are so racist."

"Stop it." I hid my face, embarrassed. "I know how it sounds, but—"

"It makes sense. Man, I…" Cleo paused for a moment. I saw the emotions gather in her brow, but she kept them down. "I wish I could ask one of my brothers."

"Maxwell does look the most like you." Exactly like her was more like it. Her eldest brother was a more muscular version of Cleo with a beard.

"I'd ask Nat," she confessed, her voice finally releasing a twinge of sadness. I leaned down and kissed her cheek.

"You played favorites," I teased her.

"No. I just think he'd be the happiest for us. Maxwell...I love him, but I think he'd have the same opinion as Mama. And Stephen would feel weird about it, like he wouldn't know whose side to choose. But I think if he got some time to get used to it, Nat would be all right."

"Did you ever think about telling them? You know, and not telling your parents."

"Yeah. I thought about it a lot. There were a few times where I thought maybe Nat would understand. Maybe we could have talked about being gay in general, but I couldn't get myself to tell him the whole truth."

I knew what it felt like to have a barrier between yourself and a family member, but I had always told Mama the truth and she had always been there for me. I didn't even have to come out to her in any official way. She just knew. I had no idea what it was like to feel like you had no one to talk to. I hated myself even more for turning my back on Cleo.

"I wish there was some way you could talk to them," I said.

"Me too. But let's focus on us."

We talked some more, and after a frank conversation about finding no shame in wanting children who favor both parents, we decided to ask Daddy to find a kind, intelligent African-American man, a reliable feeder, who would be on board with helping us in our cause. We both thought it would be best not to meet him. Legally, we would leave it up to our child and the donor to contact each other if they wanted to once our child turned eighteen.

Cleo also told me about Mary's offer for them to work together. I wasn't sure what Daddy had in mind for Cleo, but she seemed so happy about this new opportunity, I made a mental note to talk to him about it. Daddy held grudges, but Cleo would be in our lives forever. I wanted them to get along and I wanted Cleo to be happy with every aspect of our new life.

So we decided, once the weekend was over, we'd head back to campus and we'd wait.

❖

After another impromptu nap, I headed up to my room to shower and get dressed for dinner. Cleo found me in my bathroom braiding my hair. She looked great, as usual, wearing a nice gray sweater with a blue collared shirt underneath, and dark blue jeans with her white sneakers. She looked quite sharp and I told her so. As a thank-you, she grabbed my butt.

"I'm almost ready," I said.

"Take your time."

"We have reservations. I don't want to take too long."

Cleo sat up on the counter. She had this dreamy look in her eye. I blew her a kiss. Just as I started to put the finishing touched on my lip gloss, Cleo took my hand. I gazed back at her, confused until she slid a ring onto my finger. She gently let go of my hand and leaned back against the mirror. I examined the ring closely. A modest round-cut diamond was embedded deep into a hexagonal white gold setting. The metal around the band was etched with leaves and flower petals. It was old and classic and very Southern. It was simple and beautiful. I never would have picked something like it for myself. I wasn't the only one who came into the weekend armed with surprises.

I swallowed, doing my best to keep the tears to a minimum even though my eyes began to mist up. "When did you—"

"Omi helped me. She knows a guy." Cleo shrugged like it was no big deal.

"It's...I...It's perfect."

She flicked my braid on my shoulder, then gently swept my bangs to the side. "You already said yes, so, ya know."

I grabbed her hand and laid a full kiss right on the center of her palm. "I love it and I love you."

"When we get back from dinner you can show me."

I looked down at the ring again. "Oh, I will."

❖

Cleo's face when we arrived at the restaurant could only be described as priceless. We walked, fingers intertwined, to the front door.

"What's the punch line, B?"

"Nothing." I laughed. "I remember a lot of things too."

"The Melting Pot, though?" Once upon a time, she'd told me that it was her favorite restaurant, though she'd only been there once. Maxwell had decided to go there for his graduation dinner, but Cleo's father vowed they'd never return once he got the bill. Fondue for six was a little expensive. Daddy didn't know it yet, but he was picking up the bill for tonight.

"If I had done things right the first time, this would have been our first date." I opened the door for her. "After you." She leaned down and grabbed my ass. I giggled as she gave me a gentle nudge inside ahead of her. I gave the hostess my name.

"Good evening, Miss Jones. The rest of your party is waiting for you."

I thanked her and ignored the strange look I knew Cleo was giving me. The young woman led us to the back of the restaurant, to a large table surrounded with our friends. I'd invited everyone I knew Cleo would want to see. Tokyo I did not invite for obvious reasons. Kina and Camila promised me that she would stay at the house.

"You've been busy scheming, huh?" Cleo said.

"This is how it should have been," I replied. "With our friends."

"Lemme see. Lemme see," Amy squeaked. She almost ripped my shoulder out of its socket as she tried to get a look at my ring.

"Did you tell her?" I asked Cleo.

"No," she grumbled. "I told Camila, though."

"I told Ginger."

"And I told Amy."

We both glared at our friends. Could no one keep a secret? Cleo took my jacket and I slid into my seat next to Ginger.

Ginger reached over and lifted my hand. "It's gorgeous," she said.

"It's not as big as that leprechaun's testicle Camila gave you, but I like it," Cleo replied.

"So do I," I added. She had a point. Ginger's wedding ring highlighted an emerald the size of a golf ball.

"Faeth, you couldn't scrounge up some tail to bring with you?" Cleo asked.

"I did." She pointed to Andrew. "He's a great date, yeah."

"How you doing, baby boy?" Cleo asked him.

"Good," he replied with his dreamy smile. Cleo had stuck to

her promise and cut her time with Andrew down a lot to spend more time with me, but I appreciated their relationship more now and I saw just how much she loved him. I was able to see, too, that he wasn't a threat.

As the night wore on, I snuggled closer into Cleo's side. I let her feed me when she wanted to and I didn't pass up the chance to steal a kiss at every opportunity. I was so in love I thought I might burst. Finally, we packed it up before they kicked us out, but soon the conversations resumed in the parking lot. Eventually, our friends were ready to go. As was I. We said good-bye to Danni and Amy before they hopped into Danni's Jeep. Camila, Ginger, and Faeth headed toward a slightly wooded area beside the restaurant so they could vanish.

"Andrew, kid. We're heading back to the city. You need a lift?" Kina asked. Monica jiggled the keys to her car. He glanced nervously between us. I had already called him that afternoon and told him to pack an overnight bag, but I wanted to see how Cleo felt about my idea first.

I gripped her hand. "I thought Andrew could come home with us. We can show him the new house?"

"You want to?" Cleo asked him, pleased.

"Yeah." He shrugged bashfully.

"Home it is."

CHAPTER TWENTY

Benny

Waking up with a man in my bed was another first for me. We didn't have a crazy threesome or anything close to that. But after we introduced Andrew to Mama and showed him the town house, we decided to watch movies. I tried to play off just how exhausted I was, but I didn't make it very far into our on-demand selection. I woke up in bed with my arm slung over Cleo's stomach and my head on her chest. Andrew was reclining on her other side. They were watching *South Park*.

We had a lazy start to the next day. Neither Andrew nor I was in a rush to get back to campus. There was something nice about getting away every now and then, especially when you have more than forty roommates. Before lunch, Andrew slipped into the bathroom. I watched Cleo as she put up her hair and stepped into her sneakers.

"Whose turn is it to feed today?" I asked.

"His. Why?"

I'd thought so, but I wasn't sure. "I was just thinking."

"I was going to wait until we got back to campus."

"You don't have to. If it's okay with him."

She finished securing her hair and walked over to where I sat on the bed. "Are you sure? The group is, you know, one thing. But I know how you feel about the one-on-one feedings. The last time we tried that, it didn't turn out so well." It wasn't an encounter I'd forgotten. We'd been studying one night in Cleo's bedroom. It was her turn to feed Camila and she asked me to stay, to watch. I was uncomfortable with the whole situation. I could barely handle the thought of Cleo having to feed Camila out of necessity. Witnessing their intimacy firsthand was too much for me to handle. But instead of telling Cleo, I stayed. I played off the panic attack I suffered near the end of their coupling as a sudden need to pee. I'm sure I gave us away to Camila even though she never brought the incident up again.

Cleo and I lacked a great deal of communication at that time. Andrew would be with us after graduation, and where Cleo would probably leave the house to meet with her other feeders, her feedings with Andrew would most likely always be under the roof we shared. Everything Andrew had told me about his relationship with Cleo was true. They loved each other, that much was obvious, but it wasn't in any way romantic. Cleo was relaxed with him in a way she wasn't at ease with other people, besides myself. She talked to him, really talked to him. I wanted to see what they were like together when it came to a blood offering.

The bathroom sink shut off.

"Ask him," I said with a little more confidence as he came back into the bedroom.

"Ask me what?"

"Would it be cool if I fed here?" Cleo said.

"Yeah. If Benny's okay with it, I don't mind," Andrew replied. "You want to do it now?"

"Sure," Cleo said. "Why not?"

I slid back on the bed to give them some room while Andrew started digging through his bag. I frowned at him when he produced two condoms.

"What are those for?" I asked before considering my words more carefully.

Andrew smiled like he knew what I was getting at. "Just a catching mitt of sorts. I come a lot."

Cleo agreed with a reluctant nod of her head. "He does."

"So? Do you wear one every time?" I asked Andrew.

"No, but—"

"Don't use one now. It's fine."

"Okay." He tossed the condoms back on top of his bag, then took a seat on the bed beside me. Cleo stepped between his legs and unbuttoned his jeans.

"Baby, move right here." She patted a spot on the sheets slightly behind Andrew. I realized as I shifted into place that I was in the perfect position for Cleo to look me in the eye as she fed. They had a quick discussion where Cleo told Andrew to "hold it." I could only assume she meant his erection.

The rest of the dance I knew well. I watched as she gently gripped his neck and tilted his head to the side. She licked his throat as she did with the rest of us, quickening his pulse through his arousal, stroking the pounding of his blood closer to the surface. Andrew groaned as she struck, a deep baritone grunt that I could feel in my own stomach. He cupped himself. I was sure to catch the onslaught of his first ejaculation.

Cleo's eyes held mine, burning and glowing as she took what she needed from him. Her purring grew stronger, as did Andrew's grunts and groans. He trembled at regular intervals. Just as I caught an unfamiliar scent, which I thought was his cum, spilling into his hand, Cleo reached out for me. I held my breath until her warm fingers brushed my skin. She touched my cheek first and then my chin. Her hand moved lower and I inched closer, eagerly moving forward until I sat up on my knees. She cupped my face and slid her thumb into my mouth. My moans matched Andrew's as I sucked her hand with enthusiasm.

I opened my mind to her.

"I want you."

She growled and took her final drag from Andrew's vein. He shuddered one last time. After she sealed her bites, Cleo moved out of Andrew's way. He turned just enough that I saw that the front of his T-shirt was covered in his cum. He was still erect.

"I'm gonna shower and change," he ground out, still trying to catch his breath. I knew his pain. He was just getting keyed up. One of the curses and blessings of being a feeder. The drawing of blood is just the start. You want more. You want to finish things.

Andrew shut himself in the bathroom as Cleo and I eyed each other. I'd closed my mind again. We both had to work for it. There was cum on her shirt too and a little on her pants, but it didn't bother me. She started shucking her clothes off anyway.

"He's gonna be in there a while," she said. "You should be naked."

"Is that how you want me?"

Cleo's head cocked to the side. Anger touched her brow as her demon teetered toward its limit. She wasn't used to waiting.

Cleo grabbed my ankles and pulled me to the edge of the bed. My pajama pants and my underwear were ripped off with one quick tear.

When she flipped me on my stomach, I was able to scramble a whole foot away before she was on top of me, grinding her wet heat against my ass. I arched back, forcing my leg between hers just as she got a good grip on my hair.

She pulled my head to the side. "Is this what you want? You want me to ride you rough?"

I thrust back, rubbing myself against her thigh. She tugged my hair a little harder. The perfect amount of pain. "Say it."

"I want you so fucking bad it hurts."

"Well, fuck me, then."

Cleo was on top, her hips posed behind my body in the perfect position to guide every moment and every movement between us, but instead she bumped me hard, once, twice, encouraging me to take the lead. She released her hold on my hair and I dropped myself to the bed, raising my ass and pussy against her thigh and her crotch in a shameless, prostrating display. I rubbed myself against her, wiggled my pussy up and down, feeling my juices slide along her skin, and I felt her heat and her wetness too.

She slapped my ass. "You can do better than that."

"I'm trying," I whimpered, feigning desperation and fear. I could feel it in her grip on my waist. I was doing exactly what she wanted.

"You're not trying hard enough." Forcing my stomach flat against the comforter, Cleo rode me, using my body to stroke her clit. I arched back at every opportunity, rubbing myself along her skin, skirting that thin line, needing just one final push to make me explode. I felt Cleo's tongue on my neck before I could ask for it. Her fangs inside gave me that extra shove. The rush of the shower running was lost, scrambled among the sound of my screams.

❖

That Tuesday was my last Tuesday as president of the Alpha Chapter of Alpha Beta Omega sorority. I opened my door for a final hour of sister counseling. A few girls poked their heads in to say hello, but I think knowing that Amy and I would be passing on our responsibilities in a short twenty-four hours might have dissuaded them from striking up a fresh session. We still had our scheduled meeting with our sister-queens, but this time we'd be finalizing the ballots for the chapter elections.

I was finishing my reading for my media and culture class when I heard a soft knock on my door. Jill was standing in the hallway. "Hey, Benny. Can I come in?"

"Hey. Yeah." I pointed to my vanity stool.

Jill grabbed it and dragged it over to my desk, grinning at me with her mouth full of metal. Those braces made her look so young, but just as sweet as she really was, once you got to know her. "Hi. Did you see the e-mail from Professor Fitzer?" she asked.

"I did."

"She's out for the whole week. I'm so excited."

"I'm just hoping she doesn't stick it to us when she gets back."

"She might." Jill laughed and started nervously rubbing her knees. I knew she didn't stop by to talk about our German professor taking a week off to take care of her sister. "So I've decided to run for health and wellness chair."

"That's a great idea," I replied.

"I know the sister-queens take care of us, but I want to do more campus outreach. I had some ideas for a freshman sex-ed program. I thought if I could get the whole chapter on board and maybe even the guys, we'd show that Alpha Beta Omega can have a positive influence on the whole school."

"Jill, that's great."

"So you've made it official with Cleo?" She wouldn't look at me then.

"Yeah." I thought I should hug her, but I stayed where I was.

"Can I see?"

I held out my hand. She took my fingers and turned my palm to the side. "It's a really pretty ring."

"Thank you, Jill."

She let go of my hand and everything about her seemed to deflate. She sagged in her seat, staring at the floor, and a few moments later, her chin began to tremble. "I'm really going to miss you."

I leaned forward and put my hand on her knee. "We can still be friends. I'll only be an hour away, and I'll be back to see Ginger and Camila." I didn't know what else to say, which always seemed to be the case with Jill. I did care about her now. She was a good girl. Over-the-top in so many ways, but she was a good person, with a huge, pure heart. Sometimes, though, one person's happiness, no matter her intentions, is another person's pain. When she jumped out of her chair and threw her arms around my neck, I didn't have a choice but to hug her back. It didn't feel like an obligation this time. I wanted Jill to be happy. I cared about her.

"I won't call you or anything. I know you guys will want your time alone. But do you promise you'll come visit?" She sniffled.

"I promise. An hour is much closer than you think."

"Hey, ladies." I looked up to see Amy cautiously creeping into my room. "It's meeting time."

Jill wiped her eyes and made a quick break for the door. "I'll see you later."

"Hey." She stopped and looked back at me. "Breakfast tomorrow. Just me and you."

Like that, her face lit up, even though her eyes were still wet. "Okay. I'll see you then."

❖

That Thursday night, the girls elected Kendall, a junior econ major and one of Natasha's feeders, to the office of chapter president. I handed over my copy of *Robert's Rules of Order* along with a goodie bag of upper-level chapter swag. Kendall loved the engraved ABO iPad case I'd picked out for her. Camila was nice enough to put an iPad in it. Jill won the post of chapter health and wellness chair. I promised her I would come back to support any of her community programs.

I saw the rest of the semester through. The second week of May, Amy, Samantha, Anna-Jade, Ruth, Maddie, Gwen, Laura, Melanie, Irene, Ebony, Kyle, Julia, and I graduated. We all wore a red rose on our gowns for Ginger. Though she couldn't walk across the stage with us, she was there, perched on the closest power line with seven other blackbirds, looking down as each of us made our way across the graduation stage. Mama was there with Douglas and a rather unhappy miniature pinscher who looked like he was anxious for sundown.

After commencement, we all met back at the house for a small reception with friends and family and our sisters who'd decided to stick around. Douglas and the movers had already packed up my room. The girls would be passed on to their new demons over the course of the summer, just in case some plans changed here or there. Before I left, I gave my ruby necklace back to Camila. We both managed not to cry.

CHAPTER TWENTY-ONE

Benny
The Second Saturday in June

Mama and Mary sure knew how to put on a wedding. The sun was down. My hair and makeup were done. My dress fit perfectly. Everything was going so smoothly, my whole side of the wedding party was running way ahead of schedule. I stood patiently, letting Mama and Ginger fuss over me as we ran down the clock. It was hard to imagine, but in less than an hour I would marry the most important person in my life.

Cleo and I officially belonged to Daddy's nest. He'd accepted her, begrudgingly, unbinding her from her pledge to serve Alpha Beta Omega. Now she served Daddy solely, and worked side by side with Mary to help keep the existence of their kind a secret. I wore her charm around my neck, a princess-cut ruby. Unfortunately, a dark cloud, gray and black with its ominous truth, seemed to follow us no matter how much we tried to ignore it.

I'd learned to live with Paeno's mark. Every day, it had grown darker, the color and texture sharpening little by little. Every day. The swirls and lines were black now, raised off my skin in sharp relief. I'd stopped asking Daddy when it would go away, fade, or just disappear. His answers were cryptic, but Mama kept telling me not to worry. We had a wedding to plan. When Daddy didn't try to hold up the process, I figured Mama was right. Still, I wanted the mark gone. I belonged to Cleo. After we made things as official as possible, I didn't want the slightest hint of another demon touching our bond, or our marriage.

"Flowers!" Mama lightly thumped herself on the forehead. She looked lovely in her black dress. "Your flowers are down in the kitchen. Let me just go grab them."

"I can go," Ginger said.

"No, sweetheart. Let me go. I need to burn some of this energy. I'll be right back." As Mama nearly ran from her bedroom, I turned to look at myself in the mirror. Mama had pitched me all sorts of gowns. Dresses to enhance my shape, some to tone it down. There had been so many veils. Even a few tiaras fit for a princess. In the end, the decision was mine. I skipped the veils and the tiaras.

"I still can't believe you're wearing blue," Ginger said. She playfully fluffed out the skirt of my gown. The lightly ruffled fabric below the empire waist floated back toward the ground. I felt like a princess.

"It didn't make much sense for me to wear white."

"You are a dirty slut, aren't you?"

"The dirtiest," I said. Then I admitted the truth. "It's Cleo favorite color."

"You look so beautiful."

"Thank you, Ginger. You don't look so bad yourself." As my only bridesmaid, I put her in a black dress that nearly matched my own. Mama was a little shocked by my chosen color scheme, until I reminded her that with our guest list composed mostly of the undead, there would be no pictures.

"I'm gonna cry," Ginger said. She fixed my necklace. She couldn't stop the fussing.

"What's wrong?"

"Not now, but when you come down the aisle. Buckets, I swear."

"Well, good thing *you're* not wearing white."

Her eyebrows went up suddenly. "Oh, the master approaches." I turned just as Daddy walked into the room. He'd toned his demon down, only letting his horns and fangs show. He looked extremely handsome in his tux.

"We're almost ready," I said. "Mama is just grabbing my flowers. How is everything downstairs?"

"Your guests are arriving and your Cleo has not tried to escape."

I rolled my eyes. "Thanks, Daddy."

"My Ginger, a moment alone. Please."

"Sure. Of course. I'll go help your mom," she replied, then vanished from the room.

Daddy stepped closer and took my hands. "What's going on?" I asked.

"Paeno would like to speak with you."

I'd been calm all day. Trying my hardest to relax, breathing deep when Mama started getting a little overexcited. But now my heart took off, pounding frantically. "But, Daddy, I thought—"

"She only wishes to confirm your final decision in person."

I closed my eyes and focused on my breathing again. This was not the time to pass out. Or throw up. I wanted to believe that she would come all this way just to speak to me. But I couldn't help but think that she'd planned to murder me on my wedding just to prove some point. It appeared I didn't have much of a choice. "Okay. Where is she now?"

"She is here."

Paeno appeared near Mama's chaise, nude in her full demon form. Her horns almost touched the high ceiling. She nodded once to Daddy, who dropped my hands. He slowly backed away from me. He almost walked into Mama as she came back into the room. Out of the corner of my eye I saw her hands tighten around the bouquets. She wasn't expecting Paeno to drop in either.

Paeno turned to me then, and got right to the point. "You wish to dishonor our tu'lah."

"I—things changed with the person I was in love with all along. We're getting married tonight."

"She is here."

"Yes."

"You will bring her to me."

I all but silently screamed for Cleo.

"B, what's wrong—oh." Cleo appeared in such a rush, her dress shoes slid a few inches across the carpet. She swallowed when she saw our new guest, eyes wide, and stepped closer to me. "You're Paeno."

"She wanted to meet you," I said.

Paeno looked at Cleo very carefully. I could feel that she was reading her, gathering every bit of information she could from Cleo's mind, her demon, even the scents she carried with her. She read our bond too. It angered her somehow. "You have taken from me."

"Technically, yes. But Benny was mine to begin with. And now she chooses to be with me."

"I do."

Paeno seemed to ignore my words. She was focused on Cleo.

I looked up at her and could tell that they were doing some sort of mental tango. Perhaps Paeno was threatening her, or simply probing her mind in a way Cleo didn't like. I couldn't break their connection, but I grabbed Cleo's hand. She had to know I was with her.

Paeno turned to Daddy. "You will fulfill your tu'lah."

"Yes, kri'ah. Blood for blood. Body for body."

Paeno nodded, dipping her heavy head in a slow motion. "She will be unmarked." She held out her talons for me. Reluctantly, I let go of Cleo's hand and crossed the room. I took hold of Paeno's outstretched claw and turned my forearm upward. Our eyes locked, and for one moment, the impossible happened. She overtook my bond to Cleo. My whole body flooded with heat. My tongue grew thick in my mouth and my pussy ached. I could hear Cleo growling somewhere behind me, but I couldn't look away from Paeno's face. She smiled, a slight parting of her lips that showed off the tips of her fangs. The words came in her human voice, sweet and pleasing. "You would have been happy with me."

And then, as if she'd poured a whole bottle of acid on my arm, her mark melted away, taking a few layers of my skin with it. I crumpled to the floor, crying out and sucking air through my teeth as my mind tried to process the agonizing pain. There was no blood, but my skin had peeled back on itself, leaving a large chunk of my forearm raw and exposed. Paeno vanished as Cleo rushed to my side. She gently took my hand to check out the damage.

"Motherfuck—" Cleo shoved her suit sleeve up her arm and scored her wrist. "Here. Drink." I took what she offered, sucking down her blood as fast as my throat could manage. My skin started to heal instantly, returning to normal in seconds, but I still felt the pain. Paeno wanted me to remember what it felt like to cross her.

"Are you okay?" Cleo asked. She was checking me all over, looking for more invisible scars.

"Yeah, I'll be fine." I was still shaking. "It's fine."

Cleo turned to Daddy. "Get out," she said. He didn't argue.

I let her help me off the floor and we sat together on the settee. There were a few flecks of her blood on my dress, but the tiny stains were further proof of how much she loved me and what we were both willing to do for each other. I scooted closer as she wrapped her arm around my waist. Her scent and her breath helped.

"We don't have to do this tonight," she whispered against my temple before she kissed me.

"No. I want to. She's out of our lives for good now. I want to marry you tonight."

"Okay, baby. Can I just hold you a few minutes longer?" I wiggled as close as I could get, resting my hand in Cleo's lap and my head on her shoulder. I wouldn't let Paeno ruin our night. I wouldn't let my anger with Daddy ruin it either.

"Okay. I think I'm good." I looked up at Cleo and gave her my most convincing smile.

"You're sure?"

"Just give me a few minutes. I'll meet you downstairs." Cleo kissed me one more time, then walked, not vanished from Mama's bedroom.

Mama handed me a glass of water. She checked my arm, gently stroking my skin, and then set about checking my hair. More fussing. "I might kill your daddy."

"Can it wait?"

She smiled and touched my cheek. "Yes, angel. It can. Let's get you hitched."

Cleo

Omi and Mary found me in the driveway. I had to catch my breath. I couldn't stop seeing the way Benny's skin had rotted away. I couldn't unhear the sound of her screams. Omi wanted to know what had happened, why I was suddenly panicking, but I couldn't put what had just gone down into words. So I showed them both. I showed Omi and Mary how Paeno had stripped my mind bare. She'd probed my whole life, torn through all my memories, things I'd forgotten or chose to ignore. She set off little bombs, reminding me of every moment I'd wanted to open up to Mama but couldn't.

She dug through every second Benny and I had been apart. She showed me all the things she could do to me if she wanted. She told me that it was her mercy that would get me through the night, not the begging and pleading of her brother. She was letting Benny marry me and she wanted me to be grateful. And when I wasn't, she burned my baby. Lord Jesus, the look of her arm. I knew I would never forget it.

I couldn't fathom how the hell Dalhem could send Benny off to be bound to such a creature. "How could he—"

"Listen to me." Omi placed her fingers under my chin and urged me to look at her. "You must never think of our master as one of us. Do you hear me?"

"I know. I don't. I just—he loves Benny. He loves Leanne. Why would he want that for her?"

"He is not human. He is real. He has a heart and a very strong mind. He loves, but hate is his nature. He was born of nothing but evil. You have to remember that. Their whole world is bargains and rituals and deals. Even his love for Leanne grew out of revenge, out of his hatred for her ex-husband. His hatred for you is not paternal; it's his nature."

Maybe with time I would fully understand, but I knew that Omi was telling the truth. Dalhem and Pacno were not some predictable beings who played by human rules. They made their own rules, existed by their own code, and all I could do was stay out of their way. The look on Benny's face flashed through my mind again. I wanted to be sick.

"You will always be safe with him because the consequences for him are too dire, but never forget what he is. Accept that you cannot understand their ways," Omi said.

Mary laid her hand on my shoulder. "Benita is your focus now. Paeno can't touch her any more. She has released her to you for good. Benita's part of the tu'lah is broken." I wasn't so sure about that, but I nodded anyway.

"Are you ready?" Omi asked.

"Yeah. Yeah. Let's do this." I took another deep breath, and as Mary and Omi turned for the backyard, I vanished to the kitchen where Andrew was waiting for me. I'd left him with my other feeders, his new boyfriend, Bruno, and Nancy, but they had gone to take their seats. Andrew didn't get a chance to ask if Benny or I was all right. I saw the fear in his eyes.

"I'll explain tomorrow. Okay?"

"Yeah. Okay."

I fixed his boutonniere and he straightened my tie. "You look good," he said, that dreamy smile of his reminding me again what I was living for.

"Thanks, baby boy. You're looking pretty sharp as well. Let's go."

Having no other choice but to force Paeno from my mind, Andrew and I made our way out to the backyard. Less than thirty chairs split the lawn. We walked around our guests to the preacher standing at the front. Of course Leanne had a Baptist preacher who was also a feeder on speed dial. Reverend Masey offered me a wink and a nod. Then he cued the violinist.

There was not a single young female relative among any of our friends or sister-queens, so we let Jill act as our flower girl. She handled the position with pride, strolling down the aisle in her black dress, her big smile showing off her braces.

Ginger followed, her eyes on Camila nearly the whole time. Then I saw my baby, my bunny, and I felt like I was seeing her for the first time. I'd already seen her flowing blue gown, twice, but knowing that she was walking toward me to finally be my wife, everything about her was new, head to toe. Inside and out.

She walked arm in arm with her mama. There was no ceremony in giving her away. Leanne had already told me she was gaining a daughter, not losing one. She placed Benny's hand in mine. Then she kissed both of our cheeks. She told us both that she loved us and took her seat beside Dalhem. I was doing my best to ignore that he was even there.

Reverend Masey kept things brief. He talked about the special nature of our love and the uniqueness of our blood bond. He talked about our separation and how it was God that had brought us back together. I held on to that idea as I wiped a few tears from Benny's face. Paeno might have thrown us a few curves, but she still had to answer to a higher power. She did not have the final say in our love or in our lives.

Samantha read a beautiful poem, by the end of which tears were streaming down Benny's face. Ginger was sobbing so loud Andrew offered her his handkerchief.

It wasn't much of a question, more of an obvious statement of fact. I said my I do. I promised Benny everything within my power. My heart, my body, and my love. She did the same. Then the rings and my lips on her perfect lips. There was clapping and hoots and whistles, but for me there was only Benny's smile and the soft scent of her skin.

We danced all night. When the first hint of sunrise sent that telltale tingle up my back, our friends vanished back to their homes. We sent Nancy off to get some sleep. Andrew and Bruno headed back to Bruno's place, assuring me that they'd be available for me to feed as soon as I could pull myself away from Benny. I estimated it would be a few days. We'd fly out the following evening for our honeymoon, but in the meantime, I led my bride across the street to our new home, down to our bedroom. I made love to Benny all day long.

CHAPTER TWENTY-TWO

Cleo
Thirteen Months Later

The memory was easy to find, but not as easy to fix. This young girl had seen a lot. Her name was Sierra. Her mom had been letting a vampire named Julian feed from her on and off for a few months now. Sierra had walked in on one of their feedings. I had to alter Julian in her mind. It was a multi-step process. First, the sight. I had to change the way Julian appeared to her. Not completely, but little things like his hair color, the shape of his nose and the appearance of his fangs.

I sat on Sierra's bed, holding her lightly by the shoulders. Mary stood by the door.

"Good," she said. "Now run it back." I replayed the entire encounter, through every blink and stored image. His new look was consistent. "Good. Keep going."

Mary waited patiently as I altered the smells in the room that night, and then the sounds. Blood has a very distinct smell, and Julian was a sloppy eater. Noisy too. I had to make Sierra forget the sounds of his snarls and growls.

I finished with the memory, then erased any sense that Mary and I had been in her room. She went back to sleep without a problem. When I finished, Mary did a final check. She gave me an A+ and then we vanished back to my front steps.

"Okay. Finish your story." Mary leaned against the iron banister.

"It wasn't much of a story. She just rolled over. Man, you should have seen it. B and I were freaking out and Jillian had the biggest smile on her little face. I'm sorry. Let me shut up."

"No. It's so cute. You can gush about her any time you like. You know I want to hear it."

"Thanks. Just eighteen more years and I swear I'll shut up."

"Don't make promises you can't keep, darling."

"True. Let me get inside. Give the other mama a little break."

"I'm sure she'd appreciate that." Mary kissed me on the cheek, then vanished. I headed inside. Straight for my girls.

I found Benny in our bedroom, sound asleep on our bed. She hadn't even tried to get under the covers. I didn't hear a peep from the nursery, but I had to go take a look.

Our daughter, Jillian Joy Jones, was born on Easter Sunday. She came early in the morning, way before the dawn. She was kind enough to give our midwife enough time to get over to the house before she executed her speedy arrival. She was perfect. Squishy and purple, with the shape and color of Benny's eyes and her wide lips. She had a full head of curly black hair. Her little nose, we decided, had to come from her father, a man whose identity we decided we didn't want to know. I had to applaud Dalhem for his connections when it came to finding a donor. Jillian was perfect.

At the moment, she was wide-awake in her crib.

I whispered my, "Hey," and gave in to my need to scoop her up. Benny's pregnancy had been difficult on us both. Her health was fine, but I couldn't feed from her, and if she was ever injured, I was afraid to give her my blood. Ginger had been born with vampire blood in her system, but we didn't know how it would affect our own kid.

But we pushed through. No incidents. No injuries, and now we had this amazing four-month-old. Benny was fucking fantastic. Leanne helped when she could, but Benny was the rock star. I'd found my place in our family routine. I'd learned not to breathe through my mouth during diaper time and I learned that I could also do this mother thing.

I kissed Jillian's cheeks—I couldn't get enough of her chubby baby cheeks—and chatted her up with nonsense as I walked our usual circuit around the nursery. And then Jillian decided it was time to fill that diaper. Benny hated how hard I laughed at her I'm-about-to-poo-face. And poo she did. I made it to the changing table in relative silence, but I had to say something about the stink.

"Baby. Sister-girl. What have you been eating?" That, of course, made her fussy. Not dropping a load in her pants, but me insulting the smell of her crap made her scrunch up her face and crank out a little whine. The slightest noise from Jillian had Benny's baby senses tingling. She was out of bed and in the nursery before I could execute wipe phase one.

"I didn't mean to fall asleep. I was waiting up for you," Benny said as she stroked Jillian's hair. "Hello, my hubby," she cooed.

"You know you don't have to do that. We have all morning."

"I know. I just missed you."

"How about I finish up here with the stinkster and then I help you get back to sleep."

"Will this so-called help involve a massage?"

"Does my bunny want a massage?"

Benny groaned and rubbed her back. "Yes, your bunny does."

"Well, bunny always gets what she wants, doesn't she?" I leaned over and kissed Benny's lips. "And how about you, my Jilli? Do you want a baby-sized massage for your baby-sized muscles?"

Jillian stuck her fingers in her mouth.

"I think that means I should shut up and get a new diaper on her bum."

Though I was quick with the diaper change, Jillian had designs on what was under Benny's shirt. So did I, but I had to wait my turn. Her feeding was long, and then there was another diaper change and then Benny walked her around for a bit until she conked out again. I knew the routine, as unpredictable as it was, wore Benny out. But despite her exhaustion, I'd never seen her this happy. Or more beautiful. Or patient. Finally, we put Jillian down in her crib and I led Benny to the bed.

She flopped forward on her face. I watched, amused, as she tried to get undressed without really lifting her arms or head. "Help me," Benny whined, trying to pull down her pants. I rolled her onto her back and helped her out of her jeans. "You're gonna have to do my feet too. They are killing me."

"I'm gonna do your whole body, baby. Just you wait." Once she was naked, I pulled down the covers, then grabbed her favorite oil. With a quick zip around the room, I lit Benny's favorite candles and put on the *Music for Massage Mix* Camila had compiled for us.

"You're not going to use the table?" she asked. Yeah, I'd bought a proper massage table too. For now it was nice and handy, a few feet away in the closet. But I had very specific plans, and the table was too narrow to accommodate us both.

"I told you, I have every intention of putting you to sleep. Come on." I scooped her up and laid her on the center of the bed. As soon as she was in a comfortable position on her side, with her pillows between her legs, I went to work on her hip and thigh. During her pregnancy, I'd become quite the master of the slow stroke prenatal massage. I used it as a ploy to get Benny into bed plenty of times, even though she was on to me. Neither of us saw a reason to stop them once Jillian was born. The baby had brought several changes to our sex life. There were ways to practice bondage safely with a pregnant woman, but I was not on board with that shit, and the more the baby continued to grow, neither was Benny, especially when her all-day sickness kicked in.

We had both missed that kinky side of our relationship, so she had the idea that I take Andrew back on. We started slowly, but over time, Benny revealed to me that she enjoyed watching, that it turned her on. I only fucked him with a strap-on, but he was happy with that. He enjoyed his time with Rodrick, but he missed having a more complete relationship with me. With the help of my blood, Benny recovered from the delivery in no time. I was glad to have both of my submissives back in full action, but Benny still got the bulk of my attention.

"Andrew sent me a text. He's home and Bruno's spending the night," Benny said as if she'd read my mind.

"I'll go check on them later," I replied, knowing that later would probably turn into tomorrow. I ran my fingers up Benny's thigh, over her hip, and slowly back down again. She groaned again, but this time in delight.

"Better?" I asked.

"So much better. I love your hands."

"They love *you*."

"I want to pounce on you right now." Benny snorted with laughter, and then she let out a sigh that morphed into a moan. "But I can't move. You're going to have to keep this pleasure moving."

"Downtown?"

"All the way downtown. I'm so glad you have a sense of humor about this. I'm so horny right now, I might burst." I stopped my massaging and got undressed. In the next second, I was on the bed behind her, my fingers resuming their stroking around her front. I slid my other arm under her head and buried my nose in the thick waves of her hair. She'd become obsessed with the weight she'd gained. A ton of times she'd bashfully wiggled out of my gasp or moved my hands if I touched her belly. She was convinced she was never going to get rid of the baby weight. She still looked beautiful to me, and at the moment all I wanted to do was touch her. All I noticed was the smell of her. Her sweet almond scent was only more appetizing to me. Her skin was so soft. I gently parted her lips with my fingers and rubbed the tip of her clit. She rested her hand on my forearm.

"How does this feel?" I asked as I stretched myself between her legs, my destination, her sweet, pulsing g-spot. I pumped my hips a few times, stretching her pussy little by little with each back-and-forth. My shifting abilities had never come in this handy before.

"It feels…Cleo. Oh God."

"Tell me," I purred.

"It feels really good. Really good."

I kissed every inch of skin I could reach. Her shoulder and her cheek. Her neck and her hair. Her soft lips until we were both gasping for air.

I nudged her head up, and once her neck was fully exposed, I bit into her skin. Rubbing my tongue against the meter of her beating heart, I retracted my fangs the fraction of an inch necessary for the blood to flow into my mouth, holding her in the tight grip of my jaws while her body clenched and latched on to mine. I came in the moments that followed, my clit tingling as her muscles massaged my length into submission. The tremors continued, and I started to feel her orgasm rush through me, radiating out from my chest. I pulled my fangs free from her vein and sealed her skin before more than a few drops of blood could seep out, drops I savored on my lips. I lay with her, my heart thumping in rhythm with hers, loving the feeling of her skin as she rubbed her cheek against my arm.

"Babe," Benny said, trying to catch her breath. I kissed my way down her neck before I answered.

"What is it, sweetheart?"

"I will pay you to get me a glass of water. I'm so thirsty."

I nudged her cheek and licked her skin some more. "How about water's on the house and I throw in a spanking? And then I'll fuck you again."

Benny tilted her head back and nipped my bottom lip. "Sounds perfect to me."

❖

I stayed with her in bed until she was breathing lightly. I was restless, though, and had to move around the house.

I leaned over Benny and kissed her forehead. "You sleeping?"

"Yes." She reached up and gently mushed my face away. I laughed behind my clenched teeth and slipped out of bed.

The blinds in the nursery were open. I watched the moon over the street that separated us from our in-laws. Nights like this, when everything was perfect, when I knew Benny and Jillian were safe and Andrew was happily in the arms of his man, I only thought of one thing. Mama and Daddy. It's a strange place your mind goes when things are as they should be. When you're used to the pain, parts of you still search for it, even when you know it's the wrong thing to do.

I had Omi and Mary. They'd been there for me through everything; times when Leanne was going a little overboard with decorating or shopping for baby clothes, or when Dalhem, who had lightened up a little, felt like being particularly dickheadish, they were there for me to vent. Andrew was thriving in his teaching position. The kids loved him and half the parents were in love with him, but those wonderful things didn't stop Mama and Daddy from popping into my head. I knew Daddy was still drinking; he had to be. A strong relationship with the bottle didn't just fade over time, and Mama wasn't the type to ask for a change. Turning a blind eye was a way of life for her. She had Maxwell and his wife and children to focus on, Stephen to brag about, and Nat to still boss around, and she had the church. What more could she need?

I didn't want my human life back, but I wanted a way to reach her. I wanted to get through to my mama in some way, for Daddy's sake. I wanted to show her how good life was for me and I wanted to hear from her mouth that I had done okay, that she was proud of me for making the best of everything that had been thrown at me.

I latched on to little things then, the good memories like the sound of her laugh or the looks Daddy would secretly shoot me when Mama was going off on one of her gossipy tirades. I missed being with my brothers. I wished they knew Benny the way I did. I wished they had gotten a chance to meet their niece. I missed them so much it was hard not to pick at the scabs. I didn't want to forget about them.

I caught Benny's scent before I heard her soft steps over the carpet. I looked over my shoulder just as she slipped her robe on.

"What are you doing up?" I said quietly.

"I missed you."

I leaned down and kissed her full lips, cupping her cheeks.

"I have to tell you something," Benny said. "You are an amazing mother."

"You think so?"

"Yes. I mean, I'm her favorite. That much is obvious. I come loaded with food, but I see the way she looks at you and the way you look at her. You have no idea what it means to have you both."

"You're sneaky, Benita. Always knowing the right thing to say."

"What's wrong?"

Honesty was our first policy, even though we both learned pretty quickly that wording does matter. "I was just thinking about Mama and Daddy."

"Go." She nodded toward the window. I stared back at her in shock. I didn't expect that command from her.

"Go," she said again. "I know what Omi told you, and she was right in a way, but if you have to check in on them sometimes, I understand. Go."

Before either of us talked me out of it, I got dressed. Cloak or not, I didn't need to show up in my mama's yard in my underwear. Benny watched me as I tied my sneakers.

"I love you," she said with slight smile.

"I love you too." I kissed her one more time before I vanished to Virginia.

❖

The night air was muggy as I appeared within the trees beside Mama and Daddy's house. I entered through Daddy's den. I found him there in his chair. *Sanford and Son* was on the TV. Daddy was oddly still. I leaned down and put my finger under his nose. Accidentally, I brushed his mustache just as I felt his breath across my finger. He twitched twice before flopping back into his sleeping position. He reeked of booze. All it took was a quick glance around his chair and I found a bottle of rum that had toppled just out of the reach of his fingers. It was almost empty.

I touched him again, intentionally this time. I patted his hand. "I'm here, Daddy," I whispered. He snorted again. That's when I heard Mama's voice. I followed it into the kitchen, glancing at the clock as

I stopped next to the fridge. It was almost three a.m., and she was on the phone. There were papers stacked on the table in front of her. I recognized my little brother's face.

"No, no. Thank you, sister. I know it's been real hard for you too. Lord knows we appreciate your help." She was quiet for a moment as she rubbed her forehead. "Maxwell is heading down to Atlanta with a fresh batch of posters. I'm praying we find something. I know we will."

Securing my cloak, I tiptoed closer. Mama glanced up briefly, but there was no recognition in her eyes. She'd seen right through me.

I scanned the missing poster as she continued with her conversation. She moved on to church business, gossip rather. Who was still helping and who wasn't. From the information I could read, Nathaniel had been missing for over a year. I stared at his picture, one he definitely posed for for the church directory. His shirt and tie were crisp, his facial hair nicely trimmed, and his smile as big and genuine as I'd remembered it.

The posters were old. They had to be. There was no way my brother was still missing. I vanished up to his room.

Nat's room was oddly sterile and cold. A few things seemed out of place, but I could tell from the dust on his desk that nothing had been disturbed in a long time. I vanished out to the driveway, but Nat's car wasn't there. It was in the garage. He never parked his car in the garage. Daddy didn't like moving his truck every time Nat had to run out somewhere. Back in the kitchen, Mama hung up the phone. I watched her as she sat at the table. She ran her fingers over the fresh stack of fliers. When she finally left the kitchen and headed toward her bedroom, I snatched the poster off the top.

I knew one cop real well. Dewy Richwright had been sweet on Mama since they were kids. When we were growing up, every week, he and his wife could be found in the third row with their three kids. Dewy would know something. I vanished to his house and found him sound asleep. I crouched down on the floor beside his bed.

I grabbed Dewy's hands in my face. He was deep in a REM cycle, which would make things a lot easier.

"Do you know where he is?"

Dewy shook his head.

"Are you still looking?"

"I am," he said sluggishly. "But the case has been pushed to the side. Bosses think he's dead." I knew that wasn't true. Blood is blood, and I would have felt something if one of my kin had gone.

"What do you think, Dewy?"

"He's dead." Drool ran out of his mouth and onto my palm. I wiped it on the sheets. "But I'm gonna find him. I hafta do that much for your mama. I told her I'd bring her baby home."

"Can you find him?"

"No. Not this way. Not enough time. I need more time. Your folks do what they can, but I need more help." Of course he would.

"Go back to sleep, Dewy."

"Okay. Bye, Cleo." His reaction to me would have been humorous under any other circumstances, but this was no fucking joke. I needed to find Nathaniel. But I needed to find him alive.

When I appeared back in our bedroom, I could barely breathe. Benny was still wake, watching TV in bed. She'd waited for me. I stared back at her, seeing the worry as it quickly spread across her face.

"Babe? Cleo, what's wrong?" She slid over the bed as I held out the flier to her.

"I have to find him, Benny. I have to."

"Of course." She blinked in disbelief, looking over the details there in black and white. She looked back up at me, her wide, blue eyes mirroring my own grief. "Of course. We'll find him."

❖

My sister-queens took all of five minutes to rally and get over to our house. We'd woken Andrew and Bruno with the commotion, and they joined us on the bottom floor of the house to avoid the impending sunrise. They passed the flier around the room. I sat with Benny on the couch, keeping my hand busy, gently rubbing the knots in her back as she cradled a snoozing Jillian.

"He's not dead," I asserted. "I would know. He's not dead." My sister-queens had all died at different points in their lives, but many of them left behind no family members and none of them held on to their connections the way I did.

"She's right," Faeth spoke up. "I felt it when my dad passed away. I think she'd have some indication of his death when it happened."

Kina nodded to me in agreement. It was good to know I wasn't talking crazy.

"I know shit happens. I mean, look at all of us. Shit fucking happens, but I can't do this to my parents. The way I died, I don't think my daddy will make it if they lose Nat for good. He'll drink himself to death, and I don't know what that will really do to my mama." She was tough, but some things people couldn't withstand. There was only so much loss a person could handle. "Between us and, Lord knows, Dalhem, I know we can find him. Maybe we can get some demons in Virginia to help too. Maybe some feeders knew him."

We didn't keep track of unbound humans. Rules dictated that we stay away from them under most circumstances. Only demons who proved they knew how to conduct themselves without revealing their true nature moved freely around humans, and even then they left plenty of work for Mary and me. But with our numbers and our powers and connections, we had to be able to find him.

"We'll help you any way we can," Camila said. "We'll get all the files on the case and you tell us everything you know about him. All his friends, where you think he would go, where you think he would be last. We'll get our brothers to help. We *will* find him."

"None of what you believe is necessary." I froze at the sound of Dalhem's voice. He appeared behind Natasha, then stepped to the center of the room. His cold eyes fixed on me, but I glared right back.

"What do you mean it's not necessary? I have to find my brother."

"Your brother does not wish to be found."

Every drop of blood in my body rushed to my face. I pulled my arm from Benny, and I walked right up to our master. "What does that mean?"

"I have told you, Cleopatra. Your actions have consequences you could not begin to comprehend. You owed a debt, and you have paid it with your brother's life."

"Daddy." I heard the air rush from Benny's lungs. "How could you?"

He answered Benny's question, but he addressed me. "You have what you wanted. And now her Nathaniel is no longer your concern."

"You motherfucker!" I rushed him, but a force I could not see crushed against my chest, holding me back. I felt my ribs would crack at any second when Dalhem dropped me to the floor. Wincing, I rubbed my sternum. Everything was in place, but the pain still throbbed up and across my collarbone. "What did you do to him?"

"I will repeat myself. He paid your debt."

"Daddy!" I looked at Benny as she cased to the edge of the couch, her hands soothing their way down Jillian's back right back down to earth. I scrambled back to her side. Jillian whined a little, but slid back to sleep.

"What is it, B? What the hell is he getting at?" I asked.

"I…He gave Nathaniel to Paeno."

I closed my eyes and let the truth sink in. The asshole loved talking in riddles, but clearly, this pact with his sister was written in something stronger than stone. I'd taken Benny from Paeno, and her place in the demon queen's life needed to be filled. Problem was, I didn't steal Benny from her life and her family. She chose me. Snatching Nathaniel off the street did not constitute any sort of eye-for-an-eye-type situation. When I opened my eyes again, Dalhem was staring me down, daring me to charge him again. Instead, I filled my head with every evil thing I was thinking about him. He was fucking dead to me at this point. I didn't care what *he* thought about that.

"Master." Camila addressed Dalhem in a tone I'd never heard before. Her voice seemed to break him of our heated gaze. "Think of your brother-spawned. Think of *your* family. Do this for Benny and for me."

"I will arrange a meeting, but I will not promise his return. He belongs to Paeno now. He is hers." Once he disappeared, he left us all speechless. I held Benny as tears began flowing down her cheeks.

"This is my fault."

"Shh, no. Please, baby. Deep breaths and relax." I took Jillian from her and pulled Benny tight against my side.

Ginger came over and knelt in front of us. She took Benny's other hand. She looked between us both. "This is not your fault. Everything will be okay. We'll get him to calm down and then we'll talk to Paeno. I'm sure if she knows the details, she'll let him go."

Dalhem returned as the word left Ginger's mouth. "She will see you." He stepped toward me and pressed a burning finger to my forehead. I handed the baby back to Benny. "Think of her Nathaniel and she will lead you to him." I did as he told me, and when I opened my eyes, I was someplace unfamiliar and bright, filled with sunlight. The stone entrance to Paeno's temple.

CHAPTER TWENTY-THREE

Cleo

Of course, Dalhem would zap me to a part of the world where the sun had yet to go down. I dropped to my knees and prepared to shift, but a wonderfully powerful force stopped my body from changing its form. I looked up, shielding my eyes from the slanted rays of sunlight coming through the engraved slats of the temple walls. But for some reason I didn't burst into flames.

I stood slowly, allowing my eyes to adjust. Four years without natural light in your human eyes is a long-ass time.

"This light is artificial sunlight. You will not be burned."

I looked up into Paeno's creepy white eyes. She sat atop a wide throne on a wide altar at least twenty steps above me. Her partially human body was wrapped in blue and green silk. Two beautiful and naked Chinese women accompanied by two Bengal tigers stretched out at her feet. I knew she was different from Dalhem, who did his best to commit to a human persona. And based on her royal setup, I really had no idea how he could possibly think Benny would be happy or comfortable here, in this place or with this demon bitch.

Paeno's sheer power was palpable. From the first moment I met her, I could see, feel, hear, smell why she controlled our demon population. I could sense with every cell in my body why Dalhem had to follow her orders, but even he did not have her frigid energy. Paeno did not know how to connect with humans, but she knew how to possess and control them. She knew how to hurt them. There was no way I was leaving without my brother. Paeno and Dalhem would have to strike up some other deal with some other human they thought they could just barter like cheap clothing.

She eyed me with disgust, if I read her correctly, but I wasn't here on a social visit. Her grimace grew heavier as she probed my thoughts.

"Where is he?"

"You think he has been harmed." Her voice was strange. It seemed to vibrate through the air.

"I want to see him with my own eyes. I want to talk to him without you messing with his head." Her presence dropped from my mind as she rose from her seat.

Paeno handed off the tigers' chains to one of the women and slowly walked down from her dais. I braced myself for the worst. She'd probably turn me inside out and make me watch my bones do the cha-cha before she let me die, just because she could. But this wasn't about fear. This was about knowledge and acknowledgment. No matter what I did or where I was, Paeno could touch me.

"Where is he?"

"He comes." Paeno calmly took a seat on the bottom stair, and that's when I heard the voices coming down a long hallway.

"Where are we going?" I heard Nathaniel say. His voice sounded strange, hollow.

"We're going to see your sister," another man replied. He spoke English, but his voice was heavily accented.

"I have a sister?"

"Remember? You told me all about her. Her name is Cleo."

"Right, right. She's dead to me." Tears stung my eyes as he said those words, but I held them back. Nathaniel and a Chinese man, a demon, rounded the corner. Though they held hands, I sensed the bond between them immediately. Nat was this man's feeder. They were dressed alike, both shirtless, wearing black silk pants and no shoes.

He stopped walking a few away from me and stared blankly at my face for a moment. He looked healthy, well fed. He'd grown out his hair a little and had a goatee that matched the one Maxwell had rocked for years, but something was wrong with his eyes.

"Nat?"

He kept staring, not saying a word. And then he lunged at me, going right for my neck. I moved quick enough to dodge his gasp, spun him around, and put him in a head lock. He struggled, spitting through his teeth and calling me names.

"I should have killed you myself," he said.

"What is wrong with you?"

The demon he belonged to did his best not to attack me, but only because he didn't want me to hurt Nat. I released him and shoved him back into his demon's arms. Nat kept trying to come at me, swinging his arms, reaching for my throat. I backed away even farther and looked to Paeno.

"What did you do to him?"

"He is whole. I have done nothing but let him choose his demon and live his life free of your lies and his family's judgment. Xiang takes good care of him, and he can be himself here."

Paeno's voice suddenly changed. It sounded sweet and feminine; its hellish treble was gone. "Your poor brother. He had a life. He had a lover. He had to abandon all of that to cover your mistake." She looked beyond me, right into Nat's eyes. He stopped struggling. His jaw fell slack.

"Tell her, sweetheart. Tell her how it was for you."

With his eyes still glazed over, Nat addressed me. "I had a boyfriend. Deacon Fuller. He was going to leave his wife. We were going to New York together. You ruined it."

Never mind that my twenty-two-year-old brother had just confessed to having an affair with a sixty-year-old member of our church, it was apparent that he'd been ripped from the middle of his life. I spun on Paeno. "Did you just kidnap him? How did he even get here?"

Her voice snapped back to its regular layered tone. "You need no explanation."

"I know what you did," Nat said. "You left us so you could play vampire. You broke Mama's heart and ruined Daddy's life so you could marry some rich girl. Paeno told me. You used me too, so you could have your baby."

"What?"

"I didn't even know until Paeno told me she was born. You could have told us."

"What are you talking about?" I heard what Nat was saying, but I couldn't wrap my mind around it.

"You share a true kinship with your child," Paeno said.

"He's Jillian's father?" I suddenly felt lightheaded. This was too much shit to process.

"It was your wish," Paeno replied.

"Nat, I didn't know. I swear. I would have asked you first. You know that."

"Yeah? Well, you didn't." He turned back to Xiang. "Let's go, man. I don't want to look at her anymore."

"Why are you letting this happen? You're his demon. How can you see him like this?" It was clear that Paeno was deep inside my brother's head, but something wasn't connecting with Xiang. Even though I had the least of my personal relationships with Nancy, I still loved her. I would never stand by and let Dalhem screw with her head like this.

"I'm not in control here," Xiang said as his eyes strained in the strangest way. He was begging me to understand. I suddenly got it. Xiang might have been bound to Nathaniel, but Paeno was running the rest of the show. She pulled every string.

"Nat, none of that is true," I said. "I am married, but I didn't leave you guys on purpose. I died in that car wreck."

"Yeah, well, you could have said something to me or Daddy, at least. You've gone and fucked everything up."

"I couldn't. You have to know that. If I could have exposed myself, I would have come home right away."

"You all speak so of the past."

I closed my eyes and battled back the need to at least try to kill Paeno. It wouldn't get me anywhere but killed. I had to remember Benny and the baby.

"Yes, the baby. You should return to them," Paeno said, her voice sweet once again.

"You don't even want him. He's not even feeding you. Just let me take him home."

"You take from me. You give to me. Blood for blood. Body for body."

"You have to let him go."

"No! I want to stay," Nat said.

"Nat, please." If I had to beg, I would. "My parents need him back."

"Then you will fulfill the tu'lah. Blood for blood. Body for body."

I knew exactly what she was saying, but I didn't know what to do. I had three feeders. My wife and our child. I had no blood to give, no bodies to spare.

"You will speak to your master. He will help you sort things. In the meantime…" Paeno stood and walked over to Nat. Slowly her talons morphed to a woman's delicate fingers. I winced, thinking of the damage I'd seen that hand do, but she only touched him under his chin. "In the meantime, we shall enjoy the things that we have. And you shall enjoy all that is yours."

Paeno didn't give me a chance to make another case. My body was instantly pulled apart and flung back through space.

❖

When I returned to our family room, Leanne had a crying Jillian tucked against her shoulder and Ginger had a sobbing Benny at her side. I didn't know whether to hug them both or fall down on the floor and cry with them.

But once Benny saw me, she was in my arms. We sat back together on the other end of the couch just as the piece of shit that called himself our master reappeared. I ignored him, wiping Benny's tears away.

"Is Nathaniel okay?" she asked.

Her daddy answered for me. "He is unharmed."

"Dalhem, I'm telling you," I said, my voice eerily calm, "I cannot look at you right now. I don't care how much power you have over this nest and the demons in this room. You have to get the fuck away from me and my family right now or something bad is going to happen."

"You should go," Leanne said, backing me up. There were a few tense seconds where Dalhem refused to be excluded from the conversation, but finally he left the room.

"What happened?" Ginger asked. I explained our encounter as best I could. That Nathaniel had been taken or just given to Paeno by Dalhem. I tried to describe how he'd been brainwashed under Paeno's control, but that he wasn't even bound to her. I stopped speaking. There would never be a good time to tell Benny the last bit.

I looked at Jillian, snoozing again on her grandmother's shoulder in the midst of the commotion. Did she have Nat's nose, which looked exactly like mine? Were there other little bits that I was missing, obvious connections that I was overlooking because I thought half of her DNA came from a complete stranger? Before she was born, I did wonder how I would relate to her, if it would bother me that we had no biological ties.

I'd pushed the thoughts away, and they'd stayed out of my mind, especially after Jillian was born. But did my bond with her come from my love of Benny, or was it something more? Did my demon know she was my blood all along? Did it matter, when our demon masters had violated my brother in such a serious way just so we could have her?

I took a deep breath and peered at Benny. Her beautiful face was blotchy and red. When I told her the truth, my voice came out in a rough whisper.

"Nat...he's Jillian's father." Fat tears dripped from my eyes and hit the carpet between my feet. The silence in the room was terrible. I knew my sisters had heard what I said. Benny sighed and wiped my face. I knew we were thinking the same thing. We wouldn't change a hair on Jillian's head. She was an amazing gift to us, but if we'd known, we'd never have gone about it this way.

"We *will* deal with Daddy later. Trust me. What should we do about Nat?"

"She wants someone from me. Someone close to me that I care about, or she won't let him go."

"So this was payback for us being together. I told you this was my fault."

"No," Leanne said. "This is your daddy's fault."

"Either way, I don't know what to do. She did all of this so there was no way out. I have you and now she has Nat. She manipulated Nat and now we have Jillian. She planned all of this so she could fuck with us forever."

"I'll go," Andrew said.

"No," Benny and I said at the same time. Bruno tensed at his side, but kept his objection to himself. Andrew was just too sweet to fall victim to Paeno. His heart was too kind.

"You've never met this woman. Demon, whatever. You have no idea. I'm not sending you there."

"Well, who else is there? She won't be happy with Bruno or Nancy. And other than that, there's only your other brothers. There's no one closer to you than me," Andrew said.

But we all knew that wasn't true.

❖

Benny waited three hours after our friends headed back to the house before she came to me. Andrew was sleeping and Bruno had left for work. Jillian was down for a nap and I was killing time shopping for little baby sneakers online.

Benny slid beside me on the couch.

"I have to go."

I dug my fangs into my bottom lip to keep from screaming at her nonsense. "No, you don't."

"Cleo. Look at me."

I closed my laptop and gave her the attention she asked for.

"She wants me."

"I know."

"She wants me. She's not going to let Nathaniel go until she gets me. She didn't take Stephen or Max. She took Nathaniel because she knows how much you love him."

"I know."

"She'd never be satisfied with Andrew. And she's not satisfied with Nathaniel now. Why do you think he's bound to another vampire?"

"I know."

Benny shuffled to the carpet between my feet. "Let me go."

"How can you say that shit to me?" I leaned forward and kissed her.

"Remember how you used to call me a spoiled princess? Remember how you used to tell me that I always get my way?"

"I vaguely remember saying something like that."

"Well, being spoiled leads to one having a fabulous lack of responsibility. I didn't want to own up to my part of our breakup. I didn't want to admit that I promised myself to Paeno without really thinking it through. For once, I need to take responsibility for the situations I find myself in. I can't pin this on Daddy. I've known him most of my life. I know that nothing with him is ever simple, but I took for granted how much he lets me have my way. I really thought there would be no consequences for breaking the tu'lah. And now Nathaniel is paying for it."

"Why can't we be together? Why can't we just be happy?"

"We are happy, but we have to fix this. I have to fix this."

"And what about Jillian? I just send you away and what do I tell Jillian? How do I explain where you've gone?" The thought made the blood in my stomach roll. I couldn't do it.

Benny sat back on her heels, a position she knew well. "I was yours years before our blood bond. She does not have my heart, Cleo. She never will. She can control my body and even my mind if I can't fight her off, but my heart is yours. Let me go. Let me end this and bring Nathaniel home."

"No, B. You can't."

❖

A week passed. Benny and I argued. I came with my same reply. I was not sending my wife to live with that thing. She would not become a part of her world. But Benny came with the same response—Nathaniel's missing poster.

"You know I have to go. She wants me. I have to make this right. Think of Nathaniel. Think of your mama and daddy."

I didn't say yes, but in our last argument, she took my silence as a sign that I was giving up the fight. All those things she'd said about responsibility ran through my head. I'd survived so much, beat death and was born again. I had everything I wanted. I couldn't leave my brother to pay the price for my joy.

"Come with me." Benny grasped my hand. "Let's go tell Daddy."

So it was arranged. One night a year, when Paeno took audiences with demons from other regions, I would be allowed to see Benny. Jillian, who was still pretty breast dependent, was allowed to come and go as she pleased, once she was weaned. We talked about me keeping her, but I found a speck of comfort in the thought that Benny wouldn't be across the world alone. She would have a very important piece of our family with her.

Whenever I wanted, I could visit Jillian at a secure location, away from Paeno's palace. Our baby wasn't part of the bargain, but Benny and I could only see each other once a year. Our visits would be supervised. If I tried to reclaim her, I would be killed. If I bit her, I would be killed.

I imagined the first visit would be a joyous reunion, filled with tears and catching up. I'd make love to her, supervised or not. But over time, Benny would grow more distant. The older Jillian got, she wouldn't recognize me as her mother, but just as some demon who came around with gifts and emotions, filled with guilt and longing she wouldn't understand. Paeno would get exactly what she wanted—my wife and my child.

In our last few days together, I didn't dominate my bunny. It wasn't what I wanted. I made slow love to my wife. I held her as much as I could. I took so many pictures of her, with Jillian and Leanne, even as she slept. I needed something tangible to hold on to.

We flew overnight in a private jet to Beijing. I shifted twice during the flight and slept as a cat on Benny's thigh. When I was able to hold my human form, I held Jillian. Changed her and sang to her, songs she would never remember. Walked her the length of the cabin.

A short limo ride and a long walk through the palace grounds later, the three of us arrived in a large receiving room where the switch was to go down. We were told Paeno would be with us shortly. I had to say good-bye. I held Jillian. I needed more time with her close to my heart. She was awake, blinking as she looked at our surroundings, taking it all in.

I took Benny's cheek in my hand. "I love you. Do you hear me?"

"Yes."

"I love you more than anything."

"I know, Cleo. I love you too. I will always love you." Benny reached down and grabbed my ring finger. "Remember this, okay?" Her hand moved up to my ruby pendant, which still hung from her neck. "She can take the blood bond, but she can't erase our vows. She can't change the fact the we are a family."

"Don't let her all the way in. Please. Don't let her make you forget me." My voice cracked, but I couldn't help but smile when Jillian tried to shove her fingers into my mouth. Benny laughed and freed my lip from her strong baby grip.

"Give me time. I'll come back to you. I swear. I'll be such an annoying brat, she'll want to give me back. No one wants to kidnap a spoiled princess. You said so yourself."

"What's going on?" Nat was standing in the doorway with his demon by his side. I'd caught their scents moments before, but my girls were my focus. I glanced at Nat and saw that he was dressed to leave, in jeans and light jacket and sneakers. Still, though, he was under Paeno's spell.

"I'm taking you back," I said.

"What? Why?" Nat looked frantically to Xiang. "I want to stay with you. My family doesn't love me like you do."

"No, Nat. You have to go home," I insisted.

Paeno appeared on the other side of the room, still enormous with her giant wings folded behind her back, but with the face of a woman. "You can't imagine that his life would be better here with me. That he is happy with Xiang."

"You stole him from my family," I growled.

"Or I led him to his true life and his true happiness. This sense of security, familial bonds, the entitlement of bondage between parent and child. It is false. This mother and father of yours give you physical life, but you are not alive until you seize your own control."

"Then let him say it for himself. Let him tell me what happened and what he wants, on his own."

"You may speak."

Nat squeezed his eyes shut and shook his head. It was a few moments before he looked at me again, but finally, his eyes were clear. "Cleo." It was him this time, my brother present in his own mind, the sweet kid I remembered. When he stepped toward me, he pulled me into a hug, lightly squeezing Jillian between us. "We thought you were dead."

"I know. I'm sorry." I pulled back and scanned his face. He was still present and in the moment. "I gotta get you home. Mama and Daddy—"

"I can't. Paeno was right. I have nothing to go back to. I was failing out of school. I was sleeping with a married man, and Mama… she wouldn't let me move out, but she knew about me and Deacon Fuller. She just kept her mouth shut about it. She'd rather me sin with a married man than acknowledge that her son was gay." That admission alone was so much to hear, that we had been the same for all those years, sharing the same secret, but Nat had more reasons to stay.

"You have to consider the time too. Xiang said I've been gone for a crazy long time. A year or something? How can I just go back? How will I explain how long I've been away? Where I've been? How I'm completely okay?"

"We'd give you a new memory," I said. Mary vowed to try to rewrite his experience, erase any knowledge of any demons, including myself, to help him get back to his life. If it didn't work, he'd have to become a feeder. It was the only way.

Nat shook his head and looked longingly at his demon. Clear blue tears lined Xiang's eyes. "No," Nat said. "I don't want new memories. I like the ones I have." Jillian made a little eeping noise that broke up the mood. Nat touched her curly hair. She reached out to him with her little fingers.

"I helped with this?" he asked.

"I guess so."

"What's her name?"

"Jillian Joy," Benny replied.

"Cute name. Cute kid." Nat scratched his goatee, then took Jillian's finger when she offered them again. "Take your family home. I should stay. For real. Go. I'm okay here. I mean it. I'm fine."

How could I fight such a selfless act when the most selfish part of me was telling me to take Benny and Jillian and run? "What about Mama and Daddy?"

"I don't know." He shrugged. "They think you're dead, right? Maybe it's time I'm dead to them too."

"Nat—"

"What else can I do? It's not like I can bring Xiang over for Sunday dinner. Mama would shit a duck. At least if they think I'm dead they can try to move on." He had a point, though I wasn't sure if that was altogether true.

"Can I see him again? Or is this it?" I asked Paeno.

"You have fulfilled the tu'lah if he remains. You will be granted your visit annually."

"That's good, Cleo. I can still see you. Just take her deal and let's end this."

I looked to Benny. She was just as conflicted as I was.

Xiang stepped forward and held out his hand to me. I clasped his palm. "You have my word. Demon to demon. I will continue to take care of him. To love him."

Xiang opened his mind to me, and damn if he wasn't so sincere. Paeno was a special kind of horrible bitch, but Xiang was a good man. He showed me what he could of his life with Nat, and I knew he was telling the truth. Nat was safe with him. Safe and happy. This zombie routine Paeno had Nat under was an act she only put on for me, to show exactly what she was capable of.

Again, it was impossible for me to articulate my forfeit. Could I do this to my brother? Nat made that decision for me.

"One year. Come see me. We'll show Xiang how Americans do barbecue."

"Okay," I finally said. "One year. I love you."

"I love you too, Patra." Hearing him call me by Stephen's nickname for me, I knew he was thinking clearly. That his humor was back. I knew he would be all right. I hugged him again, and Xiang, and then they left. A year was a long time, but we could make it work.

Ready to break the hell out, I grabbed Benny's hand and made for the door. Paeno blocked our exit. She seemed to have more to say.

"Your child is special."

"We know." I shifted Jillian away from her.

"You know nothing," Paeno snapped. She drew her talon down Jillian's cheek. The kid didn't seem the slightest bit afraid. "Your child is special. She is not capable of forgetting you. She is of your blood, and it is your blood that makes her special. It is what makes her soul pure. Keep her safe."

The man who'd escorted us through the palace returned just as Paeno disappeared. We didn't wait for a proper invite. We followed him right back to the car.

❖

Two days later, Mama and Daddy got the call. Nat's body had been identified as a John Doe who had died in a house fire in Rochester, New York. A feeder willingly played the part of a friend Nat had met on the Internet. The whole story was fabricated. He'd gone to visit friends. He'd taken the bus just for the adventure, and he'd died.

A week later, they put his ashes to rest. Nathaniel's memorial seemed like a twenty-four-hour affair.

I waited the whole time, switching forms as the sun traveled across the sky and set again. Around midnight, as the last of the mourners left Mama and Daddy's house, Mary and Omi found me sitting on the Montgomerys' porch.

"I'm about done here," I said as I stood from the swing. My shirt was stained from my tears, but I'd change it before Benny saw me again.

"This one time, we can help them," Mary said.

"How?"

"It's just a few simple words. She can forgive, and he can put down the liquor. They can be okay."

I wanted to say no. I had to stop trying to control the world. I had to let my parents' lives play out the way they would without any vampires interfering. Then I pictured Daddy surrounded by those bottles, and I changed my mind. They would never get their two youngest children back, but they would have each other. As a couple, they could be whole.

I rubbed my eyes, then looked up at Mary. "Please."

"I shall return."

Omi pulled me close with an arm around my shoulder. "You are a good daughter, Cleopatra Jones. A wonderful mother and wife and sister. And a phenomenal vampire. Do not forget that."

I was too choked up to respond. Omi hugged me tighter.
A few minutes later, Mary returned.

"All set." She took my other hand and we vanished home.

❖

Both my girls were waiting up for me. Gus and Leo were keeping
them company. When I popped into the bedroom, Jillian clapped from
her spot between Benny's legs. Clapping was a new thing. It was
so fucking cute I could barely stand it. I shot her the biggest smile,
clapping right back as I made my way to the bed. I flopped facedown
on the covers. My purr rolled out of me as Benny ran her fingers down
the back of my neck.

"How was it?" she asked.

I huffed out a weary sigh, then perched up on my elbows. Jillian
wanted the report too. I leaned forward and blew raspberries on her
cheeks. I needed a dose of her baby smell.

"It was nice. Everyone came out. His old friends from high school.
The deacon he was with was crying a little too much."

"Think he gave himself away?"

"Maybe. I'll e-mail Xiang in a little while. Let them know how it
went." I sighed again as I went for Jillian's little toes.

"What do you need, babe? What can I do for you?"

"Right now I just want to lie here."

"And later, my darling Cleo."

"Later? Later, I want you naked. We're going to do five, twelve,
and half of number nine."

"Only half?"

"I don't want my bunny gagged. I wanna make use of that pretty
mouth. As soon as this little boogie boo goes back to sleep." I leaned
over and nibbled Jillian's cheeks again. When it was clear she had all
she could handle, I laid my head down on Benny's thigh and slid my
hand up under her shirt. I was out cold a few minutes later. Lord knows
it was easier to sleep these days, knowing my girls were so close by and
the rest of my family was, at least, safe.

About the Author

After years of meddling in her friends' love lives, Rebekah turned to writing romance as a means to surviving a stressful professional life. She has worked in such various positions as library assistant, meter maid, middle school teacher, B-movie production assistant, reality show crew chauffeur, D-movie producer, and her most fulfilling job to date, lube and harness specialist at an erotic boutique in West Hollywood.

Her interests include Wonder Woman collectibles, cookies, James Taylor, quality hip-hop, football, American muscle cars, large breed dogs, and the ocean. When she's not working, writing, reading, or sleeping, she is watching Ken Burns documentaries and cartoons or taking dance classes. If given the chance, she will cheat at UNO. She was raised in southern New Hampshire and now lives in Southern California with an individual who is much more tech savvy than she ever will be.

You can find Rebekah at letusseeshallwe.blogspot.com.

Books Available From Bold Strokes Books

Sea Glass Inn by Karis Walsh. When Melinda Andrews commissions a series of mosaics by Pamela Whitford for her new inn, she doesn't expect to be more captivated by the artist than by the paintings. (978-1-60282-771-4)

The Awakening: A Sisterhood of Spirits novel by Yvonne Heidt. Sunny Skye has interacted with spirits her entire life, but when she runs into Officer Jordan Lawson during a ghost investigation, she discovers more than just facts in a missing girl's cold case file. (978-1-60282-772-1)

Murphy's Law by Yolanda Wallace. No matter how high you climb, you can't escape your past. (978-1-60282-773-8)

Blacker Than Blue by Rebekah Weatherspoon. Threatened with losing her first love to a powerful demon, vampire Cleo Jones is willing to break the ultimate law of the undead to rebuild the family she has lost. (978-1-60282-774-5)

Another 365 Days by KE Payne. Clemmie Atkins is back, and her life is more complicated than ever! Still madly in love with her girlfriend, Clemmie suddenly finds her life turned upside down with distractions, confessions, and the return of a familiar face… (978-1-60282-775-2)

Tricks of the Trade: Magical Gay Erotica, edited by Jerry L. Wheeler. Today's hottest erotica writers take you inside the sultry, seductive world of magicians and their tricks—professional and otherwise. (978-1-60282-781-3)

Straight Boy Roommate by Kevin Troughton. Tom isn't expecting much from his first term at University, but a chance encounter with straight boy Dan catapults him into an extraordinary, wild weekend of sex and self-discovery, which turns his life upside down, and leads him into his first love affair. (978-1-60282-782-0)

Silver Collar by Gill McKnight. Werewolf Luc Garoul is outlawed and out of control, but can her family track her down before a sinister predator gets there first? Fourth in the Garoul series. (978-1-60282-764-6)

The Dragon Tree Legacy by Ali Vali. For Aubrey Tarver time hasn't dulled the pain of losing her first love Wiley Gremillion, but she has to set that aside when her choices put her life and her family's lives in real danger. (978-1-60282-765-3)

The Midnight Room by Ronica Black. After a chance encounter with the mysterious and brooding Lillian Gray in the "midnight room" of The Griffin, a local lesbian bar, confident and gorgeous Audrey McCarthy learns that her bad-girl behavior isn't bulletproof. (978-1-60282-766-0)

Dirty Sex by Ashley Bartlett. Vivian Cooper and twins Reese and Ryan DiGiovanni stole a lot of money and the guy they took it from wants it back. Like now. (978-1-60282-767-7)

Raising Hell: Demonic Gay Erotica, edited by Todd Gregory. Hot stories of gay erotica featuring demons. (978-1-60282-768-4)

Pursued by Joel Gomez-Dossi. Openly gay college student Jamie Bradford becomes romantically involved with two men at the same time, and his hell begins when one of his boyfriends becomes intent on killing him. (978-1-60282-769-1)

The Storm by Shelley Thrasher. Rural East Texas. 1918. War-weary Jaq Bergeron and marriage-scarred musician Molly Russell try to salvage love from the devastation of the war abroad and natural disasters at home. (978-1-60282-780-6)

Crossroads by Radclyffe. Dr. Hollis Monroe specializes in short-term relationships but when she meets pregnant mother-to-be Annie Colfax, fate brings them together at a crossroads that will change their lives forever. (978-1-60282-756-1)